I was no longer alone.

The man was climbing toward me. He stood in the open, very close, yet not touching me. On one side of us was the rock wall, on the other the sheer face up which we had climbed.

I looked around. There was no one who could help me. I pressed myself against the parapet wall.

"Don't touch me," I warned. "I will fight—even if we both go off the edge."

"I won't touch you." He spoke almost pleasantly. "Because you are going to do what you have to do yourself, Dina darling. You're going to climb over that parapet. You're going to climb over it because you don't want to live any longer. Come now, Dina. I'll give you a foot up to get you over the wall. Just step into my hand—gently now."

THE
WINTER
PEOPLE

Phyllis A. Whitney

FAWCETT CREST • NEW YORK

1

I was asleep, and then I was awake, listening.

I could hear the snow hissing at the windows, hear the storm behind it and the rushing sound the wind made through the pine trees. But the sound that had wakened me was inside the house. A key had been slipped into a lock.

My hand reached automatically across the bed to find Glen, even as I remembered that after the quarrel late that afternoon he had hurled himself from the house, taken the Jaguar and gone roaring down the steep, winding drive to the road. Yet he had not been angry with me. The quarrel had been with *her*. I pushed myself up in bed, drawing the quilt around me against sharp cold and stared through blackness toward the closed door to the hall.

The sound came again. A key turning.

In the few weeks I had lived at High Towers there had never been a key in the lock of Glen's room. *Our* room— though I was still too much a bride, too unaccustomed to the house to feel at home in it. There was no other sound from the hallway. No whisper of retreating steps, no exhaled breath. There was only an intense listening on either side of the door. My side and hers. And there was the deep, frightened thudding of my heart. I knew what she had done. But I did not know why.

Soundlessly I rolled out of bed into the chill of the big

room and went in bare feet across the cold floor. At the door I grasped the china knob and turned it ever so slightly. Against pressure. Her fingers were on it too, opposing mine.

The small explosion of laughter startled me when it came—a sound of pleased triumph, probably because I had found her out so quickly. Without troubling further to be quiet, she went away down the hall to her own room and left me to turn the knob as I pleased. Helplessly.

She had locked me into the room I shared with Glen. And Glen was gone. He could not help me because he was somewhere out in the heavy snow that blew across northern New Jersey hills. Blew across the frozen lake, far below the cliff on which the house had stood in all its arrogant pretension for the last eighty years.

I found my quilted robe and thrust my arms into long sleeves, slowly fastened the small buttons, shivering in the cold. The room was not entirely dark, due to that whispering whiteness outdoors. I went to a window and pressed against the glass, trying to peer out into the storm. The branch of the walnut tree scraped against the sill, rattling in the wind, its entire length thickly crusted with snow.

Someone had left the yard light burning behind the house, and against its radiance the storm was visible. Thick flakes blew past my window, with the wind behind, hurling them horizontally, giving snow the appearance of a solid, blowing mass—a wall which shut me in, imprisoned me, just as the locked door imprisoned me and shut me away from a saner world.

Even if there were no storm at my window, there would be only the dark of a country night beyond the lamp that burned in the yard. Lake and woods and hills would be invisible, and at this hour there would be no lights in the stone house on the far side of the water.

What hour was it?

I drew the curtains tightly against the white whirling frenzy and turned back to the room. My fingers fumbled for the reading lamp beside the carved rosewood bed, and I turned the switch. My small clock on the bed table read two-thirty.

Glen had been gone nearly ten hours. And in this storm he could not get back to the house easily, even by daylight. Aunt Naomi had gone with him—as I should have done, had he let me—so that I was alone in the house with the woman who had shut me in. If she chose, she could unlock the door as easily as she had locked it and walk into my room. That would not bear thinking about.

Clumsily I set about rebuilding the fire in the grate. After a few false starts, the kindling flared, and flames licked upward into a blaze as the wood caught. I pulled a low hassock onto the hearthrug and sat upon it close to the fire, with my knees pulled to my chin, my hands held out to spears of flame. As I bent forward, my hair fell loosely over my shoulders and shone pale as silver in the firelight. Glen liked to see it loose at night. He liked to slip his fingers through its strands and bury his face in its softness and scent.

I love him so much, I thought. *I truly love him! But I don't understand him—and sometimes he frightens me.*

I began to plait my hair so that it hung in a fat braid down my back. I hated to have it all a tangle in the morning—and Glen was not here to care. In a way it was my hair that had brought me to High Towers. I had always been a little vain about it, I suppose. While other women tried to achieve its silvery blondness by artificial means, my coloring came to me from my Norwegian mother. Dad had always said that the rest of me was pure Blake—like my English grandmother, who had been small-boned and fragile. But my hair and eyes were Bernardina's. Fortunately, Dad had felt hers was much too large a name for a baby, so while they had named me after her, they'd always called me Dina. Only one person had ever called me Bernardina. Dina Blake, I had been. And now I was Dina Chandler.

Logs in the grate crackled as flame ate at them, warming me a little. Beyond the spit and snap of the fire I listened for the sound of a car. But nothing moved on distant roads, nothing came up the driveway—and I knew it could not. Outside the snow was deepening, and gusts of wind jolted the house.

Nothing moved inside either. She was safely shut away in her room, undoubtedly pleased that she had given me a fright.

How happy was I? How content in my new marriage? Of course every bride must feel doubts in the beginning, but had my love for Glen taken on a slightly desperate tinge? There was an unexpected wintry quality in him, like those freezing deeps of snow outside, which contradicted that gay and confident exuberance that hid it most of the time. An exuberance which could sweep everything before it, including me. I liked being swept away. I did not want to spend too much time thinking, because in that direction lay the past. It was the touch of winter in him which sometimes numbed me. Strangely, I thought about it most often when he was not there. When he was present he filled the room, the house, and all my mind and heart. I could only think then of how wildly and devotedly I loved him, and how I could not bear it if ever he turned away from me. Not that he had. Oh, not in the slightest! But when *she* had come there was a change. It was this that frightened me. I could not be certain what it meant. Sometimes it was necessary to reassure myself, to remember. To remember not the long ago, but the last few rapturous weeks and how it had all happened.

I buried my face in arms crossed upon my knees, closed my eyes against the firelight, and tried to recall in all its vivid detail the day when Glen had walked into the New York museum where I worked, walked resoundingly into my life.

At that moment I had been happily independent of emotional involvement. My work seemed more interesting than the men I knew. My father had been a well-known historian and university professor in California—Dr. John Blake. His books were in every library, on every reference shelf. Thanks to him, I had grown up with an interest in the historic past, though it was a different interest from his. He had cared mainly about the men and women of history, about understanding their motives and mistakes and triumphs, so they might be analyzed to serve the present. I felt that I understood something about such historical figures too, but from a different viewpoint, since I was more fascinated by the arts of the past, the paintings and sculpture, particularly—the things they had created—those men and women of other times.

I had grown up in the sunshine of Southern California, but New York had always been my Mecca. More so than ever after Father died. I had packed up the minute I was through college and come East with my mother's consent to try for the museum job I wanted. I hated to leave the golden sunshine and had no liking for the winter of the East, but I knew it was what I must do. My father was gone, but my mother was still alive. She had been the famous Bernardina Björnson—one of the great women swimmers of her day, but now she was very old and in the care of her adoring younger sister in the town where I had grown up.

Sometimes I wished I had not been born so late in my parents' life. Having so few relatives would have made me lonely, had it not been for the friends I made at the museum and the way in which I became absorbed in everything about the life there. Yet all the while underneath, without telling myself what I was doing, I marked time. I had to see *him* again some day. That was fated. It had to be. In the meantime, I watched the crowds and the turn of a head or a man's long stride that I knew so well. The sound of a voice with brusque kindness in it would make my heart beat faster, remembering his, and so would the flash of a teasing smile that reminded me of what I must forget after so much time had passed. Of course I never saw him. I read his books, I knew he lived in New York, but I lacked the courage to write to him again, or turn up on his doorstep. Old rejection—however reasonable at the time—was painful to remember. And my job kept me busy.

Not that it was an important job. I was part secretary to an assistant curator, part odd-job girl, and I liked the latter best. My favorite world was the storerooms, where treasures the public seldom saw were relegated to high rows of shelves. I helped to catalogue, to dust, to do minor repairs and keep track of where everything was kept. I had my own small walk-up apartment not far away. I dated two or three men whose company I enjoyed, but I did not go out often, because I wasn't ready to tie myself to the fortunes of any one man. I had my own fortunes to interest me first.

On the day when Glen Chandler walked in, I was engaged in a minor, rather amusing task. A bronze ballet dancer— nearly half life-size—created in Italy, and a bit on the rococo side—had been brought to the storeroom for refurbishing. The real tutu she wore—for some whimsical reason—had become gray and bedraggled. It was my duty to outfit her with new layers of tulle and I had placed her upon a long display table and climbed up beside her to finish my work. When I knelt, needle in hand, leaning past the point of her outstretched toe, my head came even with hers and I chatted to her companionably while I worked.

I knew Glen Chandler was coming. The department was somewhat atwitter because he was Colton Chandler's son. Of course the father's name was distinguished and highly respected in art circles. Though he was in his late fifties, Colton Chandler still painted portraits that had never grown dated. His portrait of Nehru and one of Sarah Churchill were among the treasures of the museum and held a place of honor in a main gallery upstairs.

All I knew about the son was that he owned and ran a small art gallery downtown which I had not seen. Artists and sculptors, students and scholars were always visiting us and I was used to distinguished callers. I had known a few in my father's home as well. That morning I had brought out the eighteenth-century Meissen figures Glen Chandler had wanted to see, and I intended to go on with my own odd jobs while he examined them. He was already a half hour late and I felt slightly impatient because my lunch hour would have to be postponed.

When I heard the outer door open, heard voices coming nearer, I hurried with my sewing in order to get the last stitch in my ballet dancer's tutu before I climbed down from the table.

Mrs. Albright brought him in, and was unsurprised to find me in my high place. "Miss Blake, will you come off your perch and show Mr. Chandler the figures you've set out for him? Excuse me, please—there's my phone!'' She dashed off and left him standing just inside the door.

I gave him a quick glance which registered only that a tall man stood near the door watching me.

''I'll be with you in a second,'' I said, and wove my needle swiftly in and out of the stiff tulle. Since he had made me wait, he could wait a little too. I had a bit of my mother's Norwegian obstinacy in me.

He said nothing and I finished my sewing before I looked at him again. Really looked for the first time.

He had not moved, but stood watching me with his dark, altogether intent gaze. Though he was still, I had an odd impression of motion arrested, of vitality held in check. His hair was a thick, dark chestnut, and rather curly, with a reddish gleam in the light. His eyes were very large—almost black—and his rather elegant, thoroughly masculine face was thin and long, with a straight, sensitive mouth. Somehow he reminded me of an old portrait I had once seen of Keats. I suppose I stared back openly because his own look was almost rude.

''I'm ready now,'' I said, to break the odd locking of our eyes across the room. I stood up on the long platform of table above him, one hand resting on the arm of my ballet dancer friend.

Glen Chandler came toward me, almost flowing into easy motion with a grace that I was to understand later came from his skill as skier, skater, horseback rider.

''Stay where you are,'' he said, his tone peremptory. ''Don't move another step. Just stand there.''

I felt suddenly self-conscious, on exhibit, a little indignant. Yet I did as he ordered while he studied me with his artist's eye—looked me over from the front and the side, and then went behind the table to complete the round. It was an impersonal inspection and therefore not as outrageous as it might have been.

''That pale gray-green smock you're wearing,'' he said, ''—it's exactly the right shade for you. It carries out the green

7

of your eyes, but your eyes are brighter and they dominate—which is as it should be. Your hair is right the way you wear it—loose with a deep dip down the back and falling simply around your face. But you've restrained it with those combs behind your ears. Take them out.''

I came to my senses and jumped down from the tabletop, thoroughly annoyed. ''The Meissen figures are over here,'' I said. ''I've put them out for you, and—''

He came toward me and there was a certain exuberance in his smile that was disarming. ''We can forget the Meissen for now. And don't look at me like that. It's foolish, you know—futile. I'm not sure what I mean to do with you yet, but it will be something. Something important. There's no use resisting.''

I like a man who can govern and decide—as my father used to do in his gently firm way—but I've never liked to be pushed around. Swept away—yes, but not with arrogant highhandedness. Yet even as I bristled, I began to see that this was no arrogance. Here was a man who was excited about something—something almost apart from me. He was not playing a game or being rude.

When he reached out with strong, long-fingered hands to remove the two silver combs from behind my ears, his touch was almost tender, and I stood hypnotized. My pale hair fell across my shoulders and he stood back with a comb in each hand, staring at me with those dark, intent eyes—eyes so much darker than the chestnut of his hair. I was glad his eyes were dark. Blue eyes troubled me.

''I can see you in alabaster.'' He was musing now, speaking more to himself than to me. ''Pure white alabaster, like ice. I think I could do it. I think I could.''

I had no idea how to deal with him. I had no intention of turning myself into a model—it wasn't the sort of work that appealed to me, and he was making me increasingly self-conscious—though he was not self-conscious himself at all.

''If you'll just look at the Meissen, please,'' I said. ''I'll have to stay here while you do, of course. But it's past my lunchtime, and—''

"What's your name?" he asked me. "I heard the Blake when Mrs. Albright introduced us. But what else? You must have Scandinavia in your blood."

"My mother was Norwegian," I said. "I was named Bernardina after her."

I always put it like that, though only one man had called me Bernardina—only one man, ever. I suppose it was a sort of test I made when I met someone new. Then I always hurried on to say that people called me Dina.

He passed the test easily, calling me Dina at once, setting me at ease.

"Dina!" He picked up the "n" sound and made it hum. "I knew it! The northern heritage shows. Yes—I could use alabaster, with your hair falling over your shoulders like that, and a tinge of ice-green throughout. Sometimes there are shadings in white alabaster."

"I'm not going to be put into alabaster or anything else, because I'm not going to stand still long enough," I said. "May I have my combs, please?"

He smiled at me again, and I felt the first twinge of a reaction I could not help. The slightly somber cast of his face brightened when he smiled, making him all the more compelling and vital. He replaced the combs in my hair without fumbling. I should have known then that he had grown up among women.

"Will you have lunch with me?" he asked. "Then I can apologize for startling you. I've been waiting for someone like you to happen to me. But of course you haven't the slightest notion what I'm talking about, or what it is that has happened. Give me a chance to explain, at least."

Without warning—or with only the warning of that slight twinge—I knew I wanted to go with him. It wasn't my mind that was guiding me now, but that familiar sense of skyrockets about to go off, of Roman candles sputtering, of something magical about to happen. At twenty-four, I'd had this occur enough times so that I knew very well how easily burned-out rockets could fall to earth, how easily sparklers faded. Yet I always welcomed it when it happened, because then for a time I stopped searching the faces of strangers in the crowd.

I said I would get my coat and be with him in a moment, and I'm sure I sounded as stunned and tremulous as I felt.

At the door, he caught me by the hand for a moment, still looking at me with that searching challenge. "Ice-white," he said. "Silver. The perfect contrast. At the opposite pole from black."

I didn't know what he meant—not then.

Over the luncheon table he told me about himself. Or at least I thought he was telling me, and I listened with my heart bumping irregularly, while I tasted nothing I ate.

Everyone knew that Glen Chandler had been a child prodigy when he was young. Even into his late teens his talent had grown—as a painter, as a sculptor. They had said the Chandler gift was his. But something had gone wrong. By the time he was twenty his talent appeared to have burned itself out. What had soared so naturally became pedestrian and difficult, he told me now. He did not give up working entirely, but for all his effort, he had only once again done what he felt he was born to do. Only once had the inspired touch returned.

"I did a piece in black marble," he told me. "But it was dark inspiration and wrong for me. I hated it after it was finished, no matter how many other people praised it. But if I could do you . . . and I believe I can . . . Dina Blake, give me my chance!"

What else could I do but agree? He was sweetly, teasingly persuasive, having seen that the high-handed alarmed me, and I was going down for the last count. The sound of sparklers sizzled in my ears, though I suspected there was no promise of anything but hurt ahead for me. Glen Chandler was in love with what he could create in white alabaster if I would pose for him, but I doubt if he saw me as a person during those first few days. Even if he couldn't really see me, my imagination was fired and I could see myself. There I'd be, posing for a great work of art, inspiring a true artist to creativity. I did not even struggle to escape. I was like a fish on a hook—swallowing the bright bait willingly, danger and all.

I moved about my job in a daze during that brief time. Glen would call for me and take me to lunch, to dinner. We did not get to work at once, though an empty weekend presented itself when I was free from my job. Perhaps Glen was afraid to put himself to the test immediately. The studio behind his art gallery waited for us, he told me, yet he would not take me into it and begin. Instead, we walked the streets of New York in brisk November weather and he talked to me endlessly. He seemed hungry for someone who would listen, and since he was never dull I gave him my fascinated attention. He told me frankly that Chandler money had bought the art gallery for him when he found he could not work with his own talent. He was proud of what he had done with it, proud of the paintings and sculpture he presented there. He was always ready to encourage young, promising artists. Several of those he had discovered were already making names for themselves.

On the third evening we were together he took me to see the gallery and opened it up for me after hours. It was a long narrow room, plain and very beautiful, with polished floors and wood panels that winged out from the walls to show the lighted pictures to best advantage. He spoke with enthusiasm of the work of this artist, that sculptor, and the soft lighting touched the red highlights of his hair as he moved, so that he looked darkly beautiful in a way that was wholly male, and I trembled a little with dread and longing.

Nevertheless, for all his enthusiasm, I sensed the pain that walked with him because it was the work of others he must show, and never his own. This was part of his appeal for me—that there was a flaw in his self-confidence so that I ached for him at the same time that I admired his courage and tenacity. He was only thirty-four. Why shouldn't it begin all over again for him? Why shouldn't he build on a more solid basis this time, not relying on inspiration alone, but combining it with the technique that was now his through almost too careful practice? I was rapt as any disciple, giddily ready to sacrifice myself to his art if I could serve him.

But now—when I think of his gallery—there is just one picture I remember. The picture which should have warned me.

It did not hang in a particularly prominent place. It was not even very well lighted, but somehow it drew my eye. The scene was of an ice-covered lake in wintertime, with bare gray trees wooding the rise above the far shore. At first glance it seemed a pretty scene, with blue skies overhead and brightly dressed figures skimming the ice. I might have looked at it briefly and moved away, if I had not seen what the picture really meant.

The style was reminiscently primitive but the little figures which inhabited this scene were not pretty at all. Each seemed to have some minute ugliness when one looked closely, for all their gay clothing, and all were engaged in actions that were anything but innocent. A line of skaters cracked the whip, and a girl at the end had been released to go sailing toward a rocky bank and imminent disaster. Beyond the skaters a bonfire burned on the shore, and a small boy was pushing another child into the flames. On the frozen lake a tall youth held a gun to his shoulder, about to shoot a small brown animal fleeing toward the safety of the wooded shore. The boy was depicted in careful detail—plaid jacket, blue jeans, checkered cap in red and black. All around his feet were the tiny carcasses of animals he had killed, and each could be identified—deer, fox, raccoon, rabbit, woodchuck.

I supposed that any hunter might be shown like this in an effort to expose a cruel truth, yet here it was more than that— and somehow evil. Each tiny horror was depicted with relish, and the effect was wicked—sick. Yet it was strangely powerful. No name had been signed to it—only scrawled initials, difficult to make out.

Glen had gone to the front of the gallery to speak to someone at the door. When the man had gone, he returned to find me staring at the scene of the ice-covered lake.

"What a dreadful picture!" I said. "Who painted it?"

He seemed to bristle, unaccountably. "In its way it's a masterpiece," he told me. "Do you see the house at the top of the hill there on the left?"

I had not noticed the house. Sunlight fell upon the lake, but clouds threw the hilltop into shadow, and the tall gray house was almost lost among the gray skeletons of winter trees. Now that I saw it, I found that here, too, were tiny details that hinted of evil—in pointed towers like pricked ears, in pale windows which wore the strange reflections of anguished faces, in the minute and grotesque carving of the era of Carpenter's Gothic.

"That is High Towers," Glen said. "I've told you about the house where I grew up. The Chandlers own all that land on the far side of the lake, so in a sense Gray Rocks Lake is ours too. Though there are those who would like to spoil it, take it away, if we don't stop them."

There seemed an eerie prickling at the back of my neck and I bent to look more carefully at the scrawled initials signed to the picture. This time I made them out: "G. C."—and I straightened to stare at Glen.

"The painting is yours, isn't it? But why, Glen—why? Is this the sort of thing you used to do?"

He pulled me angrily away. "No, it's not mine! Stop looking at the beastly thing. I own it, but I didn't paint it. Come away!"

I resisted his hand. There was something here that I did not understand and that seemed suddenly urgent for me to know.

"Why don't you want me to look at it? It's really very good, even though it sickens me a little. You needn't be ashamed of it, if you—"

His grip hurt my arm. "I've told you it isn't mine. And I don't want you to look at it because it might prejudice you against the lake and High Towers. I don't want you prejudiced, Dina, because I'm going to take you there. You will come with me, won't you?"

He swung me around to face him and I looked up into

burning dark eyes that held my own, half-challenging, half-pleading. My uneasiness grew.

"Why should I go to High Towers?" I asked.

"Because I need to begin work on the alabaster head that I'm going to do of you, Dina. I need to begin soon, before I lose this feeling that's so hard to come by."

"But I've agreed to pose for you here," I said. "You told me you would work in the studio behind this gallery. I thought we were going to start this week."

He put both hands lightly on my shoulders, and my flesh seemed to lift to his touch, yearn toward his hands. I could not help myself.

"It isn't going to work here," he told me. "The place is wrong. All I have behind me here is failure. Years of horrible failure. I can't risk it this time. At High Towers I've the right piece of stone to work with, too—clear white like ice, with the faintest hint of green. And the place is right. Emotionally right."

I found myself troubled and confused, finding it hard to deny him anything, yet uneasy, nevertheless. High Towers was in northern New Jersey. I didn't want to go to northern New Jersey, just as I didn't want Glen to have blue eyes and black hair. There's a theory that a woman who falls in love once, thereafter falls in love all her life long with the same type of man. I knew that wasn't true. I wanted to escape all likeness forever to Trent McIntyre, who had come from northern New Jersey. I wanted to forget forever that long stride which had walked away from me.

"But Glen, I have a job here in New York," I reminded him. "I've only a toe in the door of what I want to do. They'd never let me off with a leave of absence now. They'd let me go for good. I must think of me, Glen. I must!"

"No," he said, calmly and without arrogance. "This time you must think of me. Of my work. This is life or death for me, Dina. You know that, don't you?"

I knew it. He had convinced me. Yet I was afraid. What would happen to me when he had carved his alabaster masterpiece? Of what use would I be to him then? I stepped back from his hands, turned from the dark pleading in his eyes. Turned away and ran. In that last moment before utter capitulation the need for escape was paramount.

He caught me before I reached the door of the gallery and his mood had changed, as it could so quickly. He overtook me with a triumphant exuberance that whirled me down the long room, whirled me behind a protruding wing where pictures were hung, and out of sight of the street. There he kissed me, half-teasingly at first, then more demandingly. I gave up and kissed him back. None of my doubts were lifted, none of my fears had lessened, but this was where I wanted to be—here in his arms, no matter what the future held.

"We'll be married before I take you home," he told me. "We'll be married here in New York with as little fuss as possible. There's no one at High Towers now except Aunt Naomi, so we can go there for our honeymoon. Then I can start work at home. I want to show you our lake and hills. Winter's coming and there's nothing more beautiful than Gray Rocks when the snow closes us in. Not dirty city snow, but snow a girl from California has never seen."

I was suddenly quiet in his arms. "You don't have to marry me because you need me as a model," I said. "I'll go with you to High Towers. I'll pose for you there. No need to—"

"There's every need," he said and held my head against him, his long fingers caught in my hair.

A whisper went through my mind. How could I marry anyone? How could I give up my foolish dreaming? But I would not listen to such whispering. That was over long ago and there had never been a chance for me anyway. So why shouldn't I substitute new dreams? I let him press my head against him, heard the strong beating of his heart.

"I'm not buying you as a model, my darling," he said. "You're the answer to a great many things for me. You're freedom, escape, success—everything. I can't bear not to have you in my life forever."

What strange words he used—"freedom," "escape." I should have challenged them, questioned them. Though of course he would have told me nothing if I had. He was purposely telling me nothing, lest I be frightened off for good. So I gave in joyfully and did what I wanted to do. This was no matter of skyrockets and sparklers that would burn out in a little while. This was love as it should be—a generous love that I must give to someone who needed me. If I was the giver, and Glen the taker—that did not matter. Often it must be like that, and neither the worse for it. Certainly it was far better than an old painful giving to someone who did not want.

With all my heart I longed to give Glen whatever he needed to make him whole, to make him free of whatever held him back, so that he could work again. That was what he meant by freedom, I told myself—the ability to work, to recover the lost talent that would make him a whole man once more. Besides, I wanted to be free too—free of a man who had once held me in his arms, let me weep on his shoulder, and then put me quietly and firmly out of his life.

The museum was not unduly heartbroken at my resignation, and the next few days were a whirl of activity. Glen would not wait and there was little time for me to get ready properly. Apparently his assistant at the art gallery was accustomed to taking over whenever it was required, so there was no problem there.

We were married in the drab surroundings of the Municipal Building, yet I did not feel at all drab because Glen made it a gala occasion, so gay and vital and alive was he. I felt myself swept along like the tail of a soaring kite that sailed the upper atmosphere wild and scarcely fettered. Thoughts of the future were my last concern. The past I blanked out altogether. The skyrocket had gone off.

I had written my mother a long, enthusiastic letter, and had received a brief note in response. It was a loving note, but she was not able to write very clearly these days, and my aunt added her own words of congratulations, so that I had some family send-off.

Once Glen's plain gold band was on my finger—a ring I chose because I disliked the more elaborate ones he might have bought me—he sent a cable to his father, off somewhere in Portugal, painting the portrait of an exiled king. Glen's mother had died when he was five, and Colton Chandler had never married again, so there was only his one parent to notify. Glen lacked his exact address, but the American Express office in Lisbon would reach him eventually.

"What will your father say?" I asked while Glen was wording the cable. For the first time I wondered seriously what the formidable Colton Chandler, the world-renowned artist, would think of his son's sudden marriage to an unknown girl. For the first time I felt those misgivings I might have had earlier about Glen's father.

Glen wrote the last word on the form and answered my question without smiling. "Colton will be deliriously happy, and after he has seen you he will think he invented you," he said, and I heard something dry in his voice. "My father wants an heir to carry on his name, and hopefully, his far-flung fame. So far I've disappointed him."

"I'd like children," I said warmly.

Glen looked startled. "Let's take our time about that. I want you to myself for a while."

I could not quarrel with that.

When the cable had been sent we went back to Glen's apartment and he phoned "Nomi," as he called his aunt. Again I waited, while he talked to High Towers. Miss Naomi Holmes, his mother's older sister, seemed to take his news in stride, though I thought it inconsiderate of him to give her so little warning that we were coming. But I had already resigned myself to the fact that consideration and forethought were not to be expected from Glen. He enjoyed acting on lively impulse and I loved him for it.

His aunt seemed to accept his news calmly enough, and Glen talked swiftly, affectionately—coaxing her, winning her over. Nevertheless, he did not put me on the line to speak with her, and when he set the phone down he cocked an amused eyebrow.

"She'll turn the house upside down," he said. "She'll do three spring cleanings in one to welcome us."

"But what did she say?" I asked. "What did she say about your marrying me?"

"She said I was the last man in the world to take on the responsibility of a wife, but if I've chosen the right woman, she'll be glad of it. Nomi always speaks her mind. She hopes you're a sensible girl who'll see to it that I'm not given my head completely. Are you, Dina? Are you a sensible girl?"

I shook my head a bit wildly and went into his arms. "I haven't any sense at all," I told him with my lips against his cheek. "And what's more, I couldn't care less."

2

It was the last week in November on a late afternoon when we set off for New Jersey in Glen's car. I loved the drive, even though the countryside was drab and brown, with autumn colors faded, leaves hanging dead on the trees, and the snow not yet come to make everything beautiful again.

I sat beside him, feeling glamorous in the outfit he had bought me before we left New York—white wool coat, furry white wool hat, white boots that came to my knees. I'd never have dressed like this myself but he said I must not ignore my northern blood. I had never had a chance to bring it out before, but as soon as the snow came I would come into my own and I must be ready for it: "You're my winter girl. From your boots to your ice-blond hair, Dina. And don't forget it."

I didn't know about my northern blood, or all this white glamour, but my feeling was wholly one of joy. I had never been so loved, so loving, and I was filled with fine promises that I made to myself and to Glen. I meant to love High Towers and Gray Rocks Lake. Whatever Colton Chandler and Naomi Holmes might feel about Glen's marrying me, I meant to love them too, and try to please them in every way. No one could quarrel with me, disapprove of me, when I wanted so much to please. All my treasured independence was gladly tossed away. No feminine mystique for me! I was born to serve.

Glen was pleased with me. He led and I followed. I had never dreamed I could be such a chameleon, taking on his coloration, his zest and gaiety, even something of his jaunty manner. I was playmate and lover, co-conspirator—and sometimes, a little to my surprise, I was a mother as well. Glen had his dark moods when he frightened me with the depth of some despair that seemed both to drive him and hold him back. Perhaps that was when he saw the will-o'-the-wisp of inspiration vanishing, and I knew he was afraid that when he faced the block of white alabaster which waited for him at High Towers, when I actually sat before him in just the pose he wanted and he took his chisel and hammer in hand, the entire bright dream would dissolve as a rainbow dissolves when you near it. In those moments he was sure that he fooled himself most of all, and it was my task to keep the vision bright and untarnished in his mind, so that when the time came it would not forsake him.

For the most part I succeeded, and when we set out that late afternoon on the long drive to northern New Jersey our mood was zestful and merry. I loved his car, just as I loved everything else. It was a low-slung Jaguar, built for speed—a creamy white, arrogant sort of car that shouted down all other cars on the highway. Of course Glen would never have driven a dark car. He had found me to match the car, he said, and we laughed together and could not have been more carefree. Too carefree? Too heedless?

As we drove, I went on asking him questions. Learning all I could about my husband was endlessly fascinating. He had been born at High Towers, lived at Gray Rocks Lake as a boy, and he loved this country area. His memories, oddly enough, were more of winter fun and sports than of the lazy summertime. There was skiing in Sussex County, and of course skating on the lake, and sledding on the hills. He spoke of the Christmas season with special feeling, and I knew he was looking forward to that holiday this year. Yet in everything he told me I sensed a gap. Almost as though he left out something important, held something back. But if there were deliberate gaps in his story, I could hardly object when there were gaps in my story too. We weren't children.

"Is High Towers really your family home?" I wanted to know. "And for how far back?"

He laughed at me. "For as far back as Colton. An old friend of his who lived across the lake at the time—he's died since—told him about the property when it went on sale, and he bought it just before I was born. But you'd think to hear Colton that it was a Chandler who built it eighty years ago. And, by the way, you'll have to call him Colton too. He doesn't hold with much fathering."

The neon jungle of the commuting area was left quickly behind, and the towns grew smaller, less closely clustered. There were long stretches of country road winding through brown November hills. I watched the names of the towns. We passed the turn-offs to Kinelon and Smoke Rise, and a few miles later we reached Stockholm and were in Sussex County. Gray Rocks and High Towers were in Sussex.

We stopped for gas at Franklin, a town, Glen told me, that was famous for its mineral ores, and we had dinner in a comfortable restaurant that had once been a governor's mansion. It was dark when we set off again. This was Hamburg Mountain we were crossing now, he said. Like so many American towns, the place names told of early settlers—German, Swede, Englishman, Austrian—those who remembered their homes with nostalgia and named the villages in the new land for the cities they had loved.

We would make a stop in the town of Sussex, Glen said. There was an errand he must do there, but he would leave me in a warm place to wait for him. Just before we reached the town, he turned off the road into a parking place before an auto supply shop that apparently served as bus terminal as well. I stepped out into half-frozen slush, spattering my white boots. The cold dry air was bracing, and overhead stars were bright and clear.

Glen took me inside the brightly lighted shop and nodded

to the man behind the counter. "Hello, Sam. Mind if I leave my wife here for a few minutes?"

I was aware of a sudden silence in the shop. The few people who were making purchases stared at me guardedly, and the shopowner came from behind the counter to shake hands with me.

"So you've married a Chandler?" he said. I could sense that Glen was suddenly edgy and anxious to get away.

"I'll be fine here," I told him. "I'll wait for you." I did not even wonder about his errand, or question it.

Sam echoed my words. "She'll be fine," he said, and escorted me gallantly to a bench reserved for bus passengers, waving me onto it: "Make yourself at home, Mrs. Chandler." I sat down feeling conspicuous in my cover-girl white wool. Conspicuous and overdressed and out of place.

Gradually the heads turned away and I sat stiffly, with a small smile pressed onto my lips, wishing that I had waited in the car. Only one person in the shop did not cease to stare, and so intent was his look that it drew my eyes and I finally turned my head a little haughtily to return his glance. I supposed it was natural that I should be a curiosity in a small town, having newly married into a famous family, but I was beginning to feel that this particular stare was more rude than interested.

The eyes I met were those of a boy of about sixteen. He wore a checked red and black cap over a shock of dark brown hair and his long legs were encased in blue jeans, his feet in short, rugged leather boots. He had already outgrown his jacket at the wrists and his hands hung from sleeves that were too short for him. Nothing about the boy distinguished him from others his age, except perhaps his knowledgeable eyes. They were wide and dark-lashed, intensely blue beneath the upward stroke of his brows, and they were fixed upon me with the stare that a rabbit might give a cobra. Or was it the other way around? He looked avidly curious and not a little hostile. Something had to be done to break that stare. I smiled and spoke to him.

"Hello," I said. "I'm Dina Chandler. Who are you?"

He blinked brown lashes and touched his lips with the tip of his tongue, deciding. Then he came to my bench and sat beside me.

"I'm Keith McIntyre," he said—and waited, his eyes still intent, as though the name should ring some bell with me, startle me in some way.

But he couldn't have known! He could not know that to me McIntyre was a name out of the hurtful past. There were many McIntyres, and I did not so much as blink my recognition of the name.

"How-do-you-do," I said, stiffly polite. "Do you always stare at newcomers like that?"

A slow flush crept up his young smooth face, and his brows drew into a scowl. "You're a surprise," he admitted. "Does Glynis know about you?"

Everyone in the store was listening again. Not staring, after what I had said to the boy, but not talking either.

"I don't know anyone named Glynis," I told him. "Should I?"

A buzz of whispering commenced, and everyone stared, as if unable to help whispering and staring. I wished myself outside. Wished that Glen had not left me here without any warning about the stir I might cause among the townspeople.

I looked around the shop with the same pseudo-haughty regard I had given the boy, and everyone became at once very busy. The boy flung me a look of astonishment and went off to make some purchases of his own.

Relieved that curiosity had at least been momentarily veiled, I sat very still, trying to attract no further interest, wishing Glen would hurry. No one was paying any attention to me when the door opened and a man walked in. He was tall and broad-shouldered and black-haired. He wore rough country clothes, as did the boy, and his eyes were as intensely blue. A black-haired Scottish father he'd had, and an Irish mother with blue eyes. I ought to know!

He looked at me—the cover girl in dazzling white—and looked away without interest. Then back again. Recognition lightened his eyes and he came straight toward me.

"Bernardina!" he cried. "Bernardina grown up!"

It was his look of unguarded pleasure that undid me. I went hot all over, and then cold. I felt as though my face was blazing at the same time that my hands had turned to ice. My mouth was dry and my palms perspiring. The violence of a purely physical reaction was like a blow. All these pins and needles and sudden sick churning because of a man I had not seen for eight years! A man with whom I had been wildly, foolishly, headstrongly in love at sixteen! I folded my hands together, idiotically hiding my wedding ring.

"H-how did you know me?" I asked lamely, trying to still the churning, trying to catch my inner balance.

"A good question," he said, "considering that the last time I saw you, you wore an old pair of shorts you'd out-grown, a blouse you'd just torn on a nail, and you were show-ing a great deal of golden skin the color of a California peach. Now all I can see is Madame Igloo, wrapped around in white. But I knew you."

He used to talk like that sometimes, rolling words on his tongue as though he tried them out before committing them to paper.

"I wondered how you'd grown up," he went on. "I won-dered if your hair would darken—has it? I can't see under that hat. And if you'd lose your lost-little-girl look that bowled me over. Have you?"

I was beginning to collect myself in an uncertain sort of way. I hoped he had not seen too much.

"I've lost it," I said lightly. "I only looked like that be-cause you broke my heart and threw me over. All that sixteen-year-old puppy love—and you threw it away!"

"You were a darling puppy," he said gently, and I remembered his unnerving gentleness. "I was flattered that you should think yourself in love with me. I even hoped—a bit selfishly, I'll admit—that you wouldn't recover with too much speed. Did you?"

"I recovered," I said, and heard the false note in my voice. Perhaps no woman ever really recovers from first love.

She simply grows up a bit and goes on to other things. More important things, she hopes.

The boy came back from making his purchases and confronted us both. "Hey, Dad—do you know her? Do you know who she is?"

So this was the son who had been eight years old when I knew Trent McIntyre. The son about whom I had not wanted to think, and whose mother I'd hated without ever seeing her.

"Of course I know who she is," Trent said. "She's an old friend of mine—Miss Bernardina Blake."

"Oh no she's not!" The boy was emphatic. "She's Glen's wife—that's who she is. Glen Chandler's wife!"

The same odd stillness that had earlier smitten the shop settled over the boy's father. I saw the tightening of his facial muscles, the hard line of his jaw. I had never seen him look like that. He had changed too—a very great deal. His blue eyes studied me, took in my glamour-girl outfit, my high white boots already streaked with muddy slush—and it was as if a blind were pulled down somewhere behind his eyes. As if a door closed suddenly, implacably, in my face.

"She doesn't know who Glynis is," the boy said with wonder in his voice.

The man stirred and held out a hand to me—but the blind stayed down, the door was permanently closed. "Welcome to Sussex," he said. "I'm afraid my son has forgotten whatever manners he was presumably brought up with. We're your neighbors in the stone house across Gray Rocks Lake. At least my son lives there with his grandmother, and I'm home for a month or two, working on a book."

He did not mention his wife—and it made no difference. Not any more.

"I'm afraid I don't know very much about the lake yet," I said. "Or about the people who live there. Glen said it was because of an old friend that Colton Chandler bought High Towers years ago when he was first married."

Trent nodded. "Colton and my father were old friends,

25

and Dad used to bring him out here when they were boys. Small world. How long have you been married?''

''Since early this week,'' I said, somehow hating to tell him. As though, in some curious way, I had been faithless to my true love. Which was certainly absurd.

''Glynis always comes home for Christmas,'' the boy broke in. ''So you'll meet her then.''

I spoke to Trent. ''Who is this Glynis your son thinks I should know about?''

He answered me curtly. ''Perhaps you'd better ask your husband about Glynis. Come along, Keith. If you've found what you want, let's get going. We'll probably see you again, Dina.''

Dina, he called me. Not Bernardina—not ever Bernardina again. I knew that now.

The boy picked up a paper sack from a counter, but before he reached the door, Glen opened it and walked in. The two men met face to face and I sensed a leaping hostility between them before they exchanged a cool greeting. Then Trent McIntyre turned to give me a last straight look from eyes I remembered too well.

''If you find yourself lonely, Mrs. Chandler, come around the lake and call on my mother. She'll enjoy having you visit her.''

''I won't be lonely,'' I said valiantly. ''But thank you, anyway.''

He had not acknowledged knowing me in the past, and I let the chance to clarify slip by. After all—what could I say?

He and the boy went out the door, leaving a rush of chill air to pour in behind.

Glen smiled at me and held out his hand. And as suddenly as that everything was right again. My world stopped tipping uncontrollably sideways, and I knew who I was.

''Come along, darling,'' he said. ''We'll go straight home now.''

I jumped up and rushed out of the shop with him, hurrying to leave all those eyes behind, wanting to be alone with my husband. I felt relieved—so terribly relieved—because after all that churning, and burning with ice, I hadn't been sure what would happen when I saw Glen again. But it was all right. Some lost young girl in me still remembered Trent McIntyre. But the woman knew Glen Chandler. I was Mrs. Chandler.

Neither of us spoke until we were in the car. "Sorry to drop you into the enemy camp back there," he said as we turned onto the road and headed out of town. "But I had another cable I needed to send and I got it off by phone."

"What do you mean—enemy camp?" I asked.

"The McIntyres." He shrugged expressively. "Our local feud. Dora McIntyre—Pandora, we call her—is determined to open up the lake to a development she wants to build. Fortunately, she doesn't own the land—we do. Her son's aiding and abetting her, of course. He's a journalist—turns out the biography type of thing. The everything-there-is-to-know-about-the-Roosevelts sort of thing."

Indignantly, I almost spoke up. I knew those biographies—every one of his collected pieces. My father was written up—and beautifully, honestly—in his book on great teachers. Something of my joy over this homecoming to High Towers had gone out of me. I would hate this feud. I wanted no part of it.

"Forget about the McIntyres," Glen said. "There's time for all that unpleasantness another day. Dina, my darling, we're going home. We're almost there."

The road was winding again, the town lost behind us as we left the main highway and took a secondary road branching into the hills. I sat in silence, stiff and unrelaxed, somehow threatened. On either hand woods crowded the road and the car began to climb, but I could take no delight in the approach to High Towers. The name that had been spoken back in the shop kept ringing through my mind.

"Who is Glynis?" I said at last.

Glen slowed his speed abruptly and glanced at me in the light from the dashboard. "Where did you hear her name?"

"That boy back there. Keith McIntyre. He asked if Glynis knew about our marriage."

"And Keith's father? What did Trent say?"

"Nothing. He told me to ask you."

Glen laughed softly. "And he frightened you badly, I suppose? That's like him. You needn't worry, darling. Though it's because of Glynis that I stopped in town. She's in London and I sent her a cable. I wanted it to come from Sussex, not from New York. Glynis is my sister, Dina."

I couldn't have been more astonished. "Your sister? But why haven't you told me you had a sister?"

He reached across to cover my hand with his. "Wait, darling. Let Glynis go for now. This time is ours—it doesn't belong to my exotic family. Here—I want to show you something. I want to show you why I used the term feud when I spoke of the McIntyres. Our lake is out there just beyond those trees, though you can't see it in the dark. We're at the north end of it here."

We jolted over a narrow rustic bridge that crossed a stream, and Glen turned the car into a wide clearing before a long, low building that could not be High Towers. The headlights cut a swathe across the rambling, many-windowed redwood structure and came to rest upon a sign prominently displayed: GRAY ROCKS INN.

I turned in puzzlement to Glen. "But I thought you said the lake was wild, almost uninhabited?"

"It used to be," he said curtly. "Until Pandora—Trent's mother—built that monstrosity two years ago. 'Pandora's Box,' we call it. Fortunately, it hasn't done much business, though she's gaining a clientele that comes out from New York during the summer months, and she opens it up for winter party dinners when she gets an order. If she could have her way and build the development she plans along the east shore of the lake, our wilderness will be gone for good. But we still own enough of the land on both sides to stop her. Or at least my father does."

I stared at the sign in dismay. In my mind I had pictured a heavenly seclusion—woods and hills, with the lake lost among them, enclosed by their reaching arms, shutting out all the noisy world.

28

"But if you own the land so she can't go ahead, doesn't that settle it?" I asked.

"Colton is unpredictable. But the matter must be settled soon. He'll be coming home for Christmas. Then we'll persuade him to stop the McIntyres."

"And Glynis comes home for Christmas too? Your sister?"

"I don't know," he said. "She's unpredictable too." He started the motor and then slipped an arm about me, drew me close, pressing his face into the soft white wool of my collar. "At least *I* am predictable! And you know what I'm predicting for us—the beginning of a marvelous honeymoon—with High Towers and Gray Rocks all to ourselves. Our side of it, at least. What's more, tomorrow we'll start work. You'll pose for me and everything will go beautifully. It's still with me, Dina—the vision. And I don't mean to lose it this time. Before Christmas comes we'll be safe. You'll see."

Safe? Safe from what? I wondered. But I did not ask. I turned my face for his kiss, and we left the redwood inn behind and wound along a hillside road to the foot of a drive. The car bumped over muddy ruts onto its white stone surface and we began to climb steeply, winding through weedy spruce and up into tall cedars that looked black in the shining headlights.

By the time we reached a wide cleared space at the top of the hill, the moon had risen above the pines and its light shone full upon the gray house with its tall, pricked ears. As I got out of the car and stood looking up at lighted windows, at turrets and cupolas and high balconies, the imprint of the picture I had seen in Glen's gallery was sharp in my mind. I did not want to remember but I had the feeling that having seen it, I would never be free of that dreadful, wicked picture, signed with the initials, *"G.C."* Looking up at the windows, I could almost see the reflections of anguished faces pressed against the glass, peering out at me—the faces of old, never-to-be-forgotten suffering.

"Your sister painted it, didn't she?" I said. "That picture of the lake in your gallery—your sister Glynis painted it!"

He spoke to me more sharply than I'd ever heard him do. "Stop it, Dina! Glynis isn't going to touch what we have between us. Just remember that. That picture was her fantasy. It's the way her mind turns sometimes. Forget about it. This is the real High Towers, and it's waiting for *us*."

Glen's Aunt Naomi must have heard the car, for the front door of the house was pulled open to let a band of light fall across the front veranda, and down a broad flight of steps. Against the lighted doorway stood the slight figure of a woman dressed in a long gray housecoat that fell to her toes. Her white hair was piled high upon her head in intricate convolutions, and the hall light, shining through it, made it an aureole.

"Nomi!" Glen cried. He pulled me by the hand and we ran together across the white stones of the drive and up the steps. Glen caught her in his arms and swung her around upon the veranda. She patted his hands away in mock reproach, pleased and smiling. Smiling so long as she looked at him. Then suddenly grave when she turned to me.

"Welcome to High Towers," she said soberly. "Come in out of the cold. Come in, both of you."

We followed her into the narrow hallway that ran from front to back of the house, and its length was familiar to me because I had already seen it through Glen's eyes. Somehow I was thankful that his sister had not painted the interior of the house. The architect who had built High Towers eighty years ago had believed in spacious rooms, and wasted very little grace on halls and stairs. A Victorian chandelier still hung just inside the front door, lighting the foot of the steep, polished stairway, but the bulbs in its many sockets were dim and not all of them were lighted, so that one had a sense of peering into dimness where the hall vanished beyond, like a tunnel whose other end is lost in darkness.

"I've hot chocolate ready for you," Aunt Nomi was saying. "Take Dina into the drawing room, Glen dear. There's

30

a fire to warm you. You didn't give me much time, but I've done what I could to prepare.''

In the dim light of the hall I could not see her very well, but I was aware of someone who moved with dignity and grace, and with a very great reserve.

Glen laughed and caught her by one hand. ''Nomi has never learned! I'll want something stronger than hot chocolate, but I'll get it for myself. You and Dina can have the chocolate, Nomi. My wife isn't civilized. Not yet.''

Nomi disappeared at the rear of the dim hall and Glen flung open the door on our right, ushering me into the most beautiful room I had ever seen. Its size was enormous, its plastered ceiling vaulted, with a crystal chandelier dripping glass teardrops which winked in reflected lamp- and firelight. It was a room full of color. Color that shocked and yet entranced. The huge rare Chinese rug was of the palest lemon, and the four Victorian sofas the room harbored comfortably were upholstered in velvet. Two of them in apricot, two in dark purple. Several rosewood chairs were cushioned in turquoise, and everywhere there were small tables and ornaments and exquisite bibelots. One wall was solidly hung with paintings, and I glimpsed Picasso, Braque, and a Matisse—all originals. On the opposite wall was a single, honored portrait. Flames leaped invitingly in the wide grate, and across the white marble mantel marched a row of African sculptures, tall against the mirror that reflected them. The eighteenth and nineteenth centuries blended at every turn and lived together in harmony with the twentieth-century paintings.

Glen was aware of my rapt gaze. ''Glynis did this room,'' he said. ''Glynis and I together—but mainly Glynis. The African things are mine. Let me help you with your coat, Dina.''

I slipped out of the white wool coat, my eyes finding more and more detail in the room to charm me. It was a lived-in museum, and I felt unexpectedly at home. Glen flung the coat over his arm and held me off to study me in my silver-gray wool sheath that I'd belted with a linked silver chain he had bought for me at Tiffany's.

"Perfect," he said. "How was I lucky enough to find you? Enjoy the room—you belong to it now. I'll be right back."

Of course it was lovely to be admired, to be thought more beautiful than anyone else had ever found me, and to be dressed as I had never been dressed before. I was in my all-giving mood, my only intention to be everything Glen wanted me to be.

When he had gone across the hall to the dining room for his brandy, I moved about with delight, reassured in all I saw. I would like Glynis. Obviously we would have much in common. The faintly unsettling undercurrent of the auto shop was fading under new impressions, new encounters.

It was possible that Aunt Naomi was going to be more difficult when it came to finding common ground than would Glen's sister. I had been aware of her watchful attention, of a certain holding back as though she waited to test and try me. This was natural enough and I must not mind. There was no reason why Glen's aunt should receive so sudden a bride with open arms. Yet this left me with the burden of making an approach and I had a feeling that Naomi Holmes would not be an easy woman to know.

Inevitably the portrait that held an entire wall to itself drew me. This would be Colton Chandler's work, of course, and I stood before it, giving it my full attention. It was the full-length portrait of a boy and girl of about seventeen or eighteen. The bold, clear modern lines, the inner excitement that made a portrait by Colton Chandler a work of genius was there. Behind the two seated figures a thin-curtained window hinted at distant woods. His portraits were never static. The two figures in this picture leaned toward one another with an edge of curtain lifting in a breeze behind them, as if engaged in eager, and obviously lively, conversation. I saw at once that the boy was Glen—a darkly handsome youth with bright chestnut hair, dark eyes, and a straight, sensitive mouth. But it was the girl who startled me. In every respect, except for the length of her chestnut hair, she was a duplicate of Glen.

Even their clothing was similar. Both wore well-cut fawn trousers, open-throated white shirts with pale yellow sweaters flung about their shoulders. Both pairs of feet were encased in soft-cuffed jodhpur boots that came just above their ankles. Their faces showed three quarters as they bent toward each other, and the girl had reached out with a riding crop to tap the boy on the knee. The half-smile each wore, the light challenge of dark eyes, the shapely ears revealed by the girl's hair, drawn back with a yellow ribbon, and by Glen's closer cropping—all were duplicates, one of the other. Glen and Glynis were more than brother and sister. They were clearly twins, and as close to identical as a boy and girl could be.

Aunt Nomi came through the door bearing an antique tole tray laden with delicate cups and plates.

"We've no live-in household help these days," she said. "I like to do things myself with off-and-on assistance from town. Besides, that's why I came here—to keep house for Chandlers."

I hurried to clear a place for her on a coffee table before the fire, and then stood back to regard the portrait again.

"They're twins, aren't they?" I said.

She straightened from lowering the tray to the table and gave me a direct look from brown eyes shadowed with dark lashes. She had yet to smile at me.

"Didn't he tell you?" she asked.

I shook my head. "I didn't know he had a sister until a little while ago."

She shrugged gray-clad shoulders lightly and motioned me into a turquoise chair. "I'm not surprised."

I had to learn the answer to this mystery. If Glen wouldn't tell me about his sister perhaps Nomi would.

"But why? If they are look-alike twins, they probably are alike, and Glen is the loveliest person I've ever met."

She paused in pouring chocolate from a silver pot and gave me another appraising look. "Lovely is a strange word for either twin. Mind you, I'm very fond of Glen, but lovely is not the word I'd use for him. Exciting, dashing, debonair, wild—all those words fit both twins. But lovely they aren't. Just remember one thing. They *are* duplicates. Duplicates clear through and in almost every way.''

''Then I'll love Glynis too,'' I said warmly.

She handed me my chocolate in a Sèvres cup and sipped her own without comment.

I could feel time slipping away. ''Why do you like Glen and not Glynis, when they are so nearly alike?'' I asked her boldly.

She stirred the dark, creamy mixture, frowning at it. ''You'll never do,'' she said. ''Too much spunk. You won't leave things alone. You'll poke and pry and be curious. You'll try to mend things. I can tell. You must have fooled him badly.''

''Oh, please!'' I cried in dismay. ''I'm sorry if I've said the wrong thing. It's just that all this has happened to me so suddenly. I'm still trying to orient myself.''

''Yes.'' She seemed to nod to herself. ''He probably whirled you into this in a rush that took your breath away. I've been wondering why ever since he phoned me. You're pretty enough, but so are other girls. And up to now he has never married.''

''Other girls are not like Dina!'' That was Glen's voice as he came through the doorway, brandy glass in hand.

I turned to him eagerly for help. ''Your Aunt Naomi wonders why you married me. And sometimes I do, too!''

She made a snorting sound, but before she could speak, Glen came to drop a reassuring kiss on my cheek. ''Take off your hat, Dina.'' He did not wait for me to obey, but pulled it off himself, to reveal my hair. I had twisted it on top of my head, and as he pulled off the hat it fell loose around my shoulders.

Naomi Holmes stared at me in surprise. ''Good heavens, girl—you're almost as silver as I am!''

''Except that Dina's silver-gilt isn't due to her years, or to something from a bottle,'' Glen said. ''It grew that way. It's as natural as she is. As honest.''

I could feel warmth sweep into my cheeks and I smiled at

him, pleased. So he did know a little about me, after all. I liked to think of myself as honest—though that very trait sometimes got me into trouble.

"So you married her for her hair?" Aunt Nomi said tartly.

He laughed in amusement and came to sit beside her on the apricot sofa. "Only partly. Nomi, my love, this is a dream, a vision you see before you in the shape of a girl."

He toasted me with his brandy and I took refuge in my cooling chocolate, unsure of myself and troubled by this exchange.

"She's been in my mind all along," he continued. "I've been watching for her. Then I walked into a museum in New York and there she was—standing on a tabletop, waiting for me."

"In a glass case?" Nomi said.

"Not exactly, though it would have been nice if I could have found her that way. But don't you see, Nomi—she's the girl I can do in alabaster. Icy white alabaster with a hint of green. Green like her eyes. Have you noticed her eyes?"

"The alabaster that's upstairs in the studio waiting for you?" Nomi said, paying no attention to my eyes. "Oh, Glen! If only you would!"

"I'm going to," he said. "Tomorrow morning I'm going to begin."

"That's marvelous!" She did a rather surprising thing. She rose and walked to Colton Chandler's portrait of the twins and stood before it, a small, self-possessed woman in gray. "Now he'll show you!" she said, and I knew she was speaking to the girl in the picture—to Glynis who was my husband's twin sister.

"Do you know when she's coming home?" Glen asked, and I heard a faint edge in his voice.

"Does anyone ever know?" Nomi tossed over her shoulder.

Glen drained the last of his brandy and looked at me with bright dark eyes that were somehow triumphant. "There'll be time. I waited to cable her. But whatever she does, I'll be launched and this time I'll finish. I needn't have it completed before she comes. I only need to be far enough along to prove what I can do.''

He seemed to be speaking a foreign language that I didn't understand.

''Doesn't your sister approve of your work?'' I asked.

''My sister is part of my work,'' he told me.

Nomi took pity on my bewilderment. ''It isn't his work she'll disapprove of, my dear. It's you.''

''Not this time!'' Glen said quickly. ''This time it's too late.''

All my first doubts and uneasiness were back full force. I did not like the sound of those words—''this time.''

''What happens after the alabaster head is finished?'' I asked. ''What happens to me then?''

''That's a good question,'' Nomi said.

Glen laughed at us both. ''How fearful you are! Don't you have more confidence in me—you two? Doesn't a man who wants a child cherish its mother forever? Doesn't he love her for herself—not just because of the child she produced for him?''

I felt reassured, my faith in him strengthened. ''I'm not fearful, really, and I know what fine work you're going to do.''

Nomi gave me a quick look that might be approval, and came back to us. ''You've had a long drive, Dina. I'm sure you'd like to see your room. Let me take you upstairs. Glen, will you bring in your bags?''

Purposefully, she picked up my coat which Glen had laid across a chair, and I caught up my hat and went with her. Glen nodded at me, and I knew I had somehow pleased him, though I had no idea how or why.

At the foot of the stairs Nomi flicked a switch and a light came on at the top, subdued to dimness by an amber shade. Glen went out the front door to fetch our bags and I followed his aunt upstairs.

''No one has mentioned Glen's father,'' I said, climbing behind her. ''How will Mr. Chandler feel about our marriage?''

She answered me carelessly. "He'll be pleased enough. Especially if you produce another Chandler. They're a clan, you know. You'll always be an outsider. Just as I am."

"But what about *me*?" I addressed the straight back that moved to the top of the steep staircase ahead of me. "Will he like me?"

"The Chandlers aren't very much aware of other people," she said dryly and marched down the narrow, dim hall, small and defiantly erect. "I hope you'll like your room." She flung open a door. "It's really the best bedroom in the house, overlooking the lake as it does, and being the largest, as well. Colton is home so little that he doesn't mind what his room is like. He's in the attic studio most of the time anyway. Glynis hates to look at the lake, so her room is at the front of the house, overlooking the drive, and Glen's old room was next to hers, on one side. I have a lake-view room, too. I took what was left over when I came here, and I've grown fond of it, small as it is."

"Then this is your guest room you're giving us?" I asked as she touched a switch that lighted dressing table lamps across the room.

"It was my sister Elizabeth's room," Nomi said. "Colton's wife. The twins' mother. She loved Victorian things— old pieces that have been handed down in my own family. I hope you can stand the stuff. I can't."

I saw the welcoming wood fire in the grate and I was aware of dark mahogany and rosewood, an oval rug and expanses of bare floor, kept shining with wax. But it was the amazing bed that dominated the room. I knew enough about American furniture to recognize a Belter bed when I saw one. This was of his later period when he had gone wildly ornate. The rosewood was dark, almost purple, with the expected streakings of black, and I knew it was laminated work, because no ordinary wood would take this lacy carving. Nor could solid wood be molded into the undulating curves of this design. The back rose to a great carved peak at the top, curving downward like rounded shoulders to enclose the bed on either hand. The side boards dipped low and then rose to another curve that enclosed the foot. The supports were huge round pedestals, low, stubby and without beauty, intended only to hold the weight of the bed. The whole thing was straight out of history and I walked around it, examining every detail, delighted at the prospect of sleeping in such a bed. Belter had designed other furniture, of course, but beds had been his specialty.

Nomi watched me dryly and let me look. Perhaps she was relieved that for the moment I had stopped asking questions. Hers could not be an easy role in this household of Chandlers, and now I had come to add to her difficult problems.

"Good Lord!" Glen, his hands full of bags, stood in the doorway. "Nomi, angel, why on earth *this* room? And what are we to do with that mausoleum of a bed!"

"You and Glynis were born in it." The tart note was in her voice again. "Have you told Dina about the blizzard that raged the night you were born? When Colton couldn't get out, and the phone lines were down. Between us, Cook and I managed. Elizabeth lived and you twins were born unmarked and beautiful. At least outwardly. Sometimes I've wondered if that blizzard did something to you that's out of sight." But she smiled now as she lightened her tone.

"Nomi has a fantastic imagination," Glen told me. He dropped the bags and strode about the room, whistling in dismay. "I suppose it will have to do. Mother may have loved the room, but there are times when it gives me goose bumps. No matter—we can get rid of the museum aspects, and—"

"Get rid of a Belter bed?" I asked in astonishment and patted one carved shoulder lovingly.

"At least you'll have your own bathroom," Nomi put in. "And you probably won't stay here at High Towers all that long, will you, Glen?"

"If I can work, I'll stay forever!" Glen said.

"Of course you'll work, darling," I told him. "And if you like we *will* stay forever." I crossed the room, heedless of Nomi's dry observance, and flung my arms about his neck, kissed him warmly.

He must have given his aunt a look over the top of my head. "You see, Nomi? You see the treasure I've found?"

She said, "Humph," and the sound was noncommittal, unflattering. She turned her back and went to make sure of towels in the bathrooms, of fresh bars of the pine-scented soap that would always remind me of High Towers.

Glen did not release me. All the bright spirit I loved in him was evident. At least his homecoming was as it should be—exhilarating, joyful, offering promise of whatever it was he wanted most.

"Thanks for everything, Nomi," he called to her, "It's good to have someone to count on. You'll like my snow girl when you get to know her."

She gave him a smile that told of old affection. Because I was in his arms her smile might be for me as well, and I smiled back. I wanted Nomi to like me. I wanted to like her. I wanted to love everyone connected with Glen.

When she left, closing the door softly behind, Glen looked after her with a gentleness on his face I had seldom seen.

"She has always done her best for me," he said. "I can hardly remember my mother—she died when I was so young. And Colton was always away, or too preoccupied with his own work to take a really thoughtful interest in a child. But Nomi has a lot of love to give and after her sister was gone, she poured it out on me. She was always here to turn to, and in a way I didn't mind not having a mother."

I liked the way he spoke of her and I warmed to them both.

"I hope she'll like me!" I cried.

"No one could help liking you," he said, and I knew I could not ask for a happier start for a honeymoon.

3

The next morning the skies were gray, the day cold, and I had a sense of winter coming, of the dark earth waiting. Not asleep, but waiting for the winds and storms that would threaten, the snow and ice that would encase it. But the huge Belter bed had been snugly warm and I had slept soundly until Glen kissed me awake when daylight streaked the window. I moved to him sleepily, wanting my fill of love, but he left the bed as I reached for him, leaving me surprised and uncertain, as I had already been once or twice in his arms. I told myself that these were merely the adjustments of a very new marriage, and tried to put the sense of doubt from my mind.

I rose that morning filled with a curious mixture of desire to surrender my will to whatever Glen wanted of me, and at the same time a determination to fight, if necessary, for my place in this house, and my right to be Glen's wife. Perhaps the two were not contradictory, since it was only to Glen that I would be submissive. If Nomi, and the other two when they came, chose not to like me, I would hardly crawl away and die of grief over the fact.

"You're looking pretty resolute this morning," Glen said as we went downstairs.

"I'm all of that." In this brave morning light, however gray the day, I felt afraid of no one and nothing. Not of the dark, listening house, nor of Glen's formidable relatives. Such courage I had that morning—and no thought at all for the dark Scotch-Irishman across the lake.

We breakfasted in a dining room with pale cream walls, Sheraton furniture and a painting of Monet water lilies over the buffet. Dark green brocade draperies had been drawn back, and I sat on Glen's right hand where I could look out between them through a large picture window, over treetops and down toward the silvery, early morning pewter of the lake.

The three of us were surprisingly gay that morning. Nomi was adjusting well, Glen whispered when she went to the kitchen to make him a second serving of pancakes. This morning she looked less unapproachable, less the self-possessed, rather grand lady she had seemed last night. She had substituted a trim shirtwaist dress for the long gray gown, and that made her seem less formidable. Her white hair had abandoned its convolutions and was wound neatly about her head in braids that gave her a coronet and raised her height. Beneath the pale crown her face seemed untroubled—as though she might have accepted the change in Glen's life, accepted me.

I had braided my own hair this morning, to let it hang down my back, with a black velvet ribbon at the nape of my neck, holding it in place. Glen would want it loose later, but I liked it out of the way for now. At Glen's prompting I had put on my green slacks and a pale green sweater set, because it might be chilly in the attic, where we must get to work right after breakfast.

Nomi would not hear of my helping with the dishes, so the moment we left the table, Glen took me upstairs. The narrow flight to the attic was at the back of the house near our bedroom door, and Glen went ahead of me to switch on lights. Then he reached down his hand to pull me up the last few steps.

I climbed up to him with my new determination bright as a polished penny—and probably worth about as much. After all, before I could be determined about anything I must find my course of action. That Glen was in need, I had no doubt. I sensed in him a quite terrible and driving need, to which I must somehow contribute an answer. I must be the one to bend gently, but perhaps I must also lead a little, once I knew the course. I could see myself playing to the hilt this tender and generously helpful role. The picture made me glow a little.

The attic space was enormous, stretching above the entire house, with the ceiling high and peaked, so that one could walk about in comfort in most places. Dormers and gables cut into it on either side, and in three places Colton Chandler had placed skylights in the roof, so that whatever northern daylight was available shone into the room. In spite of windows and skylights, however, the place had its shadowy corners and these Glen quickly illumined with lamplight. Except for dull throw rugs here and there the expanse under foot was without covering, utilitarian, and the studio areas had been floored in vinyl tile, to be easily cleaned.

"When he's working, Colton wants as little distraction as possible," Glen said. "The entire front end of the house is his. We've installed fiber screens that can be pulled across that section when he's home and wants privacy. Glynis and I have divided up the center of the house. That's her dormer area there, and this is mine. She paints quite seriously, you know."

There was no dividing screen for the twins. On one side was the busy paraphernalia of the working artist—easel, work table smeared with daubs of paint, a stained palette, numerous brushes standing about in jelly glasses. On the other side there was very little of the workman in evidence. The sturdy worktable was all too neat and unused. An easel had been folded away against the wall. The turntable stood empty. No paints, no brushes, no tools of any kind lay ready for use, but I saw that a narrow wall between the dormers had been lined with drawers. Glen went to these and began to take out chisels, mallets, points—tools of the sculptor's art. I stood watching as he laid them in order upon the table, examining each with care, studying sharp instruments for their edge.

There was a glow about him this morning, an eagerness to be at work that promised well. For the moment he was absorbed in handling his tools, and I could only wait until he should want me, tell me what to do.

I crossed to the side where his sister worked when she was home. In Glen's twin sister might very well lie the answers to many things that puzzled me about him. Besides, if I was to make her my friend and ally, I needed to know everything about her that I could learn.

Over here paintings were stacked against the walls, some framed, some masked with cardboard mats. Apparently she was enormously prolific in her production.

"Would she mind if I looked at her work?" I asked Glen.

He scarcely glanced my way. "Do as you like. What does it matter whether she'd mind or not?"

An odd answer, but I chose a stack leaning against the wall below a dormer and picked up the top one, turning it to the light. At once my attention was caught, as it had been by that painting I had seen in New York. Again the style was pseudo-primitive, with a technique that only a first-rate artist would attain. Glynis Chandler had painted Gray Rocks Lake in the winter season. This was an eerie night scene, lighted partly by the vast stretch of snow-covered lake—snow over ice—with more of the smothering whiteness climbing the far hill beneath scrubby black spruce trees. These were not tall blue spruces—the dignified trees of my memory—but a ragged, weedy second growth. However, all this was mere background for the dramatic scene at one end of the lake where flames shot high in the air, tossing out minute, glowing sparks, casting a sickly yellow light across the snow. Greedy red and orange tongues licked high, consuming the building that was on fire. In Glynis's imagination Gray Rocks Inn was burning and she had portrayed the event in all its horrid detail.

On the bank before the inn tiny figures ran frantically about, pouring futile buckets of water onto the holocaust. A fire engine from town had just pulled up, and tiny firemen leaped from the truck, dragging out hoses that would be too late to do any good. At one window the flames had been parted cunningly to reveal a woman in a white dress who stood with her arms upflung, obviously screaming, imprisoned behind a glass frame that she could not open. On the ground below a black-haired man stood looking up at her in helpless anguish. Behind the woman the room was red and I knew there would be no escape for her, ever. All the horror and suffering of the scene came through in devastating reality.

I must have uttered some exclamation because Glen left his tools and came to look at the picture I had uncovered. At once he took it from my hands and placed it on the easel where the light was better, studying it raptly.

"What a good job! I hadn't seen this one. Glynis gets better every year."

He sounded so enthusiastic that I could only regard him in astonishment. "But it's horrible!" I cried. "I don't care how well it's done—it's a dreadful picture!"

"Nonsense! An artist has the privilege of choice. Do you think scenes like this don't happen? If she chooses to paint them, she has that right." There was reproach in his words for an outsider who did not comprehend the problems and purpose of a professional. "I can see what she put into it, because I feel the same way. Don't you understand, my innocent darling? She's painted out her feelings about this miserable inn at the end of the lake, and about the people who are destroying Gray Rocks. That woman at the window is our Pandora, of course. She's responsible for all this. And the man below the window, who knows he can't save her, is her son, Trent McIntyre. It's a beautiful picture, really. It says everything we feel—both Glynis and I, about the McIntyres."

I recalled Nomi's words—that I must remember the twins were identical in every way. I found myself staring at Glen with shock in my eyes. When he turned from the picture and saw my face he laughed, and I could not bear his laughter either. I might have turned from him and fled toward the attic stairs, trying to run away as I had done that night in the art gallery in New York, all my earlier resolutions to be what he wanted me to be tossed aside—but he put his arms about me, held me close.

"My poor, frightened darling. I suppose you feel that you've stepped into a nest of vipers. But it isn't as bad as all that. What Glynis does is therapeutic, really. When she paints out all this hostility, it helps her. Then she needn't go setting the inn on fire, or trying to burn Pandora alive, because she's done it all harmlessly on canvas. Besides, if the woman at the window had an ounce of sense, she would break the glass and drop to the ground. The inn isn't built all that high."

I pushed away so I could look into his face. "Could *you* paint like that?"

"I can't paint at all any more. But if you mean will I do something like this to you in stone—the answer is no. Glynis and I feel the same way about the lake, but we don't choose the same solutions. If I do anything about the McIntyres I'll take a more practical means."

I did not want to think about the McIntyres. I had thrust Trent McIntyre away into some deep recess and I would not easily call him out. I pressed my face against Glen's chest, not wanting to look into the brightness in his eyes—that bright delight that was for his sister's painting.

"Your Aunt Nomi said you were duplicates," I whispered.

"Duplicates in every way except possibly one, and I don't mean the obvious fact that I'm a man. There's another difference. Glynis is haunted, and I'm not. Be glad of that, Dina love, and don't be so fearful for me."

He put his fingers beneath my chin and tilted it so he could kiss my lips, reassuring me. Yet the existence of Glynis Chandler was looming all too large upon my horizon and casting a very dark shadow before it. How was I to fight what I did not understand?

"Come back here," Glen said, and led me to his side of the attic, his fingers warm upon my own, leading me toward light and an absence of nightmare. "This is what I want to show you. Now I'm ready to tell you what I mean to do with you. I want you to see this as I do before I begin.''

He pulled a sturdy three-legged turntable stand into the open, its top strong enough to hold a block of stone. Something already occupied the stand, covered by a cloth. He whisked off the covering and I saw the block of alabaster that he had told me about in New York. It stood fixed in a timber frame secured to the turntable, ready for working, and it was more than life-size, but the head that would emerge from it would be smaller. The stone was a beautiful, pure, translucent white—an icy white, with a sense of transparency about it, as though one looked into shimmering depths where there was a faint greenish cast.

''It's lovely,'' I said. ''Lovely just as it is.''

''I knew it was meant for me when I first saw it and I brought it home to High Towers to wait for the right moment. Though I won't open the actual stone until I've done a maquette first. That is, a sketch of your head in clay to give me the sense of what I want to do. The stone comes last, since there's no erasing deep mistakes, once they are made.''

I ran my hand across the cool, smooth surface. It had not yet been polished as it would be when finished, but even now it felt slippery to the touch and held a subtle gleam.

''It seems strange that stone should appeal to sculptors,'' I said. ''Strange that so much beauty can come out of something as hard and resistant as this.''

''Ah, but that's the beauty of alabaster,'' Glen said. ''It is fairly soft to carve. In fact, one has to be careful because the stone will bruise quite deeply if a tool slips. It must be treated with enormous care. Bruises make deep whitish marks that spoil the final effect. But this time there will be no slips. I have the skill—and you will furnish the inspiration. Modeling rather bores me, but I have a feeling for the stone. There's more satisfaction when a stone piece is done because the risks are greater. I've worked in stone quite often, even though the results have been pedestrian. This will be better. There's something inner which must happen to an artist so that he knows when he can truly create.''

46

The glow in his eyes warmed me with hope. What came out of this stone had to be all he wanted it to be. In whatever way I could contribute, I must. But not merely with encouragement and belief. I knew well enough that I lacked the knowledge to justify belief. Praise must come from the qualified, to matter. But if I could understand what he wanted—*be* what he wanted, I might be able to help.

"Does Glynis work in stone too?" I asked.

"No! And I'm glad of it. That's why it's safer for me. I can go my own way in this separate medium. I needn't compete on her own ground. Come here, Dina. Come close, so I can make you see what I want to do."

I stood before the block of alabaster and he turned it so that light from the sky touched its surface. Then he caught up a stick of charcoal and began to sketch roughly upon the stone.

"Do you see? There's a girl's head in there, Dina. A sort of ice dryad from Gray Rocks Lake. She's imprisoned and I'm going to help her come out. She's facing this way inside the stone, with her hair streaming down her back. The cut-off place will probably be just below the base of the throat, and the hair will fall a little below that in back."

He made long strokes with his charcoal stick and I could see the flow of hair as he indicated it. He touched in the nose, the eyes, with the proper space between, a hint of the mouth—it was all there, deep in the stone, ready to emerge as he would coax it from ice into the living, sunny world.

"Here's your platform," he said, waving me to a small dais. "And here's a canvas chair that you'll find comfortable. I'll want you out here in the middle of the floor, so I can walk around you and view you from every angle. Working in the round, every aspect has to relate to all the rest. One doesn't, for instance, do a portrait of a nose without thinking how it fits into the over-all profile and with every other feature."

He was full of his subject and all this was fascinating to me. I had loved great sculpture for a long time, but now I was seeing something of the creative work that went into the stone long before it was brought to final perfection.

I sat on the dais in the canvas chair and he tried turning my head this way and that. Everyone had a characteristic way of carrying the head, he told me, and I must not strain— we must find the pose that would portray *me*.

When he was ready he took a lump of clay from a tin and slapped it on another stand, began to build it up and work it with wire modeling tools and spatulas.

This was the part he disliked, he said. In clay you built up from the smallest mass to the larger one you wanted. In stone the mass was there and it was a matter of opening up the substance, releasing your own vision to view through the chipping away of the covering that hid it. But a maquette was helpful if you were willing to take the trouble.

He had placed a mirror on the jutting wall of a dormer to reflect the clay from the opposite side, and though I could not see his work, I could sometimes glimpse Glen's face, with its bright, absorbed, confident look.

When I tired he let me rest, but he would not show me what he had done. He kept the clay face turned away from me, since he felt that the slightest question, or hint of criticism, might throw him off at this point. Thus I saw nothing of his morning's effort and had to be content with his own assurance that all was well and the barrier that had held him for so long was broken.

It was a good morning. I felt closer to him than ever before, and the troubling events of yesterday could be forgotten. Across the lake to the McIntyres seemed very far away. Glen had driven away painful memories. He had made me happy today.

At lunchtime we joined Nomi in the dining room again, and again she served us, joining us for the meal. In the afternoon her part-time housekeeper would come out from town to assist with the housework and get dinner. When she was here alone, Nomi got her own supper, she said, but when Colton or the twins were home, dinner was a gala, candlelit meal.

As we sat at the table drinking coffee afterward, Glen surprised me. I was still bride enough to want to be with him every minute that I could, but he made it clear that this was not what he would always wish.

"I'm going for a walk through the woods to think about my work," he told me. "So I can't take along a distraction like you, Dina. If you want to explore the house, or walk about outdoors, go ahead. The sun is coming out and it's warming up to a pleasant day."

I was eager to agree to whatever he suggested, eager to play the role of handmaiden to his art. I would tread softly and do as he asked. But when he left us at the table, Nomi looked after him with a slight shake of her head.

"They're loners, both of them—the twins. Except when they have each other. You'll have to get used to that. But you puzzle me a little. Last night I glimpsed something a bit independent in you, yet ever since you came downstairs this morning, you've been acting like an echo, a shadow."

"Why shouldn't I be an echoing shadow if it gives Glen what he wants?" I asked lightly. "I only mean to help him."

Nomi had a rather sharp little nose that she rubbed when something troubled her. She was rubbing it now, and her brown eyes appraised me, much as they had last night.

"Elizabeth was like that too," she said. "She was Colton's shadow, Colton's serving maid. He thought for her, spoke for her, molded her into exactly what he wanted. And he was horribly bored with her at times. A flavoring of the unexpected doesn't hurt, you know. That's why Colton can bear to have me around. I'm no Chandler, and I'm no Chandler shadow, either. I'm devoted to Glen, who has been like a son to me. Once, I suppose, I was even a little in love with his father. But I won't be a doormat for Chandler feet, or a sounding board for Chandler voices."

I hardly listened, because I already knew Glen as a wife would know him, and as no one else could. The vision in my mind was as bright and clear as Glen's vision of the head he would do of me. No one else could know what he needed as I knew, and this was what I would give him. If it developed that he wanted me to surprise him, entertain him, then I would try to do that too. But for now I must be still and undisturbing.

"Do you think Glynis will come home soon?" I asked.

"I suspect she'll take the first plane she can catch," said Nomi sharply. "We haven't many free days left. Let me give you more coffee, Dina."

I pushed my cup toward her. "Will it matter to her that her brother is married?"

"Without her permission?" Nomi snapped. "Without having her look the girl over carefully first? She'll make mincemeat of you—if you let her."

I tilted my chin. "Then I won't let her. I've married Glen, not Glynis."

Nomi thrust a hairpin briskly back into one of her braids. "That's what you think."

"But why should she want to keep Glen from marrying?"

"Because she's frightened." Nomi set her cup down with a thump. "She has to hold onto everything around her with all her might so that her own ghosts won't catch up with her and destroy her completely. So she holds to High Towers. She even holds to the lake, though there are times when she's afraid of that too. She would hold onto Colton if he didn't slip through her fingers whenever he chooses. Me she's never held to because she's afraid of me most of all. I'm the one she least trusts. With good reason. But Glen is hers. He's part of her own flesh and blood, as a twin can be. So she holds onto him most of all. He has tried to break away—oh, many times. But he's always failed before. Now he has broken away by marrying you. That's what it is, you know—his bid for freedom. Now it remains to be seen how quickly Glynis will smash up your marriage. If you let her."

"I won't let her," I repeated stubbornly. "I'm not a sponge, and I'm nobody's bid for freedom. I'm not in the least limp and helpless. I don't believe Glen is either. It's just that he needed to meet the right person to be whole. He's not a half now. He's not a twin—he's my husband. I want

50

everything to be right for him, because if it's right for him, it will be right for me.''

"Humph!" said Nomi, unimpressed.

"Why should Glynis be afraid of you?" I asked.

With small, quick hands she began to fold her napkin neatly along its creases. "Because she knows how much I despise her." Nomi's voice was light, calm, with no intensity of feeling. It was as though she had said it was a lovely day, but later it might rain. I knew that this was not the time to ask why she despised Glynis. Perhaps she would trust me enough to tell me sometime, but not on my first day at High Towers.

"This morning I saw a picture Glynis painted," I went on, still pressing for clues to the puzzle of the twins. "It was a frightening picture of the lake—with the inn on fire, and a woman trapped at the window of a room."

Nomi nodded, her expression wry. "I've seen it. Therapy, Glen calls it. I'd call it something else. But then, I'm old-fashioned and can't boast having been to a psychiatrist. I know what I am. That's something I have to live with. Sometimes I don't care for it much, but I'm willing to accept myself." She rose from the table, putting an end to our talk. "Come along, Dina, and I'll show you about the house. I can't say you'll be mistress of it, because I mean to go right on being that. As Colton will be its master, as long as he lives. He's the only one who can handle Glynis, and I hope he will come home before she does."

I found that I liked Nomi more and more. She was forthright and there was no pretense about her. If she finally decided to accept me, I would have a friend I could trust. But she had not decided yet. Naomi Holmes would never be one to make flip, impulsive judgments.

She let me look into her downstairs sitting room—not a "decorated" room, but comfortable, with the old-fashioned cast-off furniture of a house that had stood for many years. There were sewing things about, a small loom for weaving, and a big yellow tiger cat curled upon a worn sofa. I had not seen the cat before and I crossed the room to make its acquaintance.

"That's Jezebel," Nomi said. "She's not a Chandler either. Glynis hates cats, so this one stays in my rooms when she's not roaming about outside living up to her name."

The cat looked at me from eyes only a little more amber than her fur, and after consideration let me touch her.

Under Nomi's guidance, and with the cat following us, soft-footed and slightly supercilious, I was shown Glen's old room, and, finally, the large bedroom overlooking the front of the house—the room which belonged to Glynis.

In its doorway I paused to look about with lively interest. Everything I could learn about Glen's twin, I must know. Jezebel would not cross the sill. She gave the room a haughty glance that dismissed it as beneath her attention, and left us to go downstairs, her tail aloft and curling slightly at the tip, perhaps in irritation at the very scent of Glynis's room.

Here Glen's sister had used fern-printed wallpaper in pale green. The columns of a fourposter bed were carved and reeded, its quilted spread a snowflake design in rose and green. The hangings of the tester were a solid color—the same fern-green as the wallpaper, softening the bed's outlines. But I had scant interest in the general furnishings because something at the front window caught my eye. It was the room's one modern touch. On a pedestal of dark teakwood stood the black marble head of a woman. I was drawn toward it irresistibly.

Nomi thought I was looking at the view, and she came to raise the sash, letting in the bright, warm air of an Indian summer afternoon.

"Colton had some of the trees on both sides of the house cut away so the view would be clear," she said. "But the man who built High Towers created it for a woman who wanted to be shut in. His wife was city folk—Philadelphia—and she didn't like the sight and smells of the country. All that land at the foot of the hill used to be a farm. You can still see the barns and outbuildings. But she wanted it out of sight, and she liked the trees closing in on all sides. Her husband was the son of a wealthy farmer, but he was a bit eccentric himself, so he approved what she wished and put up this Victorian creation on the hilltop. Sensible people built in the valleys in those days.''

I eyed the black marble sculpture in fascination. The view over rolling lowlands toward hills and the distant Kittatinny ridge was beautiful, but it was the black sculpture that held my attention. I remembered that Glen had told me of his one successful effort in marble. This was surely it. I put my hand upon the head and could almost feel the springy locks beneath my fingers—like Glen's thick, crisp hair. I had only touched Trent McIntyre's hair once, and it had been like heavy silk and straight. But I would not think of Trent—never again, except as he came into my life as a stranger.

"Glen carved this, didn't he?" I asked Nomi.

"Yes. It's really good, I think. Even Colton feels that it's a fine piece of work. And it's appeared on loan in several museums. Wait, I'll light it for you.''

A spotlight had been arranged on the wall, above and a little to one side of the window. When Nomi touched the switch it cast a golden patina over gleaming black marble so that the face of the woman came to life. It was the face of Glen's twin—Glen's face with a feminine cast. Yet it was something else as well. Something rather awesome in the anguish it revealed—a face distorted by naked suffering.

I turned to Nomi in astonishment. "If that is Glynis, how can she bear to have the head here in her room? I should think—''

"Glen understands her as he understands himself,'' Nomi said. "He knows that she's afraid and he knows why. He hasn't carved *her*—he has carved her grief and fear and she can bear that. Nevertheless, he has romanticized, as he does about himself. You can see that, can't you?''

I bent toward the head, studying the marvelous detail that had gone into it. When a mouth turns downward in suffering, it affects every muscle of the face. Beneath the marble surface there was more than flesh.

I shook my head over Nomi's word. "Romanticized? When he has made the face so raw with emotion?"

"Exactly! Because, while she's capable of ugliness and fear, she's not capable of such tragic suffering as this. He's left out the real things, left out what she's really like."

I heard the depth of feeling in Naomi's voice, saw her usual calm ruffled by some inner disquiet.

"Why *do* you hate her so much?" I asked softly.

This time she answered me, her voice quickly under control. "Because she killed my sister Elizabeth. She destroyed her own mother willfully—Glen's mother."

I stared in astonishment. "But she was only five, wasn't she, when their mother died? A baby. What could she have done?"

Without a word, Nomi turned and left me. She walked out of the room with her back straight, her head with its white braids held high. I heard the stairs creak as she went down. For all that she was slight and small she walked heavily.

I had been given a sudden dismaying glimpse of what Naomi Holmes was really like. Implacable hatred because of what a child had done seemed a shocking thing. I studied the marble face again and felt sudden, unexpected sympathy for Glynis. What horror had she lived with as a child that made her now a haunted woman? Perhaps, after all, I could be her friend—if only she would let me. I *must* be her friend. I must know everything about her so I would have something to offer her when she came.

I switched off the light, feeling suddenly restricted by the house, stifled by these old, desperate emotions. My own family life had been happy and bright, filled with sunlight as I remembered it. This was a house made of winter things. Harsh and bleak and bitterly cold. Winter emotions, winter people.

Outdoors winter had not yet come and there was sunlight and the lake waiting for me. I turned my back on black marble and fled down the stairs. I needed no coat on this gift of a warm afternoon, and I let myself out the front door, walked around the house to the lake side. I could see the water, placid at the foot of the steep hill, blue and quiet, in a windless afternoon. I started down through dry autumn grass, down among bare walnut trees, hickories, and slim birches, then cut to my left at a diagonal over the spongy carpet of needles that lay beneath the pine grove.

In a few moments I was down and in the open at the water's edge. It was my first complete view of the lake and I could see, far to my right, the steep gray rocks, rugged and pinnacled, that gave the lake its name. The rest of this shore, and the opposite shore as well, wore no outcroppings of rock, though it was rimmed in by hills all around. Directly across was the stone house from the eighteenth century—the house where the McIntyres lived. White ruffled curtains trimmed its upstairs windows and neat shrubbery landscaped it. Belonging to an earlier time than High Towers, it seemed a more decorous house—well-mannered, as one who has learned wisdom and courtesy with age. The pricked ears of High Towers always seemed to be listening, rudely eavesdropping.

No one was in sight across the lake, and my sometimes wayward heart did not quicken at the thought of Trent walking into view. This afternoon I was safely and wholeheartedly Mrs. Glen Chandler, and I wanted nothing else.

For the first time I thought of the boy, Keith, whom I had met briefly in the auto shop last night when Glen was bringing me home. It seemed a long while ago that he had spoken to me of Glynis. I knew more about her now. I knew who she was, but I still did not know enough, and I wondered at the boy's intense interest.

As I turned to my left in the direction away from those tall gray rocks and began to follow a rough path along the bank, I saw the redwood inn at the end of the lake. Glen had been furious when he had shown it to me last night, but now, by daylight, it did not seem to me that it defaced the lake. In fact, it had clearly been built with an eye to suiting its wild surroundings, so that it was not wholly out of place.

Still, wilderness was better. Once the Lenape Indians had roamed this area and Glen said that arrowheads were still to be found in turned-up earth. I was on the side of those who wanted to keep all this a wilderness.

Walking more briskly as the path straightened, I was strong with purpose again. I must know. I must find out. Anything and everything. I moved in the direction of Gray Rocks Inn, wanting to see it more closely. Perhaps I wanted to see how true to reality Glynis had been in her painting of the inn afire. Perhaps I needed to reassure myself that no flames leaped behind its windows, that no woman in white stood with her arms upflung in desperation.

As I followed the curve of the shore, a sharp crack exploded somewhere on the hill above. Up there in the woods a gun had been fired. It had nothing to do with me, but the sound was disquieting in this lonely place, and I began to hurry on my way to the inn.

4

No sound of gunfire came again, but the strange feeling that I was somehow involved with the inn at the end of the lake began to build in me.

It was a wide building with a shallow roof that sloped toward the water, and two strong stone chimneys at either end. The main floor had been built well above the ground and glass picture windows framed the entire front, so that diners could sit at their tables and look out over the water. But in Glynis's painting the window behind which the woman stood visible against red flames, had been narrow—the window of a small room.

I followed the glass and redwood front with my eyes, searching—and found what I was looking for. The smaller window was half hidden by a shaggy spruce, its narrow space empty now, shining serenely in the afternoon sun. Yet the queer urge was still upon me, the sense of misgiving. I wanted to know what that room was like—from inside. I wanted to look out its very window. Now who was being haunted? I wondered wryly, and went right ahead to satisfy the urge.

In the summer the sloping bank that ran from the inn down to the water would be a pleasant lawn. Now it was stubby brown grass which crunched beneath my feet as I walked across it. I rounded the far end of the building to reach the driveway and parking space, where Glen and I had drawn up in the car last night. Broad stone steps led to a generous veranda and a wide redwood door. The door stood open and I hesitated before it. No one seemed to be about. No one had stirred outside, or looked down upon me from the windows of the inn. I climbed the steps and paused just outside the door.

"Is anyone here?" I called. "May I come in?"

There was no answer and I stepped into a rustic, pine-paneled anteroom which boasted a pine desk on one side, and a small cloakroom on the other. A summer painting of the lake as viewed from this end hung directly opposite the door—a watercolor, pleasant, but without any particular distinction. The shores of the lake, green as I had not seen them, though the pinnacled rise of high rock part way down its length looked as dull and gray as it had to me this morning. No warmth of sunlight, no blue waters or green shores would ever change the cold, craggy look of that pile of rock. The very contrast it made gave the picture interest, as it gave the lake interest and emphasis. Out on the painted lake a woman sat at the oars of a small boat, and a man fished placidly. I did not need to look to know there would be no Chandler initials on this picture.

To my left, a door opened into a bar which occupied one end of the inn. The other led directly into a timbered dining room, alight with the warmth that natural, golden woods cast upon a room. Again there were paintings hung all around the paneled walls. Apparently Mrs. McIntyre encouraged the artists of the county to show their work here. Several were rather good, but I did not stop to study them now.

I wound my way among the tables, noting the view down the lake, framed in each picture window. I found swinging doors that gave upon the kitchen area, passed them by and saw the door I was looking for. A narrow hallway led from the dining room, and off this opened the door of a small office. This was the room of Glynis's painting.

No one called to me. No one stopped me, and I went through the door and stood looking around. The oak desk was neat, its papers thrust into pigeonholes, the drawers closed and orderly. A clothes tree stood in one corner and upon it hung a woman's nylon uniform. A prickling ran along my nerves at the sight of the white dress. I stepped to the window and looked down upon the sloping brown lawn, to find that the sun had gone behind clouds that rolled up the sky on a rising wind. I had yet to learn how quickly the weather could change here, how quickly mist, or snow, or sleet, could blow across the lake, dropping the temperature, shrouding the scene.

The window was closed. I knew without touching it that it would not open easily to my push, and that the lock would be balky, stuck with varnish or disuse. I stepped close to the glass, knowing very well that I was here because of the painting Glynis Chandler had done of the burning inn, and because that picture had somehow possessed my imagination.

Movement near the edge of the lake caught my eye, and as I watched a man came into view to stand looking up at my narrow window. It was Trent McIntyre. Without warning, my heart went into its renegade thudding, and I had a horrid feeling that the picture was now complete, that the key to it had been given me. Now I knew why it had haunted me from first sight. The woman in white was *I*—even though this morning I wore a pale green sweater and darker green slacks. The woman who stood against the flames with her arms upflung, while the man on the bank watched in helpless horror—was I, Dina Blake. Dina Chandler! The picture was not fact, but prophecy.

I whirled, half expecting to see fire blooming red and dangerous behind me. Instead, I found myself facing a woman with short fluffy hair that had been tinted the color of dark honey. Her eyes viewed me in lively fashion and were the same bright intense blue I had seen in the eyes of her son and grandson.

"Good afternoon," she said, and the rich lilt of Ireland was in her voice. "It must be you're the young bride Glen has brought home to our lake. Trent tells me he met you when he was working on that piece about your father out in

California. I'm Dora McIntyre—though you may as well call me Pandora—everyone does. Welcome to Gray Rocks."

She came toward me with her hand outstretched, and I took it in relief, grateful for being awakened from a bad dream.

"I'm trespassing," I said. "I called out when I came in, but no one answered."

"I was in the basement. I can never hear a thing down there. But you're welcome to look about if you wish."

She slipped out of her short gray coat and hung it on the clothes tree beside the white uniform. Her gray skirt was box-pleated, and a wide leather belt buckled sweater and skirt together at the waist with a jaunty touch of brass. On her feet were brown country brogues, meant for walking rough paths. She was of medium height, a little on the plump side, and her figure seemed to go with her cheerful, expansive manner. There was nothing drawn and anxiously thin about Pandora McIntyre.

From the hillside outdoors the crack of a rifle sounded and she turned toward the window at once.

"He's hunting again!" she cried. "How I hate hunting!"

I listened intently as the firing was repeated. "It must be on Chandler land, though I noticed when I came through the woods that the area is posted."

"That makes no difference if it's Keith." Pandora McIntyre lifted her shoulders and let them drop helplessly. "Colton has given him permission to hunt over there."

Someone crossed the inn veranda and footsteps approached the office. A moment later Trent stood at the door, regarding me with a thoughtful, rather speculative look.

"Good afternoon, Dina. Is anything wrong?"

"Wrong?" I shook my head. "Why do you think—?"

"If ever a woman gave me a frightened look, that's what you did through the window just now," he said.

I felt myself flushing as I tried to explain. "I suffer from too much imagination," I told him. "This morning I saw a picture that Glynis Chandler painted—"

Pandora glanced at her son, then turned her quick look on me, nodding. "A picture of the inn burning, it was?"

"Then you've seen it," I said. "The picture's been haunting me, and I'm afraid when I stood at that window just now—" I let my words trail into silence, finding I could not explain.

Trent did not smile. "Glynis's pictures work that sort of witchcraft. I've never been able to forget one of them myself. Though I haven't seen this inn-burning inspiration, Keith has told us about it. She showed it to him right after she painted it last winter. But the inn is still standing."

His mother put a hand on his arm—a hand that seemed to gentle him. "It's the sort of primitive thing she paints—not to be taken seriously."

"Most primitives are innocent," Trent said. "There's nothing innocent about anything Glynis does."

He spoke so harshly that I looked at him in surprise. What undercurrents stirred here? He was hardly the man I had known in California.

His mother changed the subject swiftly. "Have you seen Keith since breakfast, Trent?"

He shook his head. "He went hunting, I think. I've heard shots off and on this afternoon."

That other picture painted by Glynis Chandler flashed into my mind. The one which hung in Glen's gallery in New York and showed a boy standing on the frozen lake, aiming at a small animal that fled toward the bank. I remembered the circle of small dead things around the boy's feet. What Trent had said was true. There was nothing innocent about the scenes Glynis painted.

Pandora went to her desk, opened a drawer, and drew out a sheet of paper. "I'd better get to work," she said. "I'm opening the inn for another private dinner party next week, and I must get everything ready. If you're going to help me, Trent—"

I wished I might offer to help too, but I could not very well ignore what Glen had said about the McIntyres belonging to an enemy camp. It was certain that he would disapprove any friendship I might entertain for these two. Besides, it was better for me if I saw as little of Trent as possible. He had changed greatly, and I did not care for the change. Yet I liked Pandora. It would have been pleasant to have a woman friend away from the Chandler house.

Trent moved from the doorway to let me pass, but before I could leave the office, there came a sound of running feet as Keith dashed through the big dining room, knocking a chair or two clumsily aside, and burst in upon us. His rifle was still in his hands, and he leaned it with care just outside the office door before he faced us, a hint of defiance lacing his obvious excitement. Thick brown hair tumbled over his forehead in an untidy shock, and beneath brows as heavily marked as his father's, his eyes were that electric, Irish blue.

"They're home!" he announced. "Both of them are home—Colton and Glynis! I was on the hill above the road, and I saw her car take the turn toward High Towers."

A look sped between Trent and his mother. Then the man put one hand upon his son's shoulder.

"It's neither the beginning nor the end of the world when Glynis comes home. Is it?"

Keith jerked his shoulder from his touch. "For me everything begins when she comes home! It's hopelessly boring here when she's away."

He swung about, but Trent was beside him at once and I saw the concern in his face. "You'd better wait, Keith. She won't want you underfoot right away."

All his youthful rebellion, his resentment of parental direction, was stamped on the boy's face. "You want to keep me away from her. You've always wanted that. But I don't have to do what you say any more. I'm old enough to think for myself. She wrote me in her last letter that she wanted to see me. She said I was one of the first people she'd want to see when she came home. And I'm to go to High Towers for Christmas. Just try and stop me from seeing her then!"

Insolently he picked up his rifle, and there seemed something disturbing about the way he held the gun—almost as if it were a weapon he might use against his father.

Trent stood quietly, not moving or flinching, facing his son. Yet I had the feeling that if the boy made the slightest threatening move the man would move more quickly.

Pandora stepped between the two. "Let him go, Trent. It's true that you can't stop him."

The boy was already gone, rifle in hand. I returned to the window and saw him lope around the end of the inn and start across the lawn. What his startling news meant to me began to come home. If Glynis had returned, and Colton with her—this might mean that they had left before Glen's cables had reached them. If that were true, then neither would know of our marriage. I wondered whether I could find Glen and warn him. Without thinking, I reached for the window sash and raised it easily. The window was neither locked nor stuck, but the prophecy of the painting did not concern me now. I leaned my hands on the sill and called after the boy.

"Keith—wait for me! I need to find Glen. Can you help me find him in the woods?"

He turned to look up at me, impatient and far from gracious. "Okay—I'll wait. But hurry up."

I flung an apologetic glance at the two in the room. "I'll have to find Glen and—and let him know. He only cabled his father and sister recently about our marriage, and it may come as a surprise to them."

Neither Trent nor his mother spoke. I was aware of Pandora watching me almost pityingly. Trent's look was more remote, and put me back in my enemy camp. Yet when I started through the dining room he came with me, and on the veranda he held me back for a moment.

"I don't know much about you any more," he said, "but I know you're not Chandler-oriented. So if anything happens to trouble you, come to my mother. You'll have a friend there."

I would hardly accept such an invitation. I knew where my loyalties lay.

"I have my husband to turn to," I said, and started down the veranda steps.

He came with me, unasked and without comment, walked

around the end of the inn with me, thoughtfully silent, so that I felt uneasy, wondering what he meant by his veiled warning.

"I'll run now, or Keith won't wait for me," I told him. Then I paused and held out my hand. "Thank you, Trent. I'll be fine, you know. Of course a family of geniuses is something new for me, but I'll manage. I always do."

His handclasp seemed rough, impatient. "Perhaps you'd better be told—in case no one else has informed you. Mother was right. I can't stop Keith from seeing Glynis when he wishes. He's her son and he has that right. Colton of course is his grandfather."

The news astonished me. Glen had never given me the slightest hint that his sister had ever married. And that it should be Trent—

"Then—then you're—" I found myself stammering in bewilderment.

"No!" He contradicted me sharply before the words were spoken. "I haven't been her husband since Keith was nine and Glynis went off on her own and left him to me. She dropped my name after the divorce and went her own way. As I've gone mine."

We were on the brown lawn, moving toward the lake, where Keith waited for me near the water's edge.

"You'd better know, since you're one of the Chandlers now," Trent explained grudgingly. "Pandora has raised Keith and we've had no worry about him until recently. Glynis has paid little attention to him. Now that he's in his teens, however, she'd like him as one of her devoted following. Something I find it hard to stomach."

"I'm sorry," I managed. "I'm awfully sorry."

The words were feeble, but he seemed to accept them as they were meant. The harsh look of his mouth softened a little.

"I wouldn't worry you with past history, but I know Glynis. She won't welcome you as Glen's wife, and she's accountable to no one. She makes her own laws."

"I'm not afraid," I said, encouraging myself.

He shook his head almost despairingly, as though he thought me hopelessly foolish, and I ran down the bank to where the impatient boy waited. Before I reached him, Keith started along the path, so that I had to run after him, following single file.

In spite of my boastful words to Trent, I felt shaken and unable to think clearly. Glynis was the woman my young self had once envied as Trent's wife, though I had never seen her. Now she was my husband's twin sister and a woman I wanted as my friend. I felt bewildered and not a little alarmed. Yet out of the confusion Keith's news had thrown me into, one thought was beginning to drive me. Nothing must interfere with the work Glen had started this morning. For some reason he had seemed almost fearful about Glynis's reaction to it. He had spoken of having time enough to get well along in his work before his sister came home for Christmas. Now that time was lost. But she must not be allowed to spoil what he meant to do—if that was what he feared from her. She must not discourage him, or disparage his work. Somehow I would manage to stand beside my husband so strongly and confidently that nothing his twin sister might do or say would bring down the high crest of his inspiration.

With the sun gone the bare brown hillside caught the wind and I shivered in my sweater. Trying to warm myself, hurrying too carelessly, I tripped over a snakelike root and called out to the boy who ran ahead.

"I'm not used to the woods. You're going too fast for me!"

He paused in his headlong plunge uphill and looked back at me. A branch caught at my hair, pulled a lock loose from my braid, twisted my velvet ribbon askew, jerked me to a halt with a cruel tug. The boy leaned his gun against a tree and came to release me from the branch's hold, his touch unexpectedly light and skillful. In the woods he was less awkward in his movements than in a house.

We walked together now, as the path allowed, and I regained my breath. "Have you realized something?" I asked him. "We've each just acquired a new relative. I seem to be your aunt, and you're my nephew. I've never had a nephew before. It's rather interesting.''

A smile lighted his somber young face for the first time. ''You aren't old enough to be my aunt.''

''Aunts come all ages, and anyway I'm ancient,'' I told him. ''Twenty-four.''

He accepted that age as obviously ancient, but a more companionable climate existed between us.

''I know where Glen likes to go,'' Keith offered as we followed the shore path. ''Do you see that pile of rock rising from the lake's edge on ahead? There's a place up near the top where he goes sometimes when he wants to be alone. I can show you the way up if you like, and then I'll cut up through the woods and back to the house.''

I was grateful for his help, and as the path narrowed, I fell behind again. He walked more slowly now, and even stopped once or twice to hold back a branch which would have slapped me, seeming again a more gentle, courteous boy here in the woods than he had been at the inn.

Or so I thought, until he came to a sudden halt on the path ahead of me and raised his gun to his shoulder. Instinctively I stopped too, as quiet as he. In scrubby brown underbrush near the lake's edge two pricked ears stood up—the ears of a rabbit. The boy moved his gun, aiming.

''No!'' I cried. ''No!''

The rabbit leaped for safety, vanishing behind a bushy cedar, and the boy lowered his gun and looked around in disgust.

''What'd you go yelling for?''

''A rabbit!'' I cried, thoroughly indignant. ''Why should you want to kill rabbit?''

He snorted at me, equally indignant. ''You're what Glynis calls a bleeding heart! You should see her with a gun. She's not scary and silly.''

''Just tell me why,'' I persisted. ''I'd hate killing anything wild. Woods animals have more right to be here than we have. Why did you want to kill it?''

He pondered my question seriously. ''My grandmother

66

makes great rabbit stew. She talks about hating hunting, but she eats meat right along. Besides, farmers hate rabbits. They eat things up. Like the woodchucks do. I kill every woodchuck I see. Foxes too. There's a bounty on foxes. Farmers want them killed. I got one just last week here in these woods.''

I was far from feeling sympathetic toward the farmer just then. ''Nothing alive should be shot like that! Especially not something beautiful and wild like a fox. *Why*—tell me why, really!''

He stared at me, taken aback by my vehemence, and genuinely puzzled. Undoubtedly he thought me a stupid city girl and out of order in the country, but there was something else that drove him—something I wanted to understand. I could not forget the picture Glynis had painted of this boy—her son!—shooting a small defenseless animal, while the corpses of others he had slain lay about his feet.

''Don't give me the excuses,'' I said. ''Tell me the truth!''

He put his rifle under his arm, muzzle down, and considered my words with care. ''Marksmanship?'' The word was a question and I waited. ''I suppose that's part of it. I'm a good shot, and I enjoy proving it. Especially when something is moving and I can be faster.''

''At one moment something is alive, and the next, because of you, it's dead. A life gone from the woods just so you can prove what a wonderful shot you are. Why can't you shoot at a target?''

He looked solemn, thoughtful, but as I watched, the muscles beneath the young curve of his jaw seemed to harden, and he stared at me directly.

''Maybe this is the only way I know to play God,'' he said. ''Everyone else can push me around—but not the animals in the woods. I can control whether they live or die. Glynis understands that. She knows about playing God, though she can do it in other ways.''

''None of us is God,'' I said. But he was Glynis's son, and I turned away revolted. ''If you'll show me where to find

Glen, I'll go on alone. Then you won't have anyone around to interrupt your hunting."

He grinned at me, his eyes openly mocking. "Okay—I'll show you. Maybe Glen will come down and help you up if you call to him. If he's there he has already heard us, though he can't see us because of the spruce trees."

It was true that I could not see the rocky pinnacles from where we stood, though the massive base of gray rock rose just ahead, lifting upward from the edge of the water.

"You have to go around that bottom slab," the boy said. "It's not slippery—you can do it. On the other side there's a pathway winding up through the woods. Halfway up, the rock splits and you'll find a place around in back where you can step into a sort of saddleback between the two rock towers. After that there are notches in the rock, so you can climb to the top, if you want to. If he's up there, I wouldn't."

I regarded the prospect doubtfully for a moment, then cupped my hands around my mouth, tilting my head back as I shouted Glen's name. The echoes went clattering down the lake, shouting back at me, but no human voice answered.

"He's not up there," I told Keith.

"Maybe he is," the boy said. "Lots of times he won't answer when he's hiding out up there. It's just the way he is. You'll have to go up and see."

The boy wanted only to escape me now and reach the house to meet his mother, so I started ahead toward the place where the path ended and wet rock climbed out of the lake, changing from brown to gray as it rose into towers of stone.

"There's just one thing—" Keith said.

I turned back to him and met the hard brilliance of blue eyes. There seemed nothing young about him now. Had Glynis done the damage to this boy? Or was it his father who was responsible? After all, he had left Keith to grow up in the area.

"There's just one thing," he repeated. "When you get to the rock, go around the base as fast as you can. Don't take your time in that place at the bottom."

"Why not?" I asked.

"Because there is a lot of loose rock up there on top. Big pieces. If somebody wanted, he could push one over, right down on top of you, knock you into the water, kill you, maybe. There'll be no spruce trees to hide you there. So go around fast."

I met his look in puzzled astonishment. "If my husband is up there, he won't push rocks down on top of me."

The boy came a step closer. "Even if there's nobody up there, you go around fast. I've seen rocks come down from up there by themselves. So be smart and hurry."

"Like a rabbit?" I said. "That's what you're doing, isn't it? You're aiming at me as if I were a rabbit—to frighten me."

His grin was openly insolent. "Maybe. But if you really want to know, this isn't a good place—this part of the lake. My grandmother Elizabeth died just around those rocks. I never knew her because she died when my mother was only five. But that's where it happened."

He held my attention again. This was one thing I wanted to know. "How did it happen? From stones falling from above?"

"No." He shook his head. "It happened in winter, when the lake was frozen. Except it wasn't hard enough around there because springs feed the lake at that part. Elizabeth and Glynis were skating—and her mother went through the ice and drowned. Aunt Nomi told me. Glynis won't talk about it. Everybody blamed her afterward, I guess."

His story was shocking, but he told it as though he relished tragedy—and that was even more shocking.

"Why would anyone blame a child?" I asked.

"People have to blame somebody, don't they?"

It was a curious question, and I did not want to hear any more. I turned away from him and went quickly toward the wide base of the rock towers where they slanted up from the water. My shoes had rubber soles and they took the steep slant of the rock easily. I leaned one hand against the rough surface and climbed around the base slowly and carefully, without hurrying. No rocks came slamming down upon me from above. When I was safely on the earth path beyond, I turned and looked back. Keith stood where I had left him, watching me. I waved my arm and he waved back, grinning. At least he gave me credit for not being a rabbit. Then he went his own way, up through the spruce and cedar toward the house, moving swiftly on his way to meet his mother.

The ground was rough beneath my feet, overgrown with dry winter stubble. Twin towers of rock rose above me, flinging rugged shadows across my way. When I craned my neck, seeking the topmost rocky crags, I could see nothing—no hiding place, no face peering down at me. The rock rose irregularly, with narrow ledges here and there, where earth had collected, and grass and brush had seeded in. In one place halfway up, a tiny spruce tree clung precariously, growing in an earth-filled crevice.

I would not humiliate myself by calling out again, in case Glen was really there and deliberately refusing to answer. Climbing steeply, I followed the pathway as it wound beneath maples, oaks, hickories, mounting halfway up the brown hillside before it circled the nearest rock tower to the place where the rising hill met the rock.

Now I could see what Keith meant. The towers were all one piece at the base, but halfway up they split apart at a saddle of earth which joined them and was accessible only from behind. Where I stood on the hillside I was a little above this saddle and would have to climb down in order to stand between the twin towers. For several moments I hesitated, figuring out my approach, wishing that Glen, if he was up there, would come down for me.

Because I was still, I heard someone coming along the hillside from the direction of the house, striding with certainty through dry brush. My attention quickened. Had Keith decided to see me up the rock, after all? Or was this Glen coming toward me now? Scrubby spruce hid that part of the hillside, and I waited for whoever it was to come into view.

When she stepped from behind the last tree, I saw the girl who approached the great pile of rock and I stepped instinctively behind the trunk of an oak tree, my heart thumping in my throat. Whether I liked it or not, whether I was ready or not, the moment was upon me.

Glynis Chandler had indeed come to High Towers, and it was she who strode along the hillside toward me.

5

I would have known her anywhere as Glen's sister. Colton's genius had caught her essential spirit in the portrait he had painted of the twins when they were seventeen, but now she was more beautiful—more poised and arrogant. There was something imperious, even audacious in the tilt of her head, the lifting of her chin. Here was a woman who knew exactly what she wanted—and moved toward her goal with assurance, whatever that goal might be.

Her short hair capped her head sleekly, more red than chestnut, tinted perhaps to a brighter hue than Glen's. Her eyes were as dark as his and seemed even larger because she had enhanced them with the make-up devices of current fashion. Her lips, tinted with deep rose, smiled eagerly, as if in anticipation of this meeting with her brother. Around her neck she had flung a long knitted scarf of bright yellow, and below it her camel's hair coat was jaunty, softly belted in dark brown suede. Brown leather boots came almost to her knees and she walked in them easily, accustomed to this rough hillside that she had known all her life.

She did not see me, and for this brief respite I was grateful. At least I had the advantage of watching unseen and preparing myself for an encounter I could not postpone, in fact, no longer wanted to postpone. At this unexpected sight of Glynis Chandler something curious was happening to me. Having heard too much about her—and not enough—having been alternately timid and eager to like and be liked, all this suddenly fell away and left me armed with new strength. I had seen her now. She was real and not some witch-girl, as my imagination had begun to suggest. She was flesh and blood, and I feared her in no way. If she would have me as a friend, then I would be her friend. If not, then I did not lack the courage to fight her—for Glen's sake, if that became necessary. Something in me tingled with a new eagerness for this confrontation.

Nevertheless, for a little while longer, I waited. For the moment her attention was upon the twin pinnacles of rock. Moving with the grace of a leopard, she sprang from the hillside below me into the earthen saddle between. There she stood with her arms outstretched to either tower of rock, as though she braced them apart, her head flung back so that her eyes could follow the line of rock upward against a gray, cloudy sky. Her head, bare of covering, shone against the gray. When a spate of wind swept the lake and hillside, it caught the fringe of her yellow scarf, tossing it over one shoulder. She lifted her hand to the breeze, as though she savored its touch, and called out to her brother.

"Glen? Glen—are you there? I'm home! Come down and welcome me!"

There was a movement near the top of the pinnacle nearest the lake. From some sheltered space Glen rose. When he stood up I could see him plainly, but if he was aware of me on the hillside he did not glance in my direction. All his attention was for the girl who waited for him on the connecting earth of the saddle. He climbed down the rock backwards, as though down a ladder, moving with swift ease. In moments he was at her side and I watched the twins' exuberant greeting as each flung both arms about the other in affectionate embrace. Then Glen held his sister off at arms' length, studying her, smiling his welcome. If he had harbored any doubts about her return, they were gone now, and as I watched I knew that these two were one. They always had been and always would be. Only a little while ago I had thought I must stand beside my husband, prevent any interference in his work by his twin. But I was the outsider now. Where was my place in so obviously close a relationship?

"Colton's come home with me," Glynis ran on. "I left him at the house for Nomi to fuss over, while I came looking for you. When she said you were out in the woods, I knew you'd be here."

"You always knew where I'd be," Glen said.

Her bright head bent toward him. "Yes—but something's been wrong lately. That's why I came home when Colton did. The thread has been broken between us. Did you think I wouldn't feel it? What has happened, Glen?"

It was time for me to join in this homecoming. I could not stand hiding behind my oak tree until one of them looked up and saw me. I moved down the hillside and a twig cracked beneath my feet, a stone went rolling away. The twins turned as if they were one. Glen was only a little taller. He stood with an arm about his sister's shoulders, and her arm circled his waist. Together they watched me approach the saddleback, and again I felt sharply the sense of being an outsider. I was farther away from Glen than I would have been had Glynis been a rival, rather than a sister. In the moment during which I climbed down to where they were, I felt the full impact of what these two meant to each other. This was something I had not fully known or expected. Still, I did not hesitate. My courage was still high, and I smiled at them both as I went down to join them.

Glynis was the one who challenged, and I was close enough to see quick hostility spring into her eyes.

"Who is this?" she asked her brother.

Glen looked dismayed. "You didn't receive my cables, then? Neither you nor Colton?"

She moved away from him. "What cables?"

"Come up here, Dina," Glen called to me. "I want you to meet my sister. Glynis, this is my wife—Dina."

I had never doubted that he would acknowledge me proudly. He was my love. But it was surprising to see his eyes as bright as his sister's. It was clear that this time he had thrown down the gauntlet to her.

Glynis hesitated only a moment before she stepped to the edge of the saddleback to hold out her hand to me. I gave her my own readily, and she pulled me over to the ledge so that I stood between the two on the ridge of weed-grown earth.

"So you've done it at last, Glen," she said softly, and I noted that her voice had a husky tone to it. "I never believed you really would. Hello, Dina Chandler." But her eyes were cold as winter.

Glen relaxed into greater ease with both of us. Battle was not indicated, after all, in spite of Glynis's first look of hostility. We walked toward the house together, and Glen kept one arm about Glynis and one about me.

Now and then he would press his hand lightly against my side, his touch loving, reassuring—promising me his support, his protection, if I needed it. I was still keyed up, with my battle forces in a sense unused, and I wondered if he did the same thing with her, promising partisanship to each, so each would be reassured and there would be no interference with his relationship to either. It was a strange triangle.

Since Glynis had appeared, I had not given a thought to Keith, but as we rounded a turn in the path, bringing the house into view, we found the boy waiting for us. He must have missed Glynis when he cut back toward High Towers at the very time when she was coming along the hillside to Gray Rocks. Now he leaned easily against the brown trunk of a walnut tree, rifle in hand, its butt resting on the earth beside him. He had the alert look of a woods creature, untamed and ready for flight, watchful, yet expressionless, as we came into sight. His eyes never moved from Glynis's face.

She walked toward the boy, halting a few feet away from him. I did not know how long it had been since she had seen him, but she wasted no word on a greeting.

"That's how I'm going to paint you!" she cried. "I'll do

a portrait this time. *Boy in the Woods*, I'll call it. You'll pose for me, Keith?''

He returned her look uncertainly, neither smiling nor moving, as though she was someone he could never gauge ahead of time. She laughed in the face of such caution, flung both her arms wide and ran toward him. Swiftly he laid the rifle on the ground and then waited for her, making no other gesture in response. She flung her arms about her son, and I saw that he was as tall as she—a thin stick of a boy whose head was on a level with her own. Over her shoulder his boy's face reddened and almost timidly, he put one arm about her, let her kiss his cheek.

Glen's hand pressed my side in warning. ''She's showing us that she has someone too.''

I glanced at him, startled. ''I hope the boy means more to her than that,'' I whispered.

Glynis turned, pulling Keith with her as she faced us. ''What do you think of this great son of mine? He's grown several feet, I'm sure, in the months I've been away. He'll make a marvelous woods picture, won't he, Glen? We'll start work at once—tomorrow, Keith! I'll expect you by nine in the morning. Be sure to bring your gun. That's part of the picture. And wear what you're wearing now. No sprucing up, do you hear?''

With his eyes, the boy told her he would do anything she wished, but he did not speak as he bent to retrieve his rifle. He would have escaped down the hillside then, if Glynis had not kept her hand on his arm, drawing him along with us as we rounded the drive to the doorway of the house. Only when we reached the steps did he pull firmly away.

''I'll be here in the morning,'' he said. ''I'm not going in,''—and made his escape, running with a release of energy that I had not seen in him before, releasing his very joy into motion.

Glynis laughed as she watched him go leaping down the hillside. Then she turned to Glen and me. ''Let's go in and present the bride to Colton,'' she said lightly. ''He'll be interested, I know.''

The lift of her winged brows was mocking, but Glen smiled at me. "Yes, he will be. Come along, Dina. I want Colton to see you."

See you, he said—not *meet you*. But I did not want to be something to show off, a mere acquisition for display. I stiffened a little as I went with him up the steps, my battle forces not entirely dispelled.

The twins' father was with Nomi in the drawing room. A lively fire burned in the grate, even though several windows were open. Naomi was handing him a Scotch and soda as we came in. He took the glass and rose from the purple velvet sofa nearest the fire, staring at me openly with eyes that were almost the same shining silver as his hair. They were strange, searching eyes that saw everything about me as only a portrait painter would see it: the shape of my bones, my height, my coloring, the very texture of my skin, the planes of my face. He was a big man—larger than Glen—and he wore, rather dramatically, a suit of silky envoy gray, London-tailored, with a bright red vest and expensive red and gray tie. He regarded me with those silvery eyes, and said nothing—simply studying me until Glen gave me a slight push in his father's direction.

"I suppose Nomi has told you, Colton," he said. "This is Dina—my wife."

I waited, pinned so long and uncomfortably by that searching gaze that I had time to be aware of the others in the room and even looked about to see what each was doing, determined not to speak until Colton did.

Nomi had quietly seated herself and was watching the flames with an absorbed interest, as though there were no one in the room but herself. Yet I knew by her stillness that she listened, even if she would not look.

The twins stood together, and I saw how much alike they were—tall and slim and elegant. They had long faces with rounded chins, long slender feet, long bodies and hands. And those blazing dark eyes that could light with enthusiasm—or with passion, or anger.

As I looked at her, Glynis took a little turn down the room, chuckling to herself, as if she knew some secret joke she would not share with us. Colton paid no attention to anyone but me. At last he raised his glass, bowed slightly, drank a silent toast, then put down the glass on a coffee table. Stubbornly, I would not speak in return.

Glen slipped his arm through mine. "Stop X-raying her, Colton! I know she looks a mess, but she's been running in the woods. Her hair's loose and has leaves in it. Her face is smudged and she's pulled some threads in her new sweater. But wait until you see her after she's put together again!"

"I am silent only with astonishment," Colton Chandler said. "Where did you find anything so lovely? How did you persuade her to marry you?"

"I suppose Glen means to paint her," Glynis broke in, a hint of malice in her voice. "Or at least he'll try."

Glen glanced at his sister, then looked away. "I mean to do her in alabaster. I've already started work. So neither of you can have her. Not until I've done her myself."

Glynis whistled softly, and Colton stared at his son.

I had endured enough of this. I wanted to cry out to them that I was real—a girl with feelings of my own—not a mere subject for their art. I pulled away from Glen, walked directly across the room to Colton Chandler and held out my hand.

"I've always admired your work," I said. "But you aren't important to me as an artist right now. You're only important as Glen's father. And I hope you can see me as the girl who has married him—not just as a possible model."

In her turquoise chair Nomi turned to look at us and made a slight sound that applauded me.

Glynis was less pleased. "I'm afraid you're fooling yourself, Dina. The Coltons are a painting, sculpting clan. That's all we know and care about. Now that you've married us, you'd better learn to accept that."

I wanted to announce that I had married no one but Glen, but I had made my bid as a person in my own right, and I could only wait for Colton's answer.

He was more impressively built than either of the twins and his manner was one of confident authority. He flicked his fingers in Glynis's direction, silencing her without speaking a word, dismissing her. She stood with her brown booted feet apart, her hands clasped behind her back, the camel's hair coat hanging open over a brown wool dress. She looked rather like a sulking, well-dressed child who had received a sudden slap. She *was* like a child, I thought wonderingly. She was filled with audacity and bluff, but quickly reduced to a state of pouting by a flick of her father's fingers.

Colton had taken the hand I held out to him, and he bent to kiss it, very courtly and European. "You make us all ashamed," he said. "I'm glad you've married my son, Dina. I hope you'll be able to accept us as his family. We want very much to accept you."

It was a formal little speech, and yet I felt that as far as he could make it, it was sincere. He would not be an easy man to know and understand, but at least he had given me the beginnings of respect.

Nomi knew at once that this was the sort of speech almost impossible to answer gracefully. She stood up and moved toward the door.

"Tea will be ready soon," she said to us all. "If you'd like to prepare, hurry along to your rooms and come right down."

"I'm not hungry," Glynis said, still the pouting child. She flung herself past Nomi and ran out of the room.

Colton regarded his daughter's departure calmly. "There's a nose gone out of joint," he said to Glen. "But you did the right thing this time. There's been enough of broken engagements because your sister couldn't approve of your choice."

Glen pulled me impatiently toward the door. "Dina doesn't know about all my conquests and unhappy love affairs," he mocked. "Let's break it to her gently."

I found myself laughing a little as I went out of the room with him. Perhaps it was the laughter of nervous reaction because I had come through a difficult confrontation not altogether without honor. I could still hold up my head and cling to being myself.

79

"So I'm not the first love of your life," I said lightly as we climbed the stairs. "Not that I ever thought I was."

He said nothing until we reached our room and he had pushed the door shut behind us. Then he pulled me into his arms.

"Oh, yes, you are my first love!" he told me. "My first and only love. Don't ever forget it. You're the one I've dreamed of, the one I've waited to find. I knew you right away. So don't believe what anyone else tells you. There've been others, but this time there is something special about the girl."

When he was done kissing me, I held him off. "But broken engagements! What about those?"

"Girls I chose in order to tantalize Glynis," he said. "What else? Twins can grow too close. Sometimes one can grow too close. Sometimes one can grow too possessive—to the point of, well—cannibalizing, you might call it. When Glynis married Trent McIntyre she didn't ask me first. She ran away with him. Perhaps to escape me."

"And now you've paid her off?"

He stopped my pondering with fingers thrust into my tangled hair, pressed my face into his shoulder to silence me. "Don't think and puzzle and take things apart. Let it be. You're mine now. And this afternoon we'll get back to work."

You're mine—and we'll get back to work: I wished he had not put it like that. Yet I knew an artist must *be* his work and that if I had become a part of what he wanted to create, then I had a powerful place in his life. So I must not question too much, must not stir things around inside my head until I could no longer cope with them. Keep it simple, I told myself. Let it be. Because probably it really was simple.

Unfortunately, nothing about Glynis was simple, or ever would be. She joined us for tea, after all—no longer either a child or a jealous sister. She could be completely charming when she chose, and she charmed her father, charmed her brother—charmed me. Only Naomi remained aloof, and though the twins' aunt did not wear her feelings openly, or

80

give them full rein, there was never a moment when I did not sense her dislike of Glynis. Dislike and distrust.

Right after tea Glen took me upstairs to the attic. He posed me again and worked almost feverishly at the clay head. For an hour he worked with the door locked against Glynis. It did no good. The spell that had held him this morning was marred by outside elements, by new presences in the house. When Glen's effort grew desperate, and I could see how strained and tense he had become, I spoke to him from the low platform upon which he had posed me.

"Why don't we leave High Towers? Why not go where you can work without anyone around except me?"

He answered me shortly. "Here is where I can work. Here or nowhere. Don't worry, Dina. The thing is still with me. It's just that I must hurry now. I must have something to show before they come up here to look at what I'm doing."

Only once did someone come to turn the knob of the attic door, find it locked, and go away without remonstrance. But eventually steps mounted the stairs more firmly and the door was rattled.

"Here, here!" Colton's ringing voice called out. "We can't have this. The studios are for all of us, and I don't mean to be shut out of mine."

Glen flung down his tools and went impatiently to unlock the door. Colton and Glynis surged in past him, his sister mischievously eager. There was no chance for him to cover his work, to prevent the intrusion he had wanted to avoid. Glynis ran at once to his workstand, and Colton came with her. I sat on my dais stiffly, feeling self-conscious, artificial— as if all this was playacting which would never mean anything.

"If we may?" Colton said formally, and Glen stepped back from the clay maquette. Colton and Glynis stood staring fixedly at the head. Then they glanced at each other with meaning. Colton shrugged, Glynis shook her head, and without a word each went off to his respective section of the attic, leaving Glen and me alone.

Glen returned to his stand and with one blow of his hand

he knocked over the clay head, smashed it with his fingers. Then he strode out of the attic and down the stairs, leaving me behind. I ran after him, but he moved too quickly for me. I heard the front door slam before I reached the stairs to the lower floor.

Nomi stood at their foot, looking after him. I went down to her slowly, miserably.

"What am I to do?" I said. "It seemed to be going well, until they came home. I'm sure it was. But after they looked at his work, looked at each other and walked away, he destroyed it and ran out of the house."

Nomi's thin, bony hand caught mine and she led me back to the dying fire in her sitting room, thrust me down on a shabby, comfortable sofa. Moving efficiently she poked up the fire, added fresh wood to the embers. When new flames licked upward, she sat opposite me and folded her hands in her lap. The cat, Jezebel, uncurled herself from the heartrug and stretched her paws, yawning widely.

"Listen to me, Dina," Nomi said. "When Glen was very young he had a spectacular talent. And so had Glynis. They were prodigies, really, and they supported each other. The talent of one was part of the other's talent. They gave each other all the encouragement and belief and inspiration either one needed. Outside themselves, only what Colton said mattered because he was their tutor and critic. Together they had an outstanding gallery show in New York—before they were eighteen. Everyone said, 'Fresh, original, great promise.' But Colton was concerned. He had an instinct that Glen leaned too heavily on his sister, imitated her. This proved to be true. When Glynis married Trent McIntyre and moved to New York where her husband worked for a newspaper, Glen went to pieces. He never did anything that was out of the ordinary after that, no matter what medium he chose. He perfected his technique as a sculptor, choosing it deliberately because Glynis paints, but there's more to art than capability. She could fire him with enthusiasm, and the fire was gone. There's a mystique. I believe in it thoroughly because I've lived in this house with a very great artist, a genuine professional—Colton Chandler.''

"What happened to Glynis's work after her marriage?" I asked.

"Oddly enough, she proved not to be so dependent on her twin as Glen was on her. She moved on to greater success and Glen never blamed her for leaving him behind, though I know he suffered. After her marriage broke up and Glynis left Trent, the twins were very close again. But Glen never recovered, as an artist.''

I tried to understand what she was telling me, tried to understand these undercurrents as they applied to my husband now.

"Is it possible that Glen doesn't have the talent his sister has?" I asked.

Nomi gave me an indignant look. "They're so closely twins—their bents are the same. Of course he has it! I remember his early work. And you've seen that remarkable black marble head he did of Glynis. This is a psychological block, and it's his sister who holds him back in every way. She was always about when Glen grew interested in a girl, and it never took her long to expose what was weak, or silly, or undistinguished in any woman he looked at. Glen broke up his own love affairs as soon as he started to see the girl through his twin's eyes. This is what she'll try to do to you now. So you must be on guard. He needs you desperately. It's up to you to keep Glynis from destroying him again—this time completely. It's your responsibility.''

"But why should she want to destroy him? Why shouldn't she take satisfaction in his accomplishment?"

"That's an answer I can't give you." Nomi was in deadly earnest, leaning toward me, reaching out to me with her own intensity and quiet strength. "You'll have to find the answer yourself. But there is one thing we must accept. If the look you mentioned which passed between Colton and Glynis means that Glen's work was going badly, then it was. Neither one would pretend otherwise. If it had been good, they'd have the artist's integrity to admit it. That's why this has hit

Glen so hard. He respects their judgment. Perhaps this first effort should be destroyed. But now he must start again. And that's up to you.''

Nomi rose and went to sit before her loom, where patterned wool cloth was in the making.

There was no assurance I could give her, nothing I could say. My lovely dream of inspiring Glen, providing for him the escape from his sister's domination, was already evaporating. The ugly reality I could not deal with. Glynis was a more formidable foe than I could have imagined—so how was I to find in myself sufficient cleverness and strength to help Glen?

Nomi's words went with me through the rest of the afternoon. They were with me when Glen came home. He did not come near me, but got into his car and drove away from the house just before dinner.

Glynis, Nomi, Colton, and I dined without him, the candlelight falling upon Glen's empty place, reproaching me, warning me that I was clever at dealing with dreams, but not very clever in reality.

Nomi wore her gray housecoat again, and had combed her hair into its evening convolutions. We were served by the housekeeper, Mrs. Dixon, who had come out from town. Nomi watched over everything—watched Glynis most of all. Glen's work and my posing were not mentioned by any of us.

Toward the end of the meal Nomi turned the conversation to the McIntyres' plan for building houses across the lake, and Glynis spoke against it heatedly. Her father heard her out calmly. He looked very distinguished as he sat at the end of the table, the candlelight catching silver gleams in his gray hair, his silvery eyes bright—and somehow watchful. Of me. Whether pleasantly so, or not, I wasn't sure. When Glynis finished her tirade about the lake, he spoke without rancor. So far I had never seen him lose his temper, or even give evidence of being ruffled.

''I've been thinking about all this since I've been away, and I have about come to a decision. I believe I shall sell

Pandora the land she wants. I'm not home enough to have it matter to me what happens across the lake. And I'm sure Nomi doesn't care. You and Glen, my dear Glynis, belong to city life. High Towers is only a refuge for you at holiday times. The land lies idle—it should be used. Nor am I adverse to having the money instead of the land at this particular time.''

Glynis put down her fork and stared at him. She looked very beautiful tonight in brown lace that set off the reddish glints in her hair and made her skin glow like rich cream in the candlelight.

"Glen and I won't let you sell," she said. With her left thumb she began to stroke her left eyebrow in a gesture I had seen her make before when something disturbed her.

Colton stared at her. "You are going to stop me?"

She was not afraid of him, and she answered with spirit. "You can't spoil the lake, Colton! That dreadful box Pandora has built as an inn is bad enough. The trees would be cut down over there. We'd have noise and clutter and ugly little houses cropping up beside the water. All the wild things would be driven out."

"I suppose you mean those wild things you haven't managed to kill already," Colton said dryly.

There was sudden tension between them. The testing of wills was like a current crackling down the table.

Glynis looked down at her own strong, long-fingered hands—hands that were like her brother's. "A balance has to be kept in nature," she said more mildly. "But that's not the point."

"There are any number of points," her father agreed. "And I haven't come to an irrevocable decision. What do you think, Nomi?"

"What does it matter?" Nomi said. "Providing you leave your own land on this side and you don't tear High Towers down over my head, or send me to live elsewhere."

"This house will always be your home, Naomi, as you very well know." Colton made his small, courtly bow in her direction. "But what of our bride? What is your feeling about this, Dina?"

I did not want to be drawn into the argument between them. "Gray Rocks seems a lovely, wild place, but I'll have to let Glen speak for me. I've heard him say that if he can work here, we might stay. I think he's grown tired of city living."

"That's ridiculous!" Glynis said. "Obviously he can't work here. We've seen that before. He will only break his heart again if he forces himself to try. But whether he stays here or not, he will want to see those houses kept away from the lake."

I played with the stem of my wine glass, wishing my fingers would be still, trying not to raise my voice.

"I don't think you've given him a chance in his work yet," I said. "Today was only a beginning. He will find his way. I'm sure of it!"

Colton's look told me that he was genuinely sorry and sad because I must be disillusioned.

Glynis laughed unpleasantly. "Do you think I don't know my brother?"

I met her eyes across the table, and I managed not to flinch in spite of the scorn in hers. "I think in this case you may not know him fully," I said. "Perhaps he has even changed a little."

"Through marrying you!" Glynis's words whipped out at me.

I had been placed on Colton's right hand, and he reached out and covered my fingers with his own, smiling his approval. "Good for you, young Dina! There's a bit of Viking in you after all, in spite of that Dresden complexion. But if you're going to oppose Glen's sister, you must watch out. My beautiful leopard has claws."

Abruptly Glynis turned sullen, though not in the childish way in which she had sulked earlier. This seemed a more threatening mood. Through the remainder of the meal I was aware of her covert glances, aware that some plan was hatching behind those lovely, sullen dark eyes. I did not care. It was only Glen who mattered.

After dinner, when everyone sat before the drawing-room fire drinking coffee from delicate demitasse cups, I left them, to wander about the house. I'd had enough of Chandler company for the moment. Perhaps a book would help. I needed to distract myself.

Colton's den was also the library. I found the light switch and stepped into a small book-lined room. There was little furniture here—only a massive mahogany desk with a red leather chair behind it, a big lounger, and a table with a carafe and glasses upon it. There were hundreds of books, many of them handsome art books and volumes useful for research.

I studied titles and authors, finding that a true library order reigned. Curiously, I searched for the ''Mc's''—and found Trent McIntyre's name. Colton had several of Trent's books. There was the one on Henry Brooks Adams that had launched Trent from his job as a crack reporter into the literary field, and had won him considerable acclaim. The volume on Bret Harte was here too. I remembered it particularly because he was working on the research for it when he came to see my father in California. It was this visit which had given him the idea for a book of short pieces on great American teachers— a collection which would include John Blake. Thus his visit with us had stretched into a month while he listened to Father's lively talk and made quiet notes for later use.

The book came readily to my hand, as though it belonged to me. I took it down and turned to the chapter I wanted. I knew well enough where to find the pages on Dr. John Blake.

The big lounge chair swallowed me. I put my feet up and began to read. This was the best piece in the book—and with good reason. Trent McIntyre had been in my father's classes as a young man. He knew him both as teacher and as friend. It had been John Blake who had encouraged Trent to write, and Trent had come to visit us in California to catch up on all that had happened since he had left school. He had loved my father. And I had loved Trent. That he had a wife back in the East, that he had a son—these things did not matter to a sixteen-year-old who asked nothing for herself. I did not expect him to notice me, take me seriously. I merely wanted to worship from a distance, and this I did for the month before my father died so unexpectedly.

It was Trent who came upon him late one night, Father's head resting on his desk as though he slept. He had gone quietly with the stopping of his heart, and he had lived a full, happy life to the very end. Afterwards, my mother—the sturdy Viking!—had gone completely to pieces. She was put under sedation, given a nurse, and her sister was sent for to help us out. But before Aunt Olga came, Trent took charge because there was no one else at hand. He arranged for the funeral. He took charge, in a sense, of me, who had no one, with my mother ill.

Determinedly I began to read the chapter on my father. I wanted to remember *him*—not Trent. My father's kindly, not very handsome face seemed to swim between my eyes and the printed page. I remember very well his wisdom, his humor. He could be devastating in his criticism of a student's work and yet wielded his scalpel with such wit and gentleness that hardly any pain was felt. He always left one with the feeling that better work was possible the next time. His students were, in great part, his life. The hours he spent out of the classroom were often lived in the rich, varied world of literature—at second hand. My mother in those days was far more of a realist than her husband, and Trent had caught one amusing episode which illustrated this. An occasion when Mother had dealt resolutely with a leaking pipe, from which my father had fled to a classic storm in a favorite book. Once Trent had told me that I was too much like him—coping gallantly with the imaginary and fleeing the results of my real actions.

There—no matter which way I turned, Trent came back into my thoughts. I would never, as long as I lived, forget that rainy afternoon when we came home from the funeral and I went out in the wet side garden and flung myself down on the grass to let my tears flow as the rain flowed. It was

Trent who found me, who picked me up in his arms and carried me, mud and all, back into the house. He mopped me off and wrapped me in a big towel, held me in his lap as though I'd been ten instead of sixteen. I'd wept myself out against his shoulder while he talked to me about my father, made *me* talk about him too—so the wound would bleed freely and not fester.

I had loved them both so much that dark, rainy afternoon. They were tied up together in one huge, painful love that had possessed me completely. This had been all right as long as I had seemed a child to Trent. But I was not a child. I was growing into a woman, and suddenly I wanted more than a child would want. Trent woke up to me with rather a shock and he scolded me thoroughly. I wasn't to go wasting all this brand-new wonderful puppy love on an old married man. I was to find a boy my own age, and make first love what it was supposed to be.

But when does one ever order love? I found myself rejected, knew I deserved to be—and went right on loving him futilely for a long, long time afterward. Perhaps that young girl in me had never stopped loving him.

It was this thought that jerked me awake, made me close the book and return it to the shelf. Not for a moment was I going to allow sixteen-year-old daydreams to interfere with a very real marriage.

Glen hadn't come home, and I knew what I must do. I ran upstairs to my room, pulled on warm slacks, a sweater, slipped into my brass-buttoned navy jacket, caught up a flashlight and started quietly downstairs.

But not quietly enough. Before I reached the foot of the stairs Glynis came out of the drawing room, closing the door behind her. She prowled up and down the hall, awaiting me restlessly, and I thought of how Colton had called her his "beautiful leopard." As she moved I caught the gleam of some shiny object she held in her hands, and when I reached her level she held it out to me.

"This is for you," she said, and I heard the sly note in her voice.

I trusted her not at all, but at least I felt resolute again and I was not afraid of her. She was only a rather spoiled and jealous girl, who had grown too possessive toward her twin brother. She would probably be unpleasant to me on every possible occasion, but about this I did not care. My feeling that she and I might be friends had completely evaporated, and if I had to fight her to support Glen, then I would.

The object she handed me was a hollow ball made of greenish iridescent glass. It was about six inches in diameter and it shone when I held it toward the chandelier, giving off green-tinted rainbow colors.

"What is it?" I asked.

She smiled at me almost sweetly. "It's a witch ball. For spells and incantations, you know. People used to hang them in windows to ward off evil spirits. I've collected them for years. If you like, sometime, I'll look into it for you and read your future. You'll need it, you know, if Glen is to perform miracles after all this time. You'll need its help especially, since you've already disappointed him, failed him. I suppose he depended on you for inspiration. I could have told him better."

The sphere of glass was warm from her hands, and its surface squeaked rather unpleasantly as I turned it in my fingers. I did not like the feel of it, and I set it down on the hall table.

"I don't think Glen will have any need of spells and incantations," I said lightly.

"But they aren't for him! It's you who'll need them in this house. You'll have to work against Nomi's bewitching, won't you? I do believe she's already got to you with her own spells."

I had no desire to be baited any further. "Good night," I said, and let myself out the front door.

She did not ask where I could be going in the blackness of a country night, nor did she follow me. The door creaked shut behind me and I turned on my flash, found my way down the steps. When I reached the driveway something padded softly beside me, and I looked down to find that Jezebel had chosen to keep me company.

The night was cold—no memory of Indian summer lingered on the evening air. A strong wind blew across the hilltop and the sky was ragged with clouds. When the moon disappeared it seemed very dark, yet there was a little starlight and after a few moments my eyes began to adjust. When I started down the winding drive that led to the road below, Jezebel came with me here too, and I was grateful for her company.

Perhaps this was only a wild goose chase. Perhaps I would chill myself for nothing. Nevertheless, I kept on down the drive. Once or twice some wild thing rustled through dead leaves, and Jezebel pricked to an alert. Once a fox barked in the distance and the sound was an eerie one in the empty world the cat and I traveled. Not even the lights of the house were visible behind us now.

I kept on my way until the two stubby posts that marked the entrance to High Towers came into view. There had once been a double gate between them, but it had been long since removed and only the stone posts remained. I climbed to the top of one and perched on its flat surface, my hands thrust deep in jacket pockets, legs swinging as I waited for Glen to come home.

6

Wind whispered endlessly through tree branches above me with a sound like water rushing, touching me with fingers that warned of winter. I turned up my coat collar, pulled up my knees on the post and stared across the road toward the great dark fields that fell away below Chandler property. Here and there a light shone in the valley, but it was not densely populated and I could see no cars moving anywhere. Beside my gatepost Jezebel hunted through the brush, but she did not wander away.

In the clear night air my thoughts seemed to quicken, to clarify and throw off their dreaming quality. Yet it was not Glen I thought of now. It seemed safer to put him out of my mind until he returned and I could deal with whatever then occurred between us.

I distracted myself by thinking instead of my meeting with Pandora McIntyre, and of the strange thing Trent had said about my coming to his mother if there were any need. I considered again the surprising revelation of Glynis's marriage to Trent, and the fact that the boy, Keith, was their son. There was much that seemed troubling here—it appeared to be further evidence of the damage Glynis could do. Neither Pandora nor Trent was pleased over her late-in-the-day charming of Keith, yet they were apparently helpless to keep the boy away from her. Or were they?

I wondered how Trent felt about Glynis now. He had said nothing good about her—yet he had never remarried in the years that had slipped past since he had become a husband at nineteen and Glynis must have seemed all that any man could want in a wife. And he had never taken his son away from her influence, as one would expect him to do.

I heard the car from far away before I saw it. It was coming fast along a highway that was out of sight of the road that went past my gateposts. I heard it slow for the turn before it reached the lake, and then its headlights sped along the road toward me, growing brighter as they came.

I stayed where I was on my stone perch and the lights picked me out clearly. The car was Glen's, and he turned through the gateway and braked to a halt. His window was open, and he looked out at me. The moon had come from behind blowing clouds, and it cast shadows across his face.

"Hello, Dina." His voice was calm. "What are you doing out here?"

His tone told me that he was no longer angry, or hurt, or upset. I jumped down from my stone post and ran to the car. At once he reached for me through the window, pulled me to him by my coat collar, kissed me quickly, lightly.

"I was waiting for you," I said. "I wish you had let me come with you."

"Next time I will," he promised—though when that time came he forgot me again, under worse circumstances than these.

I went around the car, and he opened the door for me. I climbed in and sat beside him. Jezebel had vanished when the car appeared—off about her own business, with no further need of my company.

"Before I left the house tonight," I told him, "Glynis gave me a glass sphere she called a witch ball. She said I would need it."

"That's like her." Glen smiled. "If there were any real witches left today, I'm sure Glynis would be one. Did she frighten you?"

"I wasn't frightened. I don't need to ward off demons, or learn incantations."

He did not start the motor at once, and I sensed a quiet excitement in him. He reached for my hand and held it in both his own.

"I shouldn't have let them upset me," he said. "Colton and Glynis. They were right about the clay head being bad. I didn't need them to tell me. Everything went wrong this afternoon. That's why I had to get away by myself and think things out. Somehow I never think as clearly when Glynis is home. Sometimes I'm not always sure whether I'm thinking my thoughts or hers. But for now I must go my own way. And you're going to help me, Dina."

"Of course," I said. "Whatever you want of me, darling."

"It was the clay that put me off," he went on. "I'm full of the feeling that I must work in stone. Work in it the way those old fellows did who created the masterworks. I want the feeling of stone under my hands—not the poor substitute of clay."

His new elation both pleased and dismayed me. It was wonderful to see him excited again and eager to be at work, determined to let nothing Colton or Glynis might say discourage him. But at the same time, I did not know whether what he planned was wise or practical. I knew so little about carving in stone. I suppose there were writers who set off without the slightest plan and completed successful novels. But could you do that in alabaster, where no erasure was possible?

He answered my doubts as though I had spoken them aloud. "The plan is fully in my mind," he said. "That's why I don't need anything else. There's many a sculptor who works straightaway in stone, once he knows his course."

He started the car, and we drove up the hill and into the clearing before the house. Lighted windows watched us, and the fox barked his lonely call again as we went up the front steps.

Inside the house Glen spoke to no one, but climbed the

stairs, pulling me with him. He did not stop at the second floor, but went straight up to the dark attic, still drawing me along. When all the lights that were available in the big studio had been turned on, he went to work without even taking off his jacket.

"Tonight, you can watch," he said. "I don't need you for posing yet. You're buried too deep in the alabaster for that. In any case, I know the shape of your head through my very fingers. First, though, I must get rid of the concealing excess."

The alabaster of the past—mentioned so often in the Bible—had been, he told me, a harder stone than this. Modern alabaster was softer and a joy to carve. It took almost any tool you chose to use, and he could even work with wood-carving tools when he wished.

"This won't be as good a portrait of you as I could do in marble," he said, "because the translucent quality of alabaster blurs the form and wipes out shadows, but for my purpose of suggesting ice, it's what I want."

Glynis could not bear to stay away, and eventually she came up to see what Glen was doing. He did not so much as glance at her, but I stared boldly into her face, although she did not seem to see me. She watched her brother as the corners of the alabaster block were pared away, so that one could see the shape of a head emerging. Glynis did not speak until he came to a pause.

"Won't you spoil the stone—working directly like this?" she asked.

He avoided her eyes. "Do be a good girl and go away, Glynis. You don't know this piece as I do."

I felt almost sorry for her—she looked so sad and lost at his words. If he was dependent on her, she was also dependent on him. They were close, these two—no matter what interruptions came between them. Too close, perhaps, for anyone else to hold first place with either. But I did not want to come between them. I had my own place. Glen was my husband first, and I wanted to see him develop into the artist he believed he might be. I must be the wife who would help him do that.

Glynis went off without a word, moving as softly, as secretly as Nomi's cat. When she was gone, I think Glen felt only relief. He worked with concentration for a time and then paused to clean the alabaster and wipe it free of stone dust. All his attention was for the alabaster, gleaming under his hands. "Go along to bed, Dina. I'll come later. I want to finish this preparatory work so I can start in tomorrow seriously."

In the hallway I came upon Colton, standing in the door of his room listening to the sound of Glen working upstairs.

"He has more to do," I said. "To get the stone ready for work tomorrow."

He smiled at me kindly. "I'm enormously pleased. No sound of an artist working ever disturbs me. The important thing is that he has gone back to it in his own way. He hasn't let the threat of failure defeat him as he has before. You are good for him, my dear."

I could scarcely have felt more pleased. Whatever Glynis might think of me, Colton Chandler had ranged himself on my side, and I already sensed that his was the governing hand in the household. He had greater strength than the rest of us put together, except perhaps for Nomi. She had needed to grow strong to live all these years among the Chandlers.

I told him good night and went into our room. When I switched on the dressing table lights, something on the bed winked with a green iridescence. The witchball waited for me beside my pillow. I crossed the room indignantly and picked it up. Without hesitation, I went down the hall to Glynis's room and knocked upon the door.

There was no answer. I knocked again and then pushed the door ajar. There was no one there, but two lights burned in the room. One was on the bed table, the other spotlighted the black marble head. I carried the green glass ball to Glynis's bed and set it down. Let it wait beside her own pillow! I wanted no such game-playing to haunt my dreams tonight.

As I turned from the bed I saw a huge, hand-woven West Indian basket set upon a dropleaf table. A basket piled high with a collection of witch balls. They were of every size, from tiny ones that had been used as stoppers for bottles, to one even larger than the one Glynis had insisted upon giving me. They were of every color as well—amber, yellow, purple, red. But I had no time to be curious about them now. Before I left the room I had to look again at that anguished face of black marble that Glen had created.

Now that I had seen Glynis, I knew that it was indeed her likeness, yet with so much that lay beneath brought to the surface. Glen could not have shown her this way unless he knew her almost as he knew himself. The look of the carved face touched me, somehow, shook me from my state of intense dislike. Perhaps I wore too much of a chip on my own shoulder, perhaps, I, too, antagonized.

"That's not for you to look at!" Glynis spoke from the doorway and I turned guiltily.

"I brought back your glass ball." I gestured toward the bed. "I haven't any need for it, you know."

She flew past me to the bed and picked up the green ball, cradled it lovingly in her hands.

I tried to remember the self-doubt I'd felt only a moment before, tried to recapture my resolve not to antagonize.

"Glynis," I said, "isn't it possible for us to start over? You're Glen's sister and I've looked forward to meeting you, wanted you to like me."

When she was excited her dark eyes looked like shiny jet, and she was excited now, tossing the witch ball from hand to hand as though she must take out her excitement in motion.

"Like you!" she echoed. "When you're so completely wrong for him! Do you think a silly little blond thing like you could ever make the right wife for Glen!"

I moved toward the door, knowing that it was useless to stay. But before I opened it, I turned for one last question.

97

"Don't you think you'd feel exactly the same toward any girl your brother married?"

She moved so quickly that I barely had time to dodge as the green ball came flying at me. It struck the door behind me and shattered, spilling splinters of glass over my head and shoulders. If I had not moved it could have struck me full in the face. Feeling as shattered as the glass that pricked my scalp, I walked into the hall.

The explosion must have sounded loudly within the house. Both Colton and Nomi had come to the doors of their rooms. Colton understood first what had happened and he came to me swiftly, touched my cheek, drew away his stained finger.

"You've been cut," he said. "And your hair is full of glass."

The sound still rang in my ears, and I could not speak. He strode to the door of Glynis's room and looked at the scattered shards of glass that lay upon the floor. She had not moved from where she stood when she hurled the ball. Her face was quiet, expressionless, except for the wild shining in her eyes—a wild, animal shining—that I could see, even from the hallway. Before Colton could speak to her, Glen came down the attic stairs and saw us standing there.

Nomi moved toward him. "Glynis threw one of her precious witch balls at your wife," she said dryly.

Glen saw the blood on my cheek, came to brush a scrap of glass from my hair—and his own eyes were a bright, angry jet. He strode to where Glynis stood beside her bed.

"If you ever try to hurt Dina again—" he said, "—if you ever lay a finger on her, I will do to you exactly whatever it is you've done to her. Will you remember that?"

At her brother's words her face crumpled, dissolved into the pain of that usually hidden emotion that Glen had caught when he carved her face in black marble. She looked like a child bereft of everything, her defenses down, her guard destroyed, so that only torment and suffering looked out of her eyes.

For an instant I had feared that Glen might strike her, and

I did not want that. But now his hand fell to his side. His back was toward me, and I could not see his face. Colton shrugged with a massive gesture and went back to his room.

"Glen," I said, "please let it go. Perhaps I made her angry and—"

I think he did not hear me. He was looking into his sister's face, seeing there what he had once carved in marble, and she must have seen a change in his eyes. Her lips quivered, and she put out a tentative hand—then she was in his arms. He held her close, murmuring over her brokenly, as though he comforted a child. They were together, inseparable.

"Come," said Nomi, her hand on my arm. "Come along with me, and I'll bathe that cheek, help you brush the glass from your hair."

Colton's door was closed, and I went with Nomi to her medicine shelf, let her minister to me. I felt too shocked and numb to do anything but obey directions. She did not speak as she worked—as though there was nothing more to be said. I had seen how it was—and that was that. But her hands were very gentle with me, even though I had never seen her face so sternly cold. She would not forgive Glynis as easily for this new offense as Glen had.

That night I waited for a long while within the dark, curving arms of the huge bed, but Glen did not come to our room until after midnight. He did not turn on the light, perhaps hoping I was asleep. He undressed in the dark, and slipped quietly in beside me without touching me.

"I wasn't hurt," I said to him. "But I might have been."

He turned to me at once, slipped an arm beneath me so that I could roll my head into the hollow of his shoulder.

"Don't hold it against her," he whispered. "I love you very much. I need you. But we must give her time. No one has ever taught her not to explode. It's her only way to release the things that wound her. She wouldn't really have struck you with that ball. She missed you on purpose. We must forget it now. Pretend it never happened."

How could I pretend? I knew better than he what she had intended. Someone who exploded into reckless violence had to be controlled. But Glen was close to me, his lips and arms demanded my attention. I loved him very much. I loved him enough to try to understand the closeness of his relationship with his twin sister, try to accept it.

We fell asleep in each other's arms, and for a little while I was comforted.

The next morning the house bustled with activity. The weather had turned very cold overnight and there was a first coating of ice over the lake. Not one of us stepped outdoors all morning. Nomi worked about the house and did not come near the attic. Colton occupied himself in his own studio, getting a number of pictures together for a coming New York show, then went downstairs to write letters in order to borrow other pictures for the show from those who had sat for him.

Keith McIntyre arrived on time to pose for Glynis, rifle in hand, dressed in old jeans and his plaid coat and checkered cap. Glynis, quite recovered and cheerful, went to work sketching him. I had missed her at breakfast, but when we passed in the hall she said, "Good morning," to me as pleasantly as though nothing had happened, and she offered no apology.

Glen had begun to work seriously on the alabaster head. Now he was ready and eager to coax my face from the stone. Sometimes he walked about the head, to view it from every light, seeing it in the round, visualizing every feature in relation to all the others. Sometimes he would turn from the stone to walk about me, even to use calipers to get the measurements right. Sometimes he talked to me, but always about his work. It was the nose, more than anything else, that gave character to a face, he said, but the ears were the most difficult to capture. He would leave them for later—perhaps cover them entirely with the loose fall of my hair.

I became utterly fascinated by what he was doing and was grateful that he chose to educate me as he worked.

Some sort of pact appeared to have been made between Glynis and Glen, because neither one stepped across the invisible line that separated their studio areas during this time.

Neither tried to see the other's work, and all hostility seemed to have been wiped away between them.

This pleasant aura of peace lasted from day to day. After a while I ceased to watch the head as it emerged from stone because I was losing all perspective about it. I would wait—fearfully!—to see the finished work. Glen talked of how the expression of my eyes must be captured, not in the eyeball itself, but by the use of planes and indentations around it. The highlight of a plane properly placed gave life and expression to the eyes.

During this time Colton took long tramps through the woods and did little work of his own. He planned to be off again soon after the first of the year, and this was a rest and a vacation for him. Once he made a sketch of my face and I saw the genius with which he could bring a likeness to life. He signed it for me with his initials and gave it to me, but he told me not to show it to Glen. Not yet. Glen must see me in his own way, Colton said. So I put the sketch with my possessions as something to treasure, and did not let Glen know about it.

During these December weeks that moved us toward the holidays, Nomi began to make Christmas preparations. She commandeered Keith to bring her evergreen boughs from the woods, to find her holly out on the hill above the swamp that marked the far end of the lake. When I said I had no gifts for anyone but Glen, she drove me through brown Sussex hills to the nearest town where I could make a few purchases. She seemed cheerful, almost happy, and she talked to me about the white Christmases she had seen at Gray Rocks Lake when her sister was alive. I joined her in watching the skies for signs of snow.

We saw little of the McIntyres during this time, except for Keith. Sometimes Glynis kept the boy with us at lunchtime and gave herself to charming him still more completely. She began to throw out vague promises to take him with her to New York to live when she went away—promises I suspected she did not mean to keep. I watched uneasily, considering his state of probable rebellion at home when this maternal phase began to bore her and she went back without him to her city life. How were Trent and his mother to deal with what Glynis left behind? I wondered.

Often at mealtime the subject of the changes the McIntyres planned came up for discussion, and Glen and Glynis argued heatedly with their father. Nomi and I were silent, and so was the boy, though he listened avidly to everything that was said. I wondered if he took any of this discussion home to his father and grandmother. Colton simply marked time and did nothing, but I sensed that he would make a decision about the land before he left in January. The matter never seemed very real to me. I had yet to interest myself in it.

Every night the temperature dropped into the teens, and was often in the low twenties during the day. The lake was freezing and I watched the process with interest—saw that the surface of ice was never smooth and unmarked, but that a pattern of frozen ripples and cracks made designs all across it. Sometimes it seemed as though a wave had broken across the surface and frozen there. Often during the day during temperature changes I would hear the ice "talking." It would make a loud, breathy *whomp-whomp-whomp* sound that sped from one end of the lake to the other, raising echoes. All because of underwater thawing and freezing that opened cracks as the level changed.

There was still no snow, and several times Glynis and Keith went skating. Glen urged me to go with them, since he wanted to take no time from his work just now. I had no wish to skate with Glynis, or to skate alone. Several times I saw Trent out on the ice, and I wondered what it would be like if I put on my skates and went out to him. But Trent belonged to another life, and I made no effort to see him.

Glen appeared to have forgotten the incident of the witch ball and forgiven his sister entirely. In his work he seemed to be hurling himself against some invisible deadline that I did not understand. Stone could not be hurried, but he gave nearly all his waking hours to his work. And during this time I seemed to move in a state of suspension, with no real world about me, or anything solid to grasp hold of.

I saw Keith nearly every day, yet I think he was hardly aware of anyone outside of Glynis. All his eager young worship centered about his mother—a mother so little known to him that she could be nothing like other boys' mothers. She was never a parental authority, a restraining hand. She was far more like a teasing playmate, and indulgent to an extreme. Whatever youthful rebellion he felt was directed toward his father and his grandmother, and it was Glynis who encouraged his flight from the real world on the other side of the lake. There was no one to convince him that Glynis was a mirage, that the world she offered was tinsel as far as he was concerned, and something to be thrown away with tarnished Christmas decorations after the holidays.

Once or twice I tried to discuss this with Glen, but his attention scarcely surfaced during this last week before Christmas. He turned inward blindly, and I no longer had a gay, demanding companion or a lover who put me ahead of everything else. Not that I expected his interest to focus on me when his work so absorbed him. For the moment I knew I scarcely existed for him except as a model. The head that was emerging from the ice of its alabaster prison was all that was important. Later my husband would come back to me. But in the meantime I was still a bride—and lonely. Lonely and more than a little apprehensive.

I took long walks along the shore of the lake and found a winding stretch of path beyond the twin towers of gray rock that became my favorite walk. It led to the swamp area, where a narrow stream meandered into the lake. Here brown hummocks of swamp grass crouched like long-haired goblin creatures, with their feet rooted in frozen mire.

It was a time of waiting—an uneasy time because I did not know what I waited for. Sometimes when we were not working in his studio, Glen would give me a look that made me wonder if he might be listening to his sister, perhaps looking at me with a changed vision—as she wanted him to see me. Yet I had no weapon to use against Glynis in those last fateful days before Christmas.

Once, while Keith posed for his mother, and Glen and I

worked in the studio across the attic, Glynis cried out angrily and flung down her palette, scattered her brushes. She must have frightened Keith, for he ran to our side, calling for Glen. But before anything could be done, Glynis shouted to her son to go home and went storming out of the attic.

Glen spoke to the boy quietly. "Don't worry. She has bad days sometimes, when the work won't come right. Go home for now, and when you come back, pretend that nothing has happened."

The boy went away downcast, and had I been free I might have walked to the lake with him and tried to find some beginning of friendship between us. He was lonely too, and uncertain of his mother. But Glen needed me for the rest of that morning. He was working on my hair now, and I must wear it over my shoulders, loose and free. It seemed both to fascinate and frustrate him as an artist. More than once he came to lift its strands as though by sensing texture and weight in his fingers he could transfer the sense of them to inert stone.

By midafternoon that day he threw down his tools and let me off. Since the weather was bright and cold, I dressed in slacks and a warm jacket, pinned back my hair, and went down the hill for my usual walk. When I reached the path along the water, I turned away from the inn and moved toward Gray Rocks. Across the lake I saw Pandora walking the road in front of her stone house. She waved to me and I considered crossing over to visit her. Only the thought of Glen's displeasure held me back. I particularly did not want to anger him now.

Down on the ice a skater came into view, and I saw that it was Trent McIntyre. He moved with confidence, bending forward and taking long smooth strokes, yet always alert for cracks across the ice. He did not see me. I watched until he was lost to view around a bend in the lake. Apparently his working hours were at night, for when I looked out my bedroom window sometimes after dark I would see him at his typewriter, sitting before an upstairs window, and I would hear the clatter of typewriter keys—an incongruous sound to mingle with the sighing of country winds. As I walked along I wondered about his book and who he wrote about this time. When he had been working on material about my father he had sometimes read snatches and paragraphs to me, and I had been a wholehearted listener, loving to watch him as he read. It was not the same watching Glen as he worked. I wondered if I had turned into the sort of woman who could only love when she was touched and paid attention to. No—that wasn't true! I was eager for love whenever Glen wanted to give it, but lately when all his interest and excitement seemed concerned with his work, I still loved him very much indeed.

In my walking, when I came to the great protruding base of the Gray Rocks pinnacles, I crossed it easily, as I did nearly every day. The woods and lake were familiar to me now, and I gave no thought to Keith's warning about loose rock on the tower above. When the rocks were behind me and the path straightened, I moved more freely, lifting my face to a brisk wind that swept along the hillside.

The shoreline was irregular, curving out into the water, then cutting back to form small coves and inlets. As I rounded one of these turns I saw something shining in the sun of the path ahead of me. A mass of dead leaves had blown down from the hillside to lie gathered across my way, and in the midst of them lay an old soda bottle, gleaming in the sunlight. It was an odd place to find litter, but though the land was marked with NO TRESPASSING signs, strangers sometimes wandered in and left trash along their way.

I wore a new pair of green suede walking shoes that Glen particularly liked, and I suppose it was these which saved me. Because I did not want to step into that dusty litter of leaves, I picked up a branch from the hillside and reached out with it, meaning to roll the bottle to where I could pick it up, and then use the branch for sweeping the leaves out of my way into the water.

But as my stick prodded at the center of the leaves where the bottle lay, everything flew into the air with a loud, whirring clang. Something sharp grazed my ankle and the stick was wrenched from my grasp. I stared stupidly at the disturbed bed of leaves and saw that the bottle had broken in two and rolled to the water's edge, while my stick was grasped firmly in the steel jaws of a trap. An animal trap of no small size, into which I might easily have thrust my foot. I was suddenly aware of stinging pain in my ankle and looked down to see that my stocking was torn, with blood seeping through nylon threads.

Escape from having my foot crushed by those steel jaws was so narrow, that I felt shaken. I sat down on a rock and stared at my throbbing ankle. It hurt from the blow it had received, but I could move it. I didn't think any bones were broken.

A voice called to me from the lake, and I looked across the ice to see Trent McIntyre skating toward me.

"What's wrong?" he shouted as he neared the bank where I sat. "I heard something like a trap go off—are you hurt?"

"There was a trap," I said. "It was buried in those leaves, but it only scraped my ankle when it closed." I extended my foot for him to see.

He had been skating with his shoes strung about his neck, and he was out of his skates and into them quickly. He tossed the skates onto the bank and came up to my rock, knelt beside me to examine my foot. In a moment he had rolled up the trouser leg and ripped away the torn stocking to reveal scraped, bleeding flesh, and with a clean handkerchief he bound the wound swiftly and neatly. Still kneeling, he balanced my foot in the palm of his hand and looked up at me.

"Small bones," he said. "A small, narrow foot. That trap would have broken it easily."

I could hardly bear his nearness, his tenderness. He was only a memory out of the past and I had no business thinking him real just because he was kind to me.

"Don't!" I shook my head. "It didn't happen. I'm all right."

He rose and held out his hand to me. "Can you walk? I'll help you back to the house if you can make it."

I tested my foot, put my weight on it. It hurt quite a lot,

but I could manage with his arm to lean upon. When he was sure I could stand, he left me to bend over the trap, pulling it toward him by means of the branch caught squarely in its jaws.

"That seems a strange place for anyone to put a trap," I said.

Trent's dark head was bent over the steel, and when he looked up at me I saw anger in his face. "It's one of Keith's, I think. But Keith would know better than to set it out here. We've all seen you walking this path."

He turned his head to stare at me, questioning, and I stared back, knowing that we were thinking the same thing. There was only one person who might place a trap here on purpose—with me as the intended victim. For an instant I was back in Glynis's room with a green glass ball hurtling toward my face. The thing was too dreadful to contemplate.

"Oh, no!" I cried. "It can't be—"

"Oh, yes, it can be!" He was still wrathful. "Malicious injury was intended here. Come along, if you can manage. We're going up to the house."

He pulled me through the difficult places, swung me over a fallen log, and once when the hillside grew rough and difficult, he lifted me in his arms and carried me to the higher level where walking was easier. I resisted the pain, held onto him, pretending for a little while that memory was real and I had an old friend.

When we reached the house I tried to thank him, not wanting him to go in, wanting to escape, afraid he would make everything worse. But he was not the sort to listen when his mind was made up.

"I'll come in with you," he told me, and we climbed the steps together.

He knew the house well, knew the door would be unlocked. As he swung it open voices from the drawing room reached us and Jezebel hurled herself past as though she could not bear to linger in the hallway.

Trent took my hand and squeezed it lightly. "Don't worry—I'll handle this."

The drawing-room door opened at his touch. He thrust me ahead of him into the warmth of firelight, where Colton Chandler and his family were having their afternoon tea. I stood near the door, with one leg of my slacks rolled up and Trent's stained handkerchief in view, waiting while four faces turned in our direction.

7

Colton sat upon a sofa of royal purple, Sèvres cup in hand. Nomi was in her turquoise chair, pouring for Glen, who stood beside her. Glynis was there too, tall and slim in fawn-colored trousers as she stood before the painting her father had done of herself and her brother when they were young.

All four stared as I hobbled into the room. Nomi set her teapot carefully on the coffee table, and Glen put down the cup she had handed him.

Colton was the first to speak. "Good afternoon, Trent. I've wondered when I'd see you. What has happened to Dina's foot?"

Glynis swung away from the picture and came to stand beside her father, arms akimbo on her hips, her dark eyes bright with malice.

"Obviously there's been an accident," she said.

Trent glanced at her briefly, but he spoke to Colton. "It was not an accident. A trap was set for her on the shore path. It was hidden in a pile of dead leaves, so that only the merest chance saved her from being injured when it snapped shut."

Almost imperceptibly something was happening in the room. Glynis was already at her father's side, and Glen stood just beyond her. The three Chandlers were drawing together, forming a guard against all outsiders, erecting a wall to protect their own. They might quarrel among themselves, these three, but they were a clan when it came to the rest of the world.

"What do you mean—set for *her*?" Colton challenged.

Nomi made a stifled sound as though she thrust back indignation.

Trent looked at her. "You're right, Nomi. Keith wouldn't have set it there. But I think we know who did."

Glynis gave her father's arm a slight pat and came toward Trent. It was not I who interested her now. A flush tinted her cheeks, and she challenged Trent's gaze with her own.

"Dina has a talent for finding knights errant, hasn't she? Fancy your coming upon her in the woods in time to rescue her and bring her home!"

"You got the trap from Keith," Trent accused. "You set it on that path yourself."

"Oh, come off it!" Glen broke in. "We know you resent the Chandlers, but this sort of wild claim—"

"Your wife could be in the hospital with a broken foot," Trent snapped. "I suggest that you take better care of her after this."

He touched me lightly on the elbow and for an instant his eyes softened. "Bernardina," he said. I did not want his pity and I was afraid I might cry. As he let himself out of the drawing room and out of the house, I had the feeling that I had lost everything that might protect me against the Chandler clan.

Glen put an arm about my shoulders, lowered me gently into a chair, and knelt to examine my ankle.

"It's not a hospital matter, Dina. An abrasion, I would think, perhaps a bruise."

I felt impatient, a little angry as I had not been before. "Of course it's not a hospital matter! Trent only said that it might have been. The trap grazed me when it snapped shut on a branch I poked it with."

"And why should you go poking at a trap?" Glynis asked.

I met her look, and if there had been any doubt left in me, it was gone. She was baiting me now, just as she had baited the trap with that empty pop bottle which any stroller would retrieve to dispose of. Though no one strolled down there but me. First the witch ball in sudden anger. Then the trap, with more calculated intent.

"Your sister wants to be rid of me," I said to Glen.

Again there was that sense of the Chandler tribe drawing together for mutual support against so foolish an outburst.

"If you don't mind," Colton said, ignoring my words, "I think we might continue what we were discussing when we were interrupted."

He could be as cold as his daughter, I realized. And Glen had already forgotten me at his father's words. "Yes," he said, "I'm all for the showing right away. I'm ready."

"But I'm not!" Glynis said. "I'm not satisfied with my sketches of Keith. I've tried crayon and watercolor, and I've half finished an oil, as well as doing half a dozen pencil sketches, and I'm not satisfied."

"Then this is a good time for me to see what you've done," Colton said. "I'm driving to New York early tomorrow to take in my pictures, and I'll be gone a day or two. So this afternoon we'll have one of our showings—just as we used to do. Have I been your tutor most of your lives, or have I not?"

Glynis looked sulky, but Glen turned to me in delight. "Come up to the attic, darling. There's a bit more I want to do before Colton is ready for us. Your foot won't bother you on the stairs, will it?"

Through all this Nomi had sat quietly by the fire, but now she rose and pushed Glen away, a small, determined figure, with her coronet braids giving her height. "How inconsiderate can you be? Come with me, Dina. And remember what I told you. No Chandler ever really sees anything except other Chandlers. You should hear the uproar if one of them gets hurt. Come out to the kitchen and I'll get bandages and warm water to fix up your ankle. She's not climbing stairs right now, Glen. I won't have it."

But in the end I climbed the stairs after all. When my ankle had been bathed and Nomi had finished her more expert bandaging, my foot felt a great deal better. It would probably be bruised and swollen for a day or two, but it didn't hurt me very much now, and I was already righting myself psychologically. From now on I must be on guard against Glynis, because I would clearly have little help from Glen. However, if he wanted me upstairs, then I must go. Nomi had explained to me while she bandaged my foot what was meant by a "showing."

When the twins were young and still learning to paint, their father had allowed them to be secretive about their work to a certain extent. Neither one was allowed to interrupt, or criticize, or even praise the other's work up to a point. But there was a time when the project was well launched and Colton would call what he termed a showing. He would even submit his own work in progress to the scrutiny of his children, and he would expect from them the critical eye of the professional in judging it.

"It was his way of keeping control over everything they did," Nomi said. "Though I'll give him credit for not interfering or putting his own tastes to the fore. He recognizes what is good, even if it's not to his personal liking. But he won't suffer the mediocre without chastisement, so the twins are a bit afraid of this sort of ordeal. Of course he hasn't been able to inflict it on them for some time."

It was hard for me to think about sculpture and painting at the moment. "What do you think about the trap down on the shore path?" I asked her.

She wrapped adhesive about the gauze to hold it in place, and did not meet my eyes. It was as it had been when Glynis had flung the witch ball at me—she would not talk. I wondered why she was afraid of becoming involved, of taking sides, when ordinarily she spoke her mind freely enough.

"They didn't really care about the trap," I mused in wonderment. "I don't think either Glen or Colton cared whether Glynis put it there to harm me, once they knew there was no serious damage."

"They're realists. You weren't badly hurt, so they went on

to other matters. If anyone did set the trap on purpose, they won't admit it, so they'll waste no time on that. It's lucky for you Trent McIntyre came along and helped you home."

"He's been kind to me more than once," I said. "Even though I'm a Chandler."

Nomi snorted. "You're no Chandler, and never will be. Any more than Elizabeth was. Or I will ever be. That's a good thing to remember. It will keep you from counting on protection from one of them against the others. They close forces, you know. You saw it today."

"It's not a serious hurt," I reminded her. "If it had been, Glen would have been more upset."

"I'm sure of that," she agreed. "If your foot had been broken he'd have his best model in the hospital by now. And he'd not enjoy that."

I drew away from her hands, forced my suede shoe over the bandaged foot and buckled it loosely. "That was an unkind thing to say. I don't think it's true."

For the first time I saw something soft in her face— something gentle that wavered toward tears and old pain. She patted me lightly on the cheek.

"I know, child. My tongue's had too much use as a knife and a prod. Don't let the same thing happen to you."

"I'm going to the attic," I told her. "I don't use that sort of knife. I want to help Glen, and I can make the stairs now."

He was there, working on the alabaster while he waited. His eyes lighted at the sight of me.

"How are you feeling, darling? Nomi loves to nurse us and boss us around when anything's wrong. I'm glad you let her."

I had nothing to say to that. I wanted to ask him what he really thought of the trap, but this was not the time, so I went to my chair on the dais and Glen turned me for the angle he wanted. When Glynis and her father climbed the stairs, Glen was working with a gouge and a mallet. Glynis did not glance in our direction, but went to her own studio area. Colton stood in the middle of the attic in neutral ground and boomed out his pronouncements. I could see him from where I sat.

He looked a great, handsome figure of a man with his mane of silvery hair and his strong face, with scarcely a wrinkle in it.

"The weather report promises heavy snow moving in from the west," he said. "It will be here by evening, so I'm going to New York today. By tomorrow we may be snowed in. As soon as we're done here, Glen, you can help me move the pictures down to my car. But first we'll all have a look at what you two have been working on. Come along, Glen, Dina—we'll see Glynis's work first."

I think Glynis was unwilling. She still wore her sullen look, and she made no move to bring out her work and set it on her easel until her father told her to do so. Then she placed her efforts for us to see, one by one, and I was puzzled by the sketches and paintings she presented.

Apparently she had approached Keith as a subject in various ways, but despite her talent nothing she touched had truly come to life. In the watercolor he stood against a tree in the woods much as I had seen him when he waited for her the day of her arrival. The butt of his rifle rested on the ground, and he held the barrel in his right hand. The face caught Keith's likeness, but somehow it was wrong.

"No life to it," Colton said, and turned to his son for confirmation.

Glen looked at his sister unhappily. "I'm afraid it's true, Glynis. This isn't up to you."

She showed us the oil. This time the boy stood on the path along the shore, grasping a rabbit by the ears in one hand, the gun in the other. The detail was meticulous, and it looked rather a pretty picture but—she had left the face blank, after working it over several times.

"Your landscape things are better," Glen said. "Perhaps you're too fond of the boy to paint him in your own way. You know you like to see through humanity when you paint. There's always something wicked about what you do. This is bland, flavorless."

Glynis picked up a paint brush and broke it in two.

114

"None of that!" Colton said sharply. "You've been spoiled, my dear. We've always praised you to the skies—and justifiably—but every artist has his off periods when things won't come right. This is obviously one of yours. I suggest more action to what you're doing. Both the water color and the oil are static. For you that won't do. You're a creature who moves, my dear. You prowl—you don't stand still—and your work should move."

"You could show Keith skinning that rabbit," Glen said dryly. "I'm sure the boy will oblige if you want."

Glynis wrinkled her nose. "I can't bear the butchering sort of thing. I don't like skinned animals."

"No," Glen said, "you like them better shot or trapped."

It was the first time he had alluded to the trap. Glynis removed her efforts from the easel and tore them up one by one. Her father gave her a look of distaste and crossed to Glen's side. Almost protectively, Glen moved toward the alabaster head, and I knew that he dreaded his father's criticism, his possible derision. He was far more accustomed to harsh judgments than Glynis was, but this piece meant much to him, and I was as fearful as Glen, lest his father quench the spirit that had charged him creatively ever since we'd come to Gray Rocks Lake.

We need not have worried. Colton knew excellence when he saw it. He walked around the head, his eyes shining, his face alight. He examined it from every angle, and I found that now I could look at it too. I had been so afraid for Glen, so terrified lest his high hopes should come to nothing. But now I could see what a splendid thing he had done.

Nevertheless, I could not visualize it as part of me. It was as if I'd had nothing to do with this creation, sitting there in my chair posing for him. The face was mine, and it was not mine. The head was shown with the chin lifted in an eager acceptance of transformation to flesh by this creature of ice. He had used a cut-off lower than the throat. One bare shoulder just emerged from icy alabaster, and that too was slightly lifted—as though the imprisoned dryad sprang upward and outward, freeing herself of the cold substance that held her. There was life in the face—a pure, cold life that was somehow untouched by humanity. A face beautiful and pure because life had not yet reached it. Surely it was not my face. Not even a child could be as coldly innocent as this—if what was there was really innocence.

Stone still encased the left shoulder, and I knew Glen meant to leave it that way. Stone held the left side partway up the throat, before all the rest emerged. A few strands of hair rested upon the visible right shoulder, as though touched by a breeze, and the fall of hair over the head and down the back seemed amazingly alive for stone. Much of the piece was uncompleted, but what was there was good.

"Of course it's not finished," Glen said hurriedly. "There's more to be done on the detail of the face, the entire head. And I'm still trying to get the hair to come right. Like Dina's."

Colton stilled his booming, almost as if he spoke in awe. "It's remarkable. You've found yourself, Glen. This is going to win you a name. And you won't lose your touch after this. Young Dina has helped you recover it. Hold onto her. Hold onto her and—"

"—and keep her out of traps," said Glynis behind us, her tone as cold as white alabaster. Cold white—flecked with the green of jealousy?

"That's all the time I can give to this now," Colton said, ignoring his daughter. "I must be on my way. Help me with the pictures, Glen."

Before Glen could move to his father's assistance, Glynis came close to the head and touched it lightly with long-fingered hands. What she said surprised me.

"It's good, Glen. Awfully good. The best you've ever done—except the black marble. I wonder if you know why?"

Glen turned to her so eagerly that my heart twisted. He must know by now that she could not be trusted. Or was he the only one who dared to trust her?

"Tell me what you mean," he said.

Even Colton's interest was caught, and he paused to hear what she had to say.

Gently, almost caressingly, Glynis ran her hand over the face that was mine—yet not mine—sensing its contours with her own sensitive fingers as though her eyes were blind.

"This is the opposite number from the black marble, Glen, but it's also the counterpart. It's not Dina you've caught in your block of ice. You know that, don't you?"

Glen had turned quite pale, and he shook his head vehemently. "No—no, you're wrong, Glynis. That's not what I intended."

His sister stared at him for a moment, and then quite without warning she burst into tears and fled from the attic. We could hear her clattering down the stairs, hear the banging of distant doors.

Glen's pallor was that of illness, but his father did not notice. "The pendulum has swung," he said. "She goes back while you go forward."

He came to look at the head once more, to study it in pleased surprise.

"Now that was very perceptive of her," he said. "She's cut through to the truth, whether you recognize it or not, Glen." He rested his hand on the alabaster head. "You'll never be free of each other—you two. So try not to make your sister bleed any more than you need to. Come along now and help me to the car. With that foot, Dina's of no use to us on a job like this."

Colton smiled at me vaguely as he picked up several canvases and started downstairs. For all his words of praise, I was outside the clan.

I could think only of Glen. I could see only the shock in his eyes. I moved toward him, wanting to offer my love, my belief, my reassurance.

"Don't believe what your sister thinks—" I began, but he brushed past me with a look that was almost one of revulsion and went to help his father.

While they were carrying Colton's pictures down to the car, I stayed beside the alabaster head, forced myself to look at it clearly. Yes—it was there. I knew what Glynis meant. That hint of the *un*human—that was surely not me. I knew where it came from now, and I felt as though I too were momentarily encased in ice. The face that was not my face would haunt my dreams tonight, I was sure, and I turned my back on the attic and went downstairs, wanting to get as far from it as possible.

When the pictures were loaded in the car, I stood at the front windows to watch Colton drive away. The afternoon had grown dark, and shredded gray clouds had the look of promised snow about them. Nomi joined me at the window where I reported the superficial results of Colton's "judging." I did not mention what Glynis had said. Nomi seemed more than a little pleased—both at Glen's success, and at Glynis's failure. She never let me forget that at every turn she was against Glynis, but I did not know for certain whether that put her on my side. Now, at least, having bandaged my foot, she was aware of me, and I took advantage of the fact.

"Tell me about Glen's mother," I said. "Tell me about Elizabeth."

Nomi did not answer or look at me.

Outdoors, Colton got into the driver's seat and slammed the door. He rolled the window down, waved to Glen, and wound his way down the driveway to the road. Glen stood looking after him for a moment, and then went off through the woods—probably in the direction of Gray Rocks, to find his sister.

When he was out of sight, Nomi took me by the arm, led me quietly back to her sitting room. Jezebel had found her way inside again and lay upon the shabby sofa, purring lazily.

"You'll always be safe in this room," Nomi told me strangely. "Glynis never comes here. It's too full of her mother, and she can't bear the accusations it holds."

"Will you tell me now?" I asked. "I want to understand. There's so much about the Chandlers that mystifies me. How is this room full of Elizabeth?"

"On a stormy night this is the warmest room in the house, and since Elizabeth was so often cold, we used to spend our evenings here. And often our afternoons, when the twins were young. Colton was away a great deal, as he is now, so Elizabeth wanted me with her. She was never very strong, and the children were an unruly pair even then.''

She went to a desk and opened it, while I sat beside Jezebel and stroked her fur. In a moment Nomi returned, bringing a photograph to show me. It was a softly done sepia print of a pretty, sweet-faced woman with her hair brushed into the upsweep of the thirties. Her eyes were clear, but a little troubled, and I suspected that her soft mouth would tremble easily.

"She hadn't the iron in her to deal with Chandlers," Nomi said, and put the folder away. "That's why I had to develop enough for the two of us. And I can say that I've held my own. They haven't subdued me as they'd have liked to at times.''

She rubbed her small pointed nose thoughtfully, and I smiled at her with growing affection. "I'm sure they haven't. But I'm beginning to wonder about me." I put out my foot and looked down at the swelling ankle.

"After the holidays, get Glen to take you away," Nomi said. "It's tradition that they all come home for Christmas and stay through New Year's Day. Then they'll scatter again, but Glynis may cling to her brother now, so you must insist that you won't stay in the same house with her for long."

That would depend on how Glen felt. If he was finding himself in his work, as his father seemed to think, then I must not be the one to fail him and insist on change.

Persistently I went back to the subject of Elizabeth. "Keith told me his grandmother fell through the ice out on the lake beyond Gray Rocks."

Nomi knelt before the fire and fed it several birch logs. Then she sat on her heels on the hearthrug and held out her hands to the flames as if a chill had touched her. In stark, unemotional tones she told me the story.

"It happened on a New Year's Day. Elizabeth took Glynis skating. Glynis was busy playing with some new Christmas toy and didn't want to go out. Even when she was five Glynis had an imp in her. Glen had the same perversity, but in him it takes a slightly different turn. That day, before they left the house, Glynis was teasing to skate in her favorite place. The weather had warmed, so there had been some thawing and that particular place—though it's good for skating because the surface melts early, then freezes smooth—is often doubtful as well, because it's fed by springs all year round. To make her stop her begging, Elizabeth said they would go where Glynis wanted and see how strong the ice was. Exactly what happened we'll never really know. How is one to get the truth out of a five-year-old child who has been terrified? As far as we could reconstruct from what Glynis told us later, she would not listen to her mother's warnings. She put on those little skates of hers and went skimming out over the ice that swayed under her weight. Perhaps if Elizabeth had stood on the shore and waited for her naughty child to come back, everything would have been all right. But Elizabeth must have lost her head and tried to go after Glynis to bring her back before the ice cracked through. And of course it did crack under her greater weight. She was the one caught in the freezing water, while Glynis skated safely back to shore."

Nomi fell silent. She watched the reddening birch logs as intently as though she saw the whole thing enacted there. Her face was shadowed with pain—and something more.

"So Glynis watched her mother die and knew it was her fault?" I said softly.

Nomi got up from the hearth and sat in a chair. "No. It was worse than that. Perhaps if she had run straight back to the house someone might have been in time to rescue Elizabeth. But instead the child knew she was in for punishment, and she ran away and hid. It was more than an hour before her mother's body was found. In the beginning it was thought that Glynis might be lost in the lake, but we first beat the woods for the child—and found her hiding in that cave at the top of Gray Rocks, where she was forbidden to go. When her father brought her down and carried her home she was hysterical with fright. It was weeks before we found out more or less what had happened.''

I did not want to be moved by anything which concerned Glynis Chandler, yet the story stirred me. I could feel pity for the child who had caused the tragedy. Her fault was the fault of a child, her misbehavior that of a five-year-old.

Nomi's eyes were bright, her expression harsh. Emotionally she had removed herself from the room where Jezebel and I sat, and was reliving an old and terrible experience.

"You can't keep on blaming her," I said. "How can you hate a child for something that was childish folly, whatever its outcome?"

"She was never a child." Nomi turned her chill look in my direction. "Glynis was always evil—a little monster even when she was young, and now a more dreadful one. She hasn't changed. You've only to look at your ankle for the answer to that."

"Perhaps the adults who blamed her turned her into something monstrous," I said. "What happened afterward?"

Nomi shook her head at me indignantly. "We were never cruel to her. I couldn't forgive her, but I didn't take out my feelings on her. I tried not to let her see how I suffered over my sister's death—not when Glynis was a child."

But a child would know, I thought. A child would know whether or not she was loved.

"That was when she turned even more wholly to her brother," Nomi went on. "They were already close as twin peas, and after what happened she could love and trust him as she could no one else. He never blamed her, and lacking a mother they clung to each other. Colton was no substitute. And I could only give them my care. I came to love little Glen, and I've loved him ever since. But his sister is something else. I warned you she'd break up your marriage if she could. Now it seems that she'll try to injure you physically as well. Perhaps she'll even try to use Keith against you, the way she got that trap from him. She's constantly bribing him with talk about taking him to New York, though I can imagine the sort of life she lives there—the corruption! He'd hardly be of use to her. But here—''

''Why does Trent let his son stay at the lake where he's sure to come under her influence?'' I asked.

''That's ancient history. It had to do with the divorce bargaining that went on. *He* wanted the divorce. Glynis didn't care. So the agreement was that the boy remain with his grandmother, where Glynis could have easy visiting privileges. She didn't want the boy with her, needless to say. And in the beginning it didn't matter. Now what she is doing matters a lot—yet Trent's hands were legally tied. This is another score I hold against her.''

Nomi had revealed herself more than she intended. Perhaps this was the reason why she had avoided talking about any of these things—because she knew she might betray the rage that still seethed in her and was so ugly a thing.

The sitting room made me uneasy, and once more I wanted to get away. I told her I would go upstairs for a book from my room, and I left her there before the fire with Jezebel.

I was still horrified by Nomi's story, still living in the past, pitying the child Glynis had been. I walked down the hall to the foot of the stairs, and met Glen as he burst through the front door with the grown-up Glynis on his heels, storming at him. I had never seen Glen so white-faced and furious. He passed me as though I were not there, and dashed up the stairs. The front door slammed after Glynis as she plunged into the hall. When she saw me she lounged against the newel post, her hands thrust into the pockets of her fawn trousers, her short hair ruffled by the wind that had tossed it. The look in her eyes promised me something—and I forgot the forlorn child. As she studied me for that endless moment she put her left thumbnail to her eyebrow and traced its contour again and again in that gesture which seemed to mean that she was busy once more at her plotting.

''What's the matter between you and Glen?'' I asked her.

She smiled as a cat might smile—secretly. I wondered that she did not like cats when she resembled them so much of the time. I did not like the promise of her look. Whatever

122

she was about to do, I would not want to be on the receiving end.

At the sound of Glen's clatter up the stairs, Nomi came out of her sitting room and stood watching from the back of the hall. But before I could start upstairs after my husband, Glen ran down again, having pulled a heavy jacket over his sweater. I tried to speak to him, but he brushed past me.

"I'm going out. I've got to be free of this house for a while. I don't know when I'll come back. Don't expect me till tomorrow—if then."

"Glen!" I wailed. "Glen, take me with you!"—but he was gone without heeding my words.

Nomi took action at once. She snatched a coat from the rack in the hall and put it on as she ran after him. When I hurried onto the veranda I saw her rush to Glen's car and manage to get into the front seat before he started the motor. They went off together, careening around the turns on the way down the hill.

Glynis's laughter had an ugly ring. "Nomi will take care of him, dear. My darling brother isn't pleased with us just now. But Nomi will see that he doesn't drive too wildly. Which may be a wise restraint with a snowstorm coming on. The first flakes are falling now. How I love winter! I can't breathe in hot weather. But when it's cold I can fill my lungs, get outdoors and *live*. I can hardly wait for the first blizzard— I hope this is it. I hope it will snow forever—pile drifts as high as the house!"

I looked up at a whitening sky, saw the shimmer of beginning snow.

"What did you do to him?" I demanded. "How did you upset him so?"

She started up the stairs. "Don't you think the point of the matter is what he has done to me?" she said, and ran up to her room.

As I stared after her Jezebel came out of Nomi's sitting room. She had heard Glynis's voice and tone, and every hair on her tiger's body was fluffed to twice its size. She walked

123

toward me stiffly on the tips of her claws, like a cat in a fit, and her bushy tail was erect, her yellow eyes a little mad.

I fled to the drawing room and closed the door. Except for Mrs. Dixon, who was busy in the kitchen getting dinner, I was alone in the house with Glynis and Jezebel—both of whom were a little mad. And by eight o'clock the house-keeper too would be gone.

8

Mrs. Dixon served dinner early, rushed the dishes into the washer, and was on her way. She had no wish to drive home in a snowstorm, she said, and it was getting worse outside every minute. When she had gone, Glynis and I sat in the drawing room with our coffee as though everything were as usual. All through dinner we had made some effort at conversation, for Mrs. Dixon's benefit, but there had been hardly a minute when Glynis did not watch me with that dark, veiled gaze which betrayed nothing of what she was thinking. My uneasiness grew constantly greater.

After the housekeeper had gone we sat before the fire listening to the storm buffet the house and wail about its eaves. I could imagine its pointed ears pricked intently to listening. Blasts of snow rattled against the windows, harsh as desert sand, and now and then the house shuddered under the impact.

Glynis had dressed for dinner, just as though her father and brother were there, and tonight she wore a long silk jersey print of swirling yellow sunflowers against a white ground—dramatic and bold. I had not gone upstairs to change from sweater and slacks because I had not wanted to be up there alone with her. It seemed pointless to keep up the amenities between us now that she had shattered Glen's confidence in his work. Most of the time I listened for the sound of Glen's car returning—a sound that never came.

"You asked me a question quite a while ago," Glynis said, sipping her Cointreau, her eyes speculative. "You wanted to know what had upset Glen. Do you still want to know?"

I let a space of time go by while I finished my coffee and set down the cup. "I suppose that you upset him," I said. "But how?"

"I'd like to tell you." Glynis nestled into a corner of her sofa as though this was to be a cozy family chat. "I think it might be a good thing for you to understand, now that you've married him. Neither Glen nor I are separate people. We're one, really. I've always known that, and I've always accepted it. Lately he hasn't. He has developed the curious notion that I am sucking him dry to feed my own talent, so there is nothing left for him that will be his own. Lately he has been trying to escape the tie between us and be someone totally remote and separate from me. Alone. That's why he married you. That's why he's trying to create that little masterpiece upstairs."

"From what your father says, it may very well be a masterpiece," I told her.

"Oh, it's all of that! I never said it wasn't. But he hadn't seen, until I pointed it out to him, that it is still another side of his twin that he's creating. This time in that lovely white alabaster. Underneath all that young prettiness that is you, Dina, he has created a force that is *me*. Only your face is there—something outward and superficial. The soul of the stone, the thing that is bringing him fulfillment is still me— Glynis Chandler, his twin."

The notion was absurd. I wanted to tell her that. Yet— what if it was so? When I had looked at the alabaster head this afternoon, I had sensed a quality in it that was nothing like me.

I left my chair and went to the windows, tried to peer out at the dervish dance of snowflakes, but saw only my own face and the room behind me reflected in black glass.

"How soon will the snow plows go through?" I asked over my shoulder.

"Who knows? Sometimes we've been snowed in, or iced in, for two or three days. We're not on a major road, and the plows go through first where school buses make their pick-ups. Besides, if the snow gets much deeper than it is, no one will be able to come up our driveway until we get it plowed out. That's Glen's job, when he's home. We have a snow plow tractor that he runs. Or Nomi will call up some neighboring farmer. But neither are here to take care of it now, so I expect we may be stranded."

"Can't you—?" I began.

She was so still in the room behind me that I turned around to find her watching me with amusement brightening her face. Her thumbnail traced the line of one brow lightly.

"Perhaps I could—but will I?" she murmured. "Don't you find it rather cozy here, with just the two of us? The very two who are most closely concerned with Glen!"

Little cat claws seemed to tap at the back of my neck, almost as though Jezebel was touching me with cold paws. But I knew instinctively that fear was the thing I must never show Glynis. She would enjoy it too much. She would use it, as a leopard stalks and freezes its frightened prey. I must not think now of that glass ball hurtling toward me. I must not think of a trap in the woods. I must never betray that I watched her, waiting for the leap that might destroy me.

"I've never seen a country snowstorm," I said. "Perhaps I'll go out for a walk around the house."

"Wait," she said. "There's something I want to show you first. I'd like you to see a picture I painted a year or two ago. I think it's right here."

She went to a slant-front desk and drew the top drawer open by its brass pulls. When she had shuffled through several sketches and paintings, she selected one and brought it to me. Not really wanting to look, I carried it to where the light was brightest beneath the big chandelier.

The watercolor was not a large picture—perhaps no more than seven inches by ten—and its subject held me rooted in

127

morbid fascination. It was as if Glynis had known I was thinking about traps and big cats. As if her sensitivity—or hatred for me?—gave her extra-sensory powers that let her read my thoughts.

I had no doubt that the cat she had portrayed here was Jezebel. Jezebel hopelessly snared in a portion of fish net which had been pulled tight about her tiger body, and from which she fought furiously to escape. The cat's yellow eyes burned with fury and terror, its ears lay back and its teeth were exposed in a snarl. One paw protruded through the net with claws wildly extended, and its tail was cruelly looped through another opening in the mesh.

Glynis came to stand beside me, smiling slyly. "Poor Jezebel. No wonder we can't stand each other. She'd have been all right if she hadn't struggled so. I must say she wasn't a very quiet subject for me to paint, but I think I caught her rather well, don't you?"

She was waiting for me to be shocked, watching for me to recoil, so I kept my hand steady as I gave the picture back to her.

"It's very good. Unpleasant, but good. Much better than the sketches you've done of Keith in the last few days."

It was she who astonished me by recoiling herself. She snatched the water color from me and returned it to its drawer. When she spoke she was breathing quickly.

"Exactly what do you mean by that?"

I hadn't known that I meant anything by it, but there was something a little heady about having the balance of power shift so suddenly. I had had enough of her cruelty. If I was to help Glen I could not always be the one to be hunted. This time it was I who attacked.

"Perhaps you're no more a separate person than Glen is. Have you thought that the time might come when he would draw everything he needs from you to sustain him as an artist—and leave you empty? Do you suppose being twins can be as psychic as all that? It does seem strange, doesn't it—that you should drop behind in your own work as soon as Glen moves ahead?"

She slammed the drawer of the desk shut so sharply that it twisted, and I heard the splintering of wood. She left it askew and crossed the room with the same free stride with which she walked in the woods, the sunflowers of her Pucci dress swirling about her.

"You seem to have missed the whole point in what I meant when I showed you the picture of Jezebel," she said. "I thought you'd be clever enough to see what I intended. The cat was caught in the fish net—with no one to come to its help until I was through with it. Isn't it the same with you tonight? Aren't you caught in a net, with a blizzard blowing outside and no one to turn to except me?"

The small cold paws tapped the back of my neck again. I understood very clearly indeed. I had sensed this all along—ever since Naomi had gone rushing off to Glen's car leaving me with Glynis. But I must not show her that I was afraid.

"I'm scarcely caught in a net," I said. "To begin with, I am hardly helpless. I have only to walk out of the house and not come back."

"But you won't," she assured me.

I had to show her then, and I moved too quickly, with the quickness of near panic, so that pain in my ankle stabbed up my leg. I limped upstairs to my room and pulled on my boots gingerly, flung myself into my coat, tied a scarf over my head. She was waiting when I came down the stairs. The leopard prowling again.

"I'm going over to the McIntyres'," I said.

She smiled at me sweetly. "And have Glen come home and find you gone? Because you're terrified of his twin sister you'll let him find that you've gone over to the enemy? You're as much of a fool as I suspected. Don't you think he has already noticed how fortuitously Trent rescued you from that trap—and managed to instill in you the idea that I had set it there?"

"Didn't you?" I said.

She shrugged. "It's more fun to keep you guessing. But don't think I haven't read Trent's chapter on your father. Don't forget that I was married to him when he went out to California to finish up that piece. And came home with quite a tale about a moonstruck child who thought herself in love with him. Oh, I've heard about his charming Bernardina. I read your letters, never fear. I know who Dina Blake is—if Glen doesn't. This is something I've kept up my sleeve to use when the right time came.''

I hated the sick warmth that flowed through me, hated the pain of a twisting knife I could do nothing about. Nothing could have upset me more than to learn that she had known all along of that first overwhelming love I'd had for Trent. To know that she had even read those young, innocent letters! But if it killed me, I would not let her see how much I minded her words.

"I'm going for a walk," I told her stiffly and went out the front door.

The snow was not as bad as it would be later. Not as deep, not blowing as severely. But it was already treacherous underfoot, and I slipped and fell as I went around the house, wrenching my hurt ankle again. When I limped out into the open on the lake side the wind struck me full force and sharp granules stung my face. This was sleet, and I welcomed the sting of ice pellets in my face. I would welcome anything that would wipe from my mind the picture she had created of Trent sharing my letters with Glynis, laughing over them, never meaning to answer.

The night was not as dark as I expected. Light fell through the windows of the house and lay in bright patches on the white earth. The very whiteness of the storm carried light and movement in its heart. Ahead of me the hillside fell away like a sheet of glass. I righted myself by clinging to the wet branches of a pine tree and fought my way back to the drive. There could be no going down that hill and across the frozen lake tonight—unless I wanted to slide all the way. But perhaps it would be possible by way of the road.

My foot hurt me, but on the upper driveway I could manage. When the road steepened, however, I could not stay on my feet. After my second fall I crawled back to the level and struggled across the open space where wind and sleet caught me full force, stumbled up the slippery steps to the veranda. At least Glynis had not locked the door against me. I let myself into the house, gasping in wind that cut, my face burning and my ankle throbbing.

For the moment it was simpler to face Glynis Chandler than to deal with the enmity of that foreign world outdoors, that world of ice where it seemed that all my hopes, my very life, could shatter in the glass-cold surfaces which mirrored my own fearful face. The country could be beautiful and peaceful and benign. But it could tear you to pieces if you lacked the courage to deal with its more malevolent moods.

Fortunately, Glynis was not in sight when I returned. Undoubtedly she had known I would come back indoors and had not troubled to watch my ignominious retreat from the storm. Lights still burned in the empty drawing room. I left them on and started upstairs. On the way I thought of going to Nomi's sitting room for Jezebel, bringing the cat to my room for company. But my memory of Nomi's pet, wild-eyed with fur on end as I had seen her, both in life and in the snarling, spitting fury Glynis had painted, made me decide to do with my own company until Glen came home.

In our room I fell asleep with the sound of the storm in my ears. The ice phase was over and the real blizzard was well under way, burying countryside, house, and lake under thick, drifting snow.

I fell asleep—and wakened to the sound of a key turning in the lock of my door, imprisoning me—as the fisherman's net had imprisoned Jezebel with its confining meshes. I did not know why she must do this. Whether it was to torment me, or because she planned something more dreadful, more serious, I could not tell.

For a long while I stayed awake. I sat before the fire and kept it burning. I listened for steps in the hallway. Steps that never came—or came so softly that I could not hear them, which was even more terrifying to consider. In my mind I went over it all—over everything that had happened to me since the moment when Glen Chandler had walked into the museum storeroom and swept me off my feet. I could not see—given the person I was—how I could have behaved any differently. It was so easy to accept the glamorous dream and believe it real.

But of course it was real, when I loved Glen as I did, and when he loved me. I did not doubt that he loved me, though now, because of Glynis, our very love was at stake. I longed for Glen to be with me—longed for the man he had been before his sister came on the scene. Yet I pitied and understood this other side of him. There was no one to help him but me, and now I could not even help myself.

After a long while I found I could keep awake no longer. I crept wearily back to bed and crawled beneath icy covers, pulled the quilt to my ears—and was asleep almost at once.

When I wakened again, morning had come. I sat up in the cold room and looked at my small clock. It was six o'clock, and the radiators had not yet started to heat. My hearth was cold ashes, but I emerged into the chill and found that I still wore my long robe. I went to the window on the lake side of the house and flung the draperies back, to see that the window was blocked by snow halfway up. I breathed on a frozen upper patch and rubbed it clear of frost so that I could look out.

Snow still blew across a white, strange world. No tree was recognizable and the unfamiliar earth was piled high with drifts of white. Boughs hung heavy with their burden, swaying toward the ground, and a small spruce tree under my window was bent almost double with heavy ice claws at the tip of every branch. At least there was gray daylight out there. Nothing dreadful had happened to me after all, except a rather bad night.

In the morning, at least, I always felt braver, more courageous. Now I was angry as well. I went to my door and turned the knob, found the door still locked against me. This was completely absurd. What could she possibly gain by keeping me a prisoner in my own room? If she was asleep by this time, then I would waken her and do so at once.

I rattled the door and banged on it furiously. I shouted Glynis's name and demanded that she come and let me out.

I caused such an uproar that it must have been heard through-out the house—wherever Glynis might be. Yet nothing happened. Absolutely nothing at all. There was not a sound anywhere, and I had the slow, cold feeling that I might have been locked into this room and deserted forever. Glynis would know her way around the countryside better than I. And she was accustomed to snow and ice. There were skis and snowshoes about, and stout walking boots. If she wanted to go out, she would—leaving me in a cold and empty house, locked into one room.

I found Glen's small transistor radio and turned it on while I once more tackled the laying of a fire. There was a good deal of static—country reception could be bad—but at least the familiar voice of a New York station came through, uttering doom-filled messages of clogged roads, wires down, cars abandoned, deaths from freezing in suburban areas. *The worst storm of the beginning winter . . . The worst storm of any beginning winter . . . The worst storm since . . .* I shut it off and warmed my hands at the fire, considering what I must do.

At least I had my own bathroom and I would have water to bathe in, however cold it might become, and water to drink. But unless Glynis chose, I'd have no food. If Glynis kept the furnace off, it would soon be bitter cold. I washed and dressed in warm brown slacks and double yellow sweaters. I must conserve the wood for the fireplace too.

When she finally called to me through the door her voice came so faintly that I scarcely heard her. "Dina? Dina—are you up?" The whisper had an almost eerie sound.

I flew to the door and rattled it fiercely. "You know very well that I'm up. Open this at once and let me out!"

I could almost see her shaking her head. "No, my dear. I'm not ready for that yet."

I tried strategy. "You can't be serious about locking me in, Glynis. Besides, we might need one another in a storm like this."

"People can go for quite a long while without eating," she said. "And you're much too high up to get out a window, even if you could battle the ice. So just be a good girl, and after a while I'll give you a little heat.''

"Glen will be furious,'' I warned her. "I don't think he'll approve of this prank.''

"Prank?'' Glynis echoed softly, her voice far more controlled than mine. "He didn't mind about the trap, did he? And I wouldn't call this a prank. If you really want to know why I've locked you in, I'll tell you. It's because I want more time to think, and I can't have you running off to the McIntyres' in the meantime. Or using the phone.''

"Think about what?'' I challenged her.

"Why—'' there was surprise in the soft voice, as though I should have understood, "—about what I'm to do with you, of course. There are so many interesting possibilities that I haven't been able to decide. But I'm sure I will think of something really lovely before long—something no one but you and I will ever know about. Something you'll be blamed for and I won't.''

I must not let that beguiling voice terrify me. I pounded on the door again. "You're mad, Glynis! There's nothing you can do to me. If you touch me, I'll fight you back. I'll—''

"Oh, I won't touch you,'' she said lightly. "Not in the way you might think. Not directly.''

"That glass ball was direct enough,'' I said.

The soft, eerie laughter came again. "That was a mistake, of course. A fit of temper.''

I wondered if she really was mad. Or if she was coldly sane and perversely enjoying her ability to seem mad. I didn't know which was worse.

"Keith!'' She cried the name in sudden inspiration, startling me. "Perhaps I can use Keith. You might as well go back to bed, Dina dear. There won't be anything for you to do for quite a while. I'll have to reach Keith. I'll see you later.''

"Glen will come!'' I shouted after her, but I could already hear her retreating down the hall, hear her steps on the stairs. I had a feeling that she knew very well that Glen would not come. Perhaps he would never come again in the sense of returning to me.

I paced the room, feeling boxed in and desperate. I remembered how Glen had been about the trap—how he had not really minded, how he had made light of my injury. This was another trap and even if he were here, he might merely regard it as a joke—am amusing trick of his sister's. What was I to do? Not only now, immediately—but in the future? How was I to come between this dreadful twinship? They were one. Yet they were not one because there was ambivalence here. They pulled against one another at times, though only to be drawn back into a closer relationship than ever, once the parting between them threatened to become permanent. I was the threat now, and they would not tolerate me. Glynis would destroy Glen's love for me—she might even destroy me. And I could no longer be sure that Glen would not help her when the time came. Indeed, wasn't he helping her now by driving off and leaving me behind to her mercies? He knew her every thought and reaction. He would know very well what he was leaving me to. There was no help for me there. If I was to get out of this predicament, I must help myself.

I walked about, surveying the room. There were two windows—the one I had looked out a little while earlier, with a very steep drop to the sloping hill below, and the one that opened upon a small balcony at the side. I tried the balcony window and raised it with difficulty against solid ice. Snow fell into the room, but I ignored it and stepped through the opening into deep snow that filled my shoes. I went to the balcony rail where windblown whiteness engulfed me. The wooden rail wore a thick white icing and I swept a small stretch of it and leaned over. The ground was a long way down, but there were deep drifts rising as high as the first floor windows of Nomi's sitting room just below me. Glynis had forgotten the snowdrifts.

It was bitterly cold and already my hair and eyelashes were frosted, while melting snow dripped down my face. I crawled back into the bedroom and closed the window as softly as I could, kicked off my wet shoes. Then I cast about for the next step. The obvious one, of course—bed sheets! I ripped them off the bed, twisted them into long ropes diagonally, and knotted two together.

For once I was glad of my glamour-girl outfit of white wool. It wrapped me in warmth, and the wool hat had flaps to pull down over my ears, the long boots came to my knees and helped to protect my ankle. I thrust knitted mittens in my pocket and let myself through the window. Though the balcony rail was of carved wood, it stretched between solidly planted iron posts, and it was about one of these that I tied the end of the first sheet. Out in California my mother had been good at sailing, and I blessed her for having brought me up around boats and ropes and sailor's knots.

My exit was far from graceful. I went clumsily over the rail in my bulky clothes, slipped and slid and jerked my way down the knotted sheets. The snowdrift sank beneath me as I dropped, breaking my fall, and I was into snow to my thighs. I scrambled out as fast as I could and fought my way to a shallow place at the side of the house where I could look up at the windows. No one gazed down at me. Nothing stirred except at the window of Nomi's sitting room. Jezebel was there, peering at me over a mound of snow. She patted one paw at the glass as I started down the hill. She was trapped too, but I could not help her now.

I started down the hill as fast as I could walk with the stabbing pain of my ankle. I was going to Trent. It was the only thing I could do. It didn't matter that long ago he had laughed over a schoolgirl's attachment. He'd had the right to laugh. No one understood how painful sixteen-year-old first love could be. I would have seemed ridiculous to anyone—and knew it now. But *this* was a matter of my life. Even Glen would understand what I must do.

The world I stepped into was like nothing I had ever seen before. The storm had blown itself out, but its evidence remained on every hand. Icicles hung heavy as steel bayonets from the eaves of the house, and every glistening brown tree branch dripped stalactites. Looking at the evergreens as I went down the hill, it seemed that the trees were mock Christmas trees turned cruel with their burden of real ice and snow. Every bough was frosted and glittering with rainbow lights as the sun came up across the lake. I almost wept for the first time, remembering my father's youthful love for decorating our tree. The Chandlers had turned even Christmas trees into an ice-brilliant nightmare. The Chandlers? Was I already including Glen in a pattern I was coming to fear and hate? I shook off the thought.

The storm was over, but the wind still blew, rattling frozen branches with a surprising clatter, and sending bits of ice scattering around me. The going was not as difficult as it had been last night because the worst of the slippery ice now lay deep under fresh snow. While I sank in almost to my boot tops at every step, I found that by thrusting ahead of me with my heels I could manage as I plunged down the hill. My foot hurt less than when I had first landed in the snow bank.

I descended with some speed, and it was only moments before I was out on the shore of the lake. The day was cold and snow blew like smoke down the lake, making a hissing sound. Wind had laid it in zigzag patterns across the ice, weaving it in the design of an Indian rug, while overhead mottled, ragged clouds tore across the blue morning sky.

I beat snow from my coat and hat, stamped it from my boots, and started across the frozen plain of the lake. There were bare spots that were slippery, and I had to be careful as I went. I felt terribly exposed out here, even in my snow-white outfit, and I knew how animals must feel when they cross open country. If Glynis looked out any rear window of the house she would see me, and I had the feeling of eyes burning into my back. Though I had a head start, I would not feel safe until I'd reached the McIntyres'.

Halfway across I suddenly remembered the alabaster head with a stab of misgiving. I had run away and left Glynis alone in the house with her brother's work—of which she was jealous. Balked of my presence, what if she decided to damage the stone head? But surely she would not. She was Glen's twin and artist enough to respect fine work. Practically speaking, I could not, would not, go back. It was too dangerous for me to return, and I had learned what it meant to underestimate Glynis as far as I was concerned.

The stone house loomed ahead of me, directly across the lake, and I crossed drifts like rippled water and made my way toward it. Lights burned in the kitchen, which meant that Pandora must be up early and getting breakfast. I was suddenly hungry, eager for shelter and friendly company. Trent had said I could come to his mother. He had lived with Glynis himself. He knew.

The front door wore a holly wreath with a huge red bow, and the big, uneven field stones of the house framed it in tawny cream. The walk had already been shoveled clear of snow and Keith opened the door to my knock, staring as if I were an apparition.

"How'd you get here?"

"Down the hill," I said. "Across the lake. I'm running away, so will you invite me in? Running away from your mother."

I could sound lighthearted now, sound as if it had all been a prank, as I'd called it to Glynis. Keith backed out of the doorway and let me in, though I sensed that he was reluctant. His manner had changed since my first meeting with the boy, and I suspected that his mother must have been working against me. She would have no scruples about what she told him, or how she might harm him with lies. Motherhood had never mattered to her.

Pandora heard our voices and came into the wide hallway that split the house. She carried a spatula in one hand, and wore a smile of ready welcome. She asked no immediate questions, but hurried me out of my coat, set Keith to pulling off my boots, and then called Trent: "We have company for breakfast. Come on down, dear."

On the first floor the house was divided into two long rooms, one on either side of the hall. Nearly two hundred years ago the house had been an inn, Pandora said, and this room she ushered me into had been the dining room. Across the hall I glimpsed a tall Christmas tree. A real Christmas tree that helped dispel my vision of those mock trees in the woods. Everywhere there was cheerful evidence of fragrant holiday decoration. The kitchen had been in a smoky hole in the cellar, but later dwellers had cut off one end of the dining room for an airy modern kitchen. Here a deal table was set with blue willow pattern china. There was country butter, Sussex honey, and a brown jug of milk to match the brown coffee mugs waiting at each place.

She put Keith to setting an extra place, asked me if I liked bacon with my pancakes, and went to busy herself at the stove. I sat in a strong wooden chair that belonged to another century, and tried to catch my breath. No one asked any questions until Trent came downstairs. He looked a welcome sight to me in his rough outdoor clothes—brown turtleneck and corduroy slacks, his dark hair brushed back from his forehead and still damp from the shower. I tried to look at him as a stranger, without emotional involvement from the past. I couldn't face any more ridicule.

He came to where I sat and for a moment he stood looking down at me gravely. Then he drew a chair opposite me and leaned forward, not touching me, but studying me, so that I knew I would have to tell him everything. He was never an easy man to fool.

It was a relief to talk. I had no loyalty for the Chandlers just then. I told him about Colton's "judging" of the work of both twins, and of Glen's alabaster that had restored his talent and would win a name for him in the art world. Pandora listened from across the kitchen as she worked. Keith stared at the wall.

"Glynis saw herself in what he'd done," I told them. "She destroyed Glen's sense of escape from her domination, his feeling that this was something he had created wholly out of himself. So he ran away from her. He got into his car and drove off, and Nomi went with him."

"He might have taken you along," Pandora said, indignantly turning pancakes.

"I asked him to take me, but I don't think he even heard me. During the evening Glynis started to bait me, so I went upstairs and stayed in my room. Then, in the middle of the night, she locked me into my room. This morning I was still locked in. When she came to the door and talked to me she said I'd have to stay there until she decided what to do about me. I—I suppose for a while I was a little frightened.''

Trent made an angry sound. "She's ungoverned to the point of being dangerous.''

I glanced uneasily at Keith, wondering how much we dared say before him. His face was as darkly angry as his father's, but I knew his sympathy did not lie with me.

"But why?'' Pandora said. "Why should she go to such extremes as this?''

"Partly, I think, because her own work is going wrong,'' I said. "She's been trying to paint Keith and nothing she does comes right, so that she's frustrated and she strikes out at anything that crosses her path. Mainly me, at the moment.''

Pandora set breakfast before us, and joined us at the table. I found that I was hungry and able to eat. Telling someone had been a release and a relief. Trent and Pandora were eating too. Only Keith stared at his plate, not touching his food, and when I paused he broke in with a fumbling question of his own.

"Is—is it my fault that Glynis can't paint me the way she'd like? Is it my fault that her work is going wrong?''

"Of course not,'' I began, but Trent stopped me.

"I can answer that. It has nothing to do with you, Keith. She's failing because she can't bear to have Glen do anything better than she can. And she believes the best way to stop him is to make him feel so guilty that the confidence will go out of him.''

Keith flushed darkly. "Just because you hate her—''

The ringing of the telephone stopped him, and Pandora went into the hall to answer. I listened eagerly, hoping somehow that it might be Glen calling. It was not Glen, but Glynis, and she wanted to talk to Keith. He went to the phone in the hallway, and we could not hear his mumbled replies. When he came back to the table he did not explain, but finished his breakfast hurriedly, and the moment he was through he stood up, breaking into my words again as I went on with what I had to tell. I think perhaps he had heard nothing I'd said since the telephone rang.

"She wants me to come over," he told his grandmother, not meeting his father's eyes. "She needs me for something."

Trent would have spoken to him, but the boy was gone before there was time. I saw the pain and worry in his father's face and knew his helplessness.

"You did the right thing in coming here," he told me when the boy was out of the room. "Don't stay in that house alone with Glynis. She'll never share Glen with anyone, if she can help it. She's been devouring him bit by bit ever since they were children—and if it weren't for the fact that you are the girl concerned, I'd say it was a good thing for him to break away and find himself a wife. But for you—"

Pandora reached across the table to touch her son's arm. "Hush, dear. Dina loves him. It's stamped all over her. Can't you see?"

"I can see," Trent said, and gave his full attention to pancakes and bacon.

Now I turned to Pandora for answers, for reassurance. "But if Glen and Nomi have driven to New York, what am I to do?"

"Stay here with us, of course," she said. "Though I don't think you need worry. Nobody could get far in that ice storm last night. The chances are they pulled into the nearest motel after it started and stayed there for the night. There are only two or three around here. Suppose I phone them and see if we can locate your family."

She was a wonderfully efficient and effective little person, and she moved quickly, though with an economy of motion that kept her from seeming hurried. Her small head, with its unlikely-colored crown of honey hair, tilted at me pertly as she removed me with soothing words from the ghost-ridden atmosphere of High Towers.

Trent cocked an amused eyebrow at me. "You might as

well let Pandora handle this. Mother can bring order out of any blizzard.''

Methodically she set about calling the nearest motels. On her second try she found Glen and Nomi registered, and we waited while the proprietor called Glen to the phone. I suppose I must have looked panic-stricken at the thought of trying to explain anything to him on the telephone, for Pandora nodded at me reassuringly.

"I'll talk to him—don't worry."

And talk she did. She told him gently that an emergency had arisen that had necessitated my coming over to this side of the lake. I would wait for him here. When the plows went through and Glen started home, he and Nomi could stop by and pick me up.

Glen asked no questions, and he apparently agreed, because Pandora was put to no argument. "He knows," she told me when she had hung up. "Glen knows he shouldn't have left you alone with his sister, and he can guess that she's been up to something. The plows will be on their way by now, and this road is more traveled than the side road across the lake. By ten o'clock or earlier, Glen should be able to get through."

We stood in the wide hall with its generous, hand-hewn planks under our feet, and small-paned windows at either end, filtering in the morning sunshine. The storm was really over. When Pandora put the phone down I asked the question which had been haunting me.

"Has Glynis ever really hurt anyone? I mean is she likely to—"

"Only her mother," Pandora said, the lilt gone from her voice. "And my son and grandson."

Trent answered me. "That's not what Dina means. Yes, she is likely to do almost anything if the urge in her is great enough. No one has ever been able to curb her, and she'll go her own unbridled way until somebody breaks her neck—as is likely to happen one of these days." He sounded as though he would like to break it himself, but as he looked at me his eyes were soft.

142

I turned away, both comforted and disturbed. Once I had wanted him to look at me as if I were a woman. Now it was too late.

When I offered to help Pandora in the kitchen, she shook her head. "Not a bit of it! You've been through enough for one week. Trent, why don't you show Dina around the house. It may be something new to her, for all her museum work."

It was new. I had never been inside a two-hundred-year-old house that was lived in before, and I was interested in all I saw. The huge main room boasted two fireplaces, their bricks set deep and wide enough to cook an entire roast when hungry travelers had to be served. The paneling was fine black walnut, and deep-set windows showed the thickness of the walls. Wide hemlock beams with beaded edges ran the width of the ceiling, supporting the floor overhead. Upstairs there was again a wide, broad-planked hall, and what had been two long rooms on either side.

"Travelers didn't expect private bedrooms in those days," Trent said. "When the stagecoaches stopped, guests were put into the room for men on one side, or the room for women on the other—dormitory style. But these have been cut into smaller rooms since."

I looked into each room in turn, admiring the handsome mantels and arched cupboards with their decorative carved keystones at the top of each arch. The house had something sturdy about its character. A house built for the years, with loving care and beautiful simplicity.

One room, on the side looking out toward High Towers, was obviously Keith's. A boy's things lay about and there was sports equipment of various kinds, hunting paraphernalia, and the mounted medals he had won as a marksman. Before we moved on, Trent crossed the room to a desk by the window. From it he picked up a framed picture and turned it for me to see.

It was the picture Glynis had painted of the lake, with the inn burning at the far end. That unhappy picture with the woman in white shut behind a locked window and flames bursting into scarlet plumes behind her.

"I didn't know he had this," Trent said. "She must have given it to him recently. This is the first time I've seen it."

I found it as ugly and threatening a picture as I had the first time, and I turned away.

Trent replaced it on his son's desk. "Yes, I can see why it upsets you. It's a good thing Pandora isn't given to fancies, or it might give her bad dreams. Glynis has only let the boy have it so that it will disturb us. Come along, Bernardina. I'm sorry I showed it to you."

"Bernardina!" I said. "No one else ever called me that."

Trent smiled and I realized that I had never seen him look really happy since I had come to the lake. The smile gentled the harsh lines of his face, drove the trace of cynicism from his eyes.

"I always liked it. It's a good mouthful of a name, and it smacks of your forebears. Not that you've made a very good Viking."

Everyone had always laughed at my name, except Trent. It did not fit me, as it did my mother, but names are personal things, and I had always felt absurdly touched that Trent should like mine.

I seized this gentler mood to ask him a question. "What is it you and your mother are trying to do to the lake that makes Glen and Glynis so bitterly angry?"

He led me to a hall window where I could look down the shore in the direction of the inn.

"Everywhere people are moving out from the cities, spreading out to look for land. Places like this are being used up badly with shoddy houses built too close together, spoiling the wild, natural aspects. Yet the need for a place to live is growing all the time. That's what I'm writing about in my new book—the vanishing countryside."

"Don't you do the biographical thing any more?"

"This is a sort of biography—about various places which have been ruined, or saved—by men. It's a subject that makes me angry. Because the countryside doesn't need to vanish—with a little more care and planning, more integrity in the use of it. Places like this can be opened to those who need homes, yet preserved as they are to a much greater degree. That's what Pandora plans. There'll be no cutting down of all the trees, and there'll be good acreage around each house, and restrictions as to quality in the building. Not expensive homes, but good homes. It's to be a thought-out community, where a number of families can come to raise their children in a relatively countrified atmosphere. The woods and the lake will be cared for—and allowed to remain wild in great part."

The plan did not seem objectionable, and I said so. "Then why are the Chandlers so set against it?"

"I'm not sure that Colton is," Trent said. "But Glynis and Glen are possessive about whatever they touch. They've never cared to share. They want it all, thousands of acres if they could have them. They want it to remain wild, not because of its beauty or for the sake of the animals and birds who live here—but because by every right they understand, it is *theirs*. As wild as they are, too. You can see how Glynis feels in that picture of the inn burning."

A great grumbling roar reached us from the road that ran high above the lake on this side. I looked out to see a red snowplow truck roaring toward us, shoveling snow away in spinning arcs on either side as it came.

"They're clearing the road!" I cried. "Glen should be here soon now. With Nomi."

Trent stood behind me, watching. When I turned, he spoke what he was thinking.

"What will you tell Glen about your coming here?" He was not smiling now. The hard look was in his eyes again.

"Why—the truth, of course. I'll tell him exactly what Glynis has done. That she locked me into my room and tried to frighten me."

"Do you think he'll believe you?" Trent asked harshly.

His challenge made me suddenly angry. "Of course he'll believe me! He knows I'm not a person to lie. He won't stand by and see his sister torment me. I know he won't!"

"I suppose you could refuse to pose for him," Trent said dryly. "That would twist his arm a bit—wake him up."

I flung away from the window, growing more angry by the moment. It was one thing for Trent to help me when it came to rescuing me from Glynis's tricks, but quite another when he attacked my husband. He was the outsider now.

"What are you trying to tell me?" I demanded. "Whatever it is, I won't listen if you speak against Glen."

There was nothing soft about him any more. "It's good for wives to be loyal," he said, and his tone was sharply ironic.

"Do you know what I think?" I was the challenger now. "I think something in you has corroded so that you don't believe in anything. In anyone. I've felt sorry for you because this could be Glynis's fault—what she did to you years ago. But I don't know her side of the story. Perhaps you drove her away, for all I know. Perhaps—"

There was no use in going on and I did not feel happy about what I was saying. A moment ago there had been gentleness between us, a tenderness such as I remembered. Now it was gone.

I turned back to the window, but when I pressed my face against a square pane, trying to see as far along the road to town as I could, he came behind me and swung me around, shook me by the shoulders, so that I shrank from his anger, shrank from the force of his hands.

"Don't waste any time pitying me," he said. "I'm not easy on those who victimize others. Nor am I patient with willing victims—if that's what you are. You need waking up to the present truth. But you've always been a dreamer, and it's not up to me to slap you awake."

"No, it's not!" I cried. "You did that once—and I won't ever let you again. You put me down badly. You could have answered one or two of my silly letters—you could have been a little kind, no matter how foolish and young I was!"

"What letters?" he said.

We stared at each other while comprehension grew. I spoke first.

"Glynis knew what my letters said. She implied you'd laughed over them together. She told me just this morning."

The anger that blazed in him frightened me—but it was not directed against me. "I never laughed at you. The tizzy you went into wasn't funny. It was obviously painful, and you terrified me. I didn't want to see you hurt, but I couldn't have you throw yourself at my head—and be ashamed afterwards."

"I was ashamed anyway," I said. "I kept on dying of shame for a long time. But I grew out of it. Of course I did!" Unbidden, the words of an old song went through my mind, denying, ". . . except when soft winds blow . . ."

"Of course you did." The gentleness was in him again. "And you mustn't ever think I was immune to your attractiveness. You grew up very suddenly one night, right in my arms. And you nearly threw me in the growing. Believe me, I had to get out of there fast. You were too young, and wholly innocent—though at the same time wholly Eve."

I put my arms about myself and hugged my body tightly because I had begun to shiver. "Then—then you might have answered my letters if you'd received them?"

"Of course I'd have answered. And I'd have done a good job of sounding the uncle and letting you down gently. As I could from a safe distance. I was still in love with Glynis then, still trying to save something of my marriage. But I'd never have let such a beautiful gift as you wanted to give me go without a very humble thank-you. When you didn't write, I thought you'd bounced right back and got over me."

"Oh, I did—I did!" I said, and began to weep quite openly, like a child, with tears running down my face. I tried to explain to him. "It's—it's not *me* crying! It's that girl I used to be. She's still there somewhere inside yowling her head off, and I've got to be rid of her. Because I'm in love too. I'm terribly, terribly in love with Glen Chandler."

"I know," he said. Very lightly he touched a tear from my cheek with his finger. "Do you know, I tried to get in touch with you not so long ago. I hadn't forgotten, you see, and I'd wondered about you a lot. When I was on the Coast recently I called to find out about you. But your mother's sister answered me and told me how ill Mrs. Blake was. So

I didn't want to push. Now I wish I'd found you again before you met Glen Chandler."

He turned away abruptly and strode off down the stairs. I stayed by the window, trying to recover. I was shaking with a chill, and churning inside again—and it was all too ridiculously childish to be endured.

As I stood there waiting for the tears to stop, Glen's long cream-colored car swept around the far curve, heading our way. Glen was what I needed! I mopped my face and ran for the stairs, calling out to Pandora.

"They're coming! They've been able to get through!"

I couldn't have been more relieved—and it was not just relief that my terrors with Glynis were over. I was relieved because now I could escape from myself, escape that daydreaming girl who was still trying to govern my life.

Pandora waited for me near the front door, and her eyes seemed a little sorry as they rested on me. I reminded myself that she too belonged to the enemy camp. She had no right to be sorry because I was eager to be in Glen's arms again—safely there, where he would protect me from his sister. And from a man like Trent McIntyre as well. Even from me, myself. From me, most of all.

Trent helped me on with my boots. When he touched my ankle and I winced he looked at me searchingly, but I did not answer. After my recent plunge downhill I could expect it to hurt me, but I must not accept any more of his kindness and sympathy. It was too dangerous. He held my coat for me, handed me my hat, watched me strap it on under my chin. But he had nothing more to say to me—or I to him.

By the time we heard the car door slam in front of the house, I was fully recovered. Outwardly, at least. The McIntyres had been kind to me, and I must thank them. But did they really matter, now that Glen was coming for me?

I held out my hand to Pandora. "Thank you for rescuing me. Thank you both."

I had not offered my hand to Trent, but he took it anyway, and held it for a moment before he let it go.

"Just be careful, Bernardina," he said. "And phone if you need us."

But I wasn't able to leave at once, after all. At Pandora's invitation Nomi came in with Glen. Pandora greeted them cheerfully, insisted that we all have a cup of coffee together before we left. Besides, there was something she wanted to consult with them about.

We gathered informally around her kitchen table, and the atmosphere seemed far more relaxed and cheerful than it ever did at High Towers.

"It's only a few days till Christmas Eve," Pandora said. "And we haven't had our bonfire party for years. What do you say we hold it again this year—over here on our side of the lake? We'll take care of the picnic part, if you'll bring one of your wonderful mince pies, Nomi, and—"

As she ran on I hardly listened. Glen sat with one arm across the back of my chair. He had kissed me warmly when he came in. Everything was right in my world again. His quarrel with Glynis no longer spilled over to me. He had recovered his good nature entirely, and he smiled at Pandora in as companionable a fashion as though he had never referred to the McIntyres as belonging to an enemy camp. He did not even try to cut Trent. I almost purred in the shelter of his arm because I was showing Trent the real state of affairs—how much my husband loved me, and I loved him.

"I suppose we really ought to keep you far away from Colton," Glen told Pandora. "But if you'll call a truce on talking about the land you want to buy, I think the bonfire party would be a wonderful idea. And a special treat for Dina. Colton will approve. He likes family rituals."

"What about Glynis?" Trent had said nothing till now.

Glen shrugged. "She'll do as she pleases, as usual. But I'll try to persuade her to come. Perhaps it will be good for Keith, too—for all of us to get together. We can start the fire as soon as it gets dark on Christmas Eve."

Nomi spoke stiffly, disapproving. "There'll be trouble."

"Don't play Cassandra this Christmas," Glen said. "Everything's going to be fine. Dina's our talisman for change."

149

I had a feeling that Trent agreed with Nomi, but no further objections were offered, and when we'd finished our coffee, we went out to Glen's car. I sat beside him in the front seat, and Nomi sat in back. She looked thoroughly sour and disgruntled this morning, and I suspected that she had not yet forgiven Glen for his precipitous flight the night before. When I smiled at her, she only glowered.

"Now then," Glen said as we started off on the short drive around the lake, "you'd better tell me what this is all about, Dina. I couldn't make head nor tail of what Pandora was chattering on the phone. Why did you come across the lake this morning? And how did you manage it?"

"Manage?" I said, bristling a little at the change in his tone. "I managed by knotting two sheets together and letting myself down from the balcony of our room. After Glynis locked me in."

Glen laughed, and I moved a little away from him in the front seat. "Good for you, Dina. That will show her she can't play such tricks on my wife. You'll find her sense of humor gets out of hand at times, but don't hold that against her. She's a prankish sort of creature. I am too, you know, but not to the same extent. You mustn't mind."

"I *do* mind!" I cried.

I was suddenly furious. I had been submitted to cruel baiting. I had been locked into my room, threatened with injury, and Glen had shrugged everything off lightly.

"Do you think I don't mind being a target for witch balls?" I went on stormily. "Or the prospective victim for an animal trap, or having my door locked in the middle of the night, with a promise of no food and no heat? But what I mind even more is the way she laughed about it. I think she's just a bit mad—your sister."

Glen's right hand flung out and pinned me back against the seat. The car swerved, skidded, and he let me go to bring it back to the road.

"Don't ever say a thing like that!" he told me roughly. "If you call Glynis mad, you call me mad. And we'll neither of us take that sort of thing lightly."

"Then you'd better have a look at that piece of alabaster you're working on when you get home," Nomi said. "You shouldn't have gone off and left it yesterday. I told you so on the way. How do you know what will come into your sister's sane and level head next? She's mad enough."

For Nomi, Glen had no answer. He gave his attention to the car, while I sat trembling with angry dismay beside him. The road on the far side of High Towers was barely passable, and when we came to the snow-clogged driveway we had to get out and climb the hill through deep snow, marked only with rabbit tracks frozen into the crust. Glen helped Nomi and ignored me. Thankful for high boots, I fended for myself, and gritted my teeth over the punishment to my ankle. I felt far too miserable to worry about physical pain.

When we reached the house Glen ran up the front steps to open the door. For once it was locked and as Glen waited impatiently for Nomi to rescue us with her key, I walked to the end of the veranda and looked out at snow-laden pine branches. The storm had swept on its way, and the sun made a dazzle of the enchanted landscape. Without the wind, everything seemed hushed and breathlessly still, muffled by a snowy world. As still as the boy who stood beneath one of the trees, leaning against its trunk, his rifle in hand as he watched us leave the car and go into the house. I waved to him, but he did not wave back. It seemed to me that, for all his quiet, there was an electric excitement about him. As though he waited for something unholy to happen. He was *her* son—too much her son, perhaps.

Glen had gone inside, and I hurried after him as he ran up the stairs. He did not stop at our room, but dashed ahead to the attic, and I followed up the last flight of steps.

Warm light touched the great skylights, washed across the studios. Glen rushed to the place where he had left the alabaster head. It was not where he had worked on it. For a moment he stood staring at the turntable stand, stunned to find it empty. Then he flung about the attic, searching. I tried to help him and when we found nothing, he rushed for the stairs again, shouting for Glynis as he went down. I heard her voice answer from the direction of the drawing room, but I did not follow him to the lower floor. This was between him and his sister now. Whatever had happened, wherever Glynis had put the head, I did not want to be there during the explosion that might follow.

Instead, I went to the door of our bedroom and tried to open it. The door was no longer locked, but it jarred against some heavy obstacle that should not have blocked my way. I shoved impatiently and the object—my dressing table bench—moved a little. At the same time something on it teetered and swayed. I made a desperate effort to snatch what stood upon it to safety, but I was too late. With a crash that rang in my ears for days afterwards, the alabaster head fell to the bare floor and lay there, shattered.

9

I knelt beside the splintered alabaster, sick with horror, too shocked to think clearly. I could only pick up bits of bruised, translucent stone and try vainly to fit them back into what remained of the piece. Obviously, the head was done for—smashed beyond any possible repair.

From what seemed a great distance I heard Glen calling to me, asking what had crashed. My voice seemed to crack, and no words came. Then it was Glynis who ran up the stairs and a moment later stood behind me in the open doorway, staring at what lay upon the floor.

"Oh, no!" she cried, and I looked up at her in desperation. She had done this—not I. But I would be blamed. That was the plan.

"You've managed well, haven't you?" I said.

She stared me down with her dark, slightly glittering eyes. "I? What have I to do with this? You've been jealous of Glen's work all along. Jealous because he paid more attention to his beautiful creation than he did to you. So now—"

"What has happened?" That was Glen on the stairs. I could not bear to see his face—yet I could not take my eyes from him.

It was like watching someone I loved being fatally stabbed. His expression of curiosity gave way to stunned disbelief, followed by the beginning of pain—and then agony. He pushed me aside and bent over the poor broken thing on the floor. He knelt to pick up a bit that had been a curve of mouth and chin—and the effect upon me was macabre. It was I who lay there shattered. Not a piece of cold alabaster, but my own flesh and blood. It was I who would never be put back together again. This was the moment at the window of the inn multiplied a thousand times. I would rather face fire than the death of hope in Glen's face.

When he could manage to speak, he turned to his sister, not to me. "How did it happen?"

Glynis dropped to her knees beside him and put both arms about him. "Darling—don't look like that. Don't suffer so. I can feel it inside me—the pain. What a vicious, cruel thing for her to do."

He let her hold him for a moment, as shattered in himself as the alabaster head. Then he moved away from her touch, stood up to face me, and his eyes were like hers—the same glittering black.

"You'd better tell me," he said.

I was too sick at heart to be anything but blunt. "I opened the door and the head fell over and smashed. It was propped up on that dressing table bench. Someone put it there to block the door."

Glen moved toward me, and I don't know what he would have done if Glynis had not stepped between us. "Wait, Glen! Don't do anything foolish. She's silly and young. And she has no idea what an artist's work means to him. Perhaps she didn't intend it to happen. Glen, listen to me!"

I flattened myself against the wall, listening in fascinated horror as she went on.

"Perhaps she thought she was protecting the head from me when she brought it downstairs to your room after you'd gone yesterday. And I suppose when she went out the window so idiotically this morning—running away like a child— she forgot all about it. Forgot that she would return by the door that it was blocking."

To my own ears my voice sounded more shrill than I intended. "Stop it! Stop your lying! Glen, it's not true. Not a word she has said is true!"

Glynis smiled sadly, pitying my outburst. "I don't know whether what I'm saying is true or not. I only meant to give you an out, if you wanted to take it. I'm guessing, of course."

"*She* put it there!" I cried. "I never brought the head downstairs, Glen. I never put it by the door. Why would I do such a stupid, mean thing? Someone would be sure to knock it over and—"

"Exactly," Glynis said. "If you won't take my way out, then you'd better tell him the truth."

"Wait a minute—both of you!" There was growing desperation in Glen. "Stop yammering at me. Nothing will bring it back. My work—" he paused as if to breathe, "—my lost work! But I want to know the truth of what happened."

"I've told you the truth!" I said. "You know I'm not the lying sort, Glen. Believe me—believe me!"

"Glynis?" he questioned. "Did you put the head there, Glynis?"

Her expression was one of sorrow for his loss, but there was serenity in her as well—an air of open frankness that I did not understand. She stood before her brother without touching him, but I had never seen more warmth, more *lovingness* in her. She spoke simply and convincingly. If I had not known otherwise, I might have believed her myself.

"You know we've never lied to each other, Glen. Not because we might not want to at times, but because when you've lied to me I've always known. And it's been the same when I lied to you. I'm not lying now. I haven't touched the head since you showed it to us yesterday. I certainly haven't carried it to your room, or set it up as a booby trap behind your door. No one could do that and come out through the door into the hall, as Dina would realize if she had thought her plans through clearly. This is something which could be done only by the person who went out the window. And that wasn't I, Glen dear."

He searched her face gravely—searched and accepted.

Then knelt beside the wreckage on the floor and began to gather it up, bit by bit.

"Your sister is lying, Glen." I had to say it again. "Your twin, your other self, is lying. But that doesn't really matter, Glen. It's your worth that matters. You can start another head. I'll pose for you. You can start over! Perhaps it will be even better next time."

He looked up at me coldly, remotely. "Do you think I could ever see you like this again?" He held up a fraction of eye and brow. "Do you think I could ever recapture what I felt for you?" He gathered the shattered pieces in his hands, and there was no love in him for me.

I was still dressed for outdoors in my coat and boots. I turned and without another word went out of the room and down the stairs. Nomi waited in the hallway below, but she did not try to question me, or stop me. I went past her out the front door and around the house.

The boy no longer stood beneath the sweeping branches of a pine tree. His footprints led along the lake side of the house, and then down the hill. My own tracks, left this morning, when the storm was over, were still in clear evidence. I followed them to the place below the balcony where I had dropped from the end of my knotted sheets. All the marks were there to be seen clearly. The sheets still dangled from the iron post above, flapping when the wind blew. There was no second trail, no evidence that anyone else had come down the same way and then tramped off through clean snow to leave the evidence of passing behind him.

"What're you looking for?" a voice said from the edge of the woods.

I whirled and saw Keith McIntyre standing some distance away, where pines ended and bare winter trees began. I walked toward him slowly, making no rapid moves—as though he might himself be a creature of the woods who would take off like one of the brown rabbits if I startled him. When I was close enough to see his face clearly, I spoke to him.

"I'm looking for the tracks of someone besides myself who climbed over the rail this morning."

He shook his head as if I puzzled him. "I don't know what you're talking about. Why should there be tracks?"

"I think you know," I said. "I think you must tell the truth to Glen sooner or later."

"You off your rocker?" He tossed the words over his shoulder as he turned away and started downhill, moving with a long, easy lope, the rifle with him as always.

I went back to the house. I would have to find a way to coax the truth from Keith—since his mother would not tell it. But he would only run away from me now. And in the meantime I had to learn how to live with the death of my marriage. I knew it was over, unless I could prove to Glen what his sister had done. It might be the end of it, even then, since he might not thank me, or forgive me, for such proof.

In the days that followed before Christmas Eve I did not see Keith again. My ankle improved and I tramped through the woods several times a day, always looking for a boy with a gun. I climbed down to the base of Gray Rocks more than once, but Keith took care to evade me, and I caught no glimpse of his red-checkered cap anywhere.

I would not go to his father. I would ask nothing of Trent McIntyre. All that was uprooted, done with, over. The young girl in me was silent, unable to cope with a woman's problems. I knew that Keith was under Glynis's spell, and not altogether accountable. I did not want to bring Trent's anger down upon him again. I must find Keith myself and talk to him first. There must be some way in which I could make him understand what had been done to me—what *he* had done. I had been made to smash Glen's work, and as a result my husband had turned away from me completely. Surely this boy was not so callous that he could not understand my suffering. For his own sake, too, he must be made to understand the motives of his mother. He must be made to see her without the glossy veneer his own idealism had built around her. There was tragedy in the shock of such an unveiling, but it was better if it came now before she corrupted him completely.

In small ways life went on as usual. Nomi had the driveway plowed out so that Colton would have no trouble when he came home. Christmas wreaths and boughs were hung. There was mistletoe under the drawing room chandelier—but I did not stand beneath it joyously, as I had hoped to do. Nomi was endlessly busy with Christmas baking. We shopped for the usual weekly groceries, and a large turkey besides. Gift wrapping was done behind closed doors. All normal preparations for Christmas went on, but underneath nothing at all was normal.

The day after I had been locked in, Glen moved out of the room we shared and into the smaller room he had used as a boy. I came upstairs in the afternoon to hear Glynis laughing as she helped him move his things. I knew it was she who had suggested this change, but there was nothing I could do. I could scarcely plead with Glen for a love he had ceased to give, and yet I did not wholly believe that he had lost all affection for me so suddenly. If only I could cut him off from Glynis's influence, find a way to reach the old Glen whom I knew and loved! But Keith was my only hope, and Keith had turned into quicksilver.

Sorrowfully, I wrapped the white silk turtleneck sweater I had bought for Glen in New York—and had hoped to give him lovingly. Now as I touched its soft folds I felt a little dead inside. He had scarcely spoken to me since the alabaster head had been shattered. No trace of stone remained on the floor, though the shattering had left a scar, and the key had disappeared from the door. But for Glen I was not there. I was a stranger he did not know. Often my throat ached with suppressed tears because I would not cry and humble myself before Glen or Glynis.

The twins were closer than ever during this time. A curious thing seemed to have happened. It was as if they had both failed in their work and had thus been drawn closer together—to the *one* they were—than before. But if Glen had ceased to know that I was about, Glynis never stopped watching me. Perhaps that was the worst thing of all—to have her eyes follow me slyly, watchfully, smilingly giving me the feeling that she was not really done with me yet. She had felled me with a stab in the back, but the *coup de grace* was still to come.

Nomi was my only confidante. I told her everything. I told her just what I believed had happened, but though she sat working quietly with her shuttle at her loom, and heard me out, she had nothing in the way of advice to offer. She agreed that what happened had been engineered by Glynis and that Keith was undoubtedly the instrument she had used. But there was nothing to be gained by making charges unless I had some sort of proof to back them up. Indeed, even then, Nomi said, it might do me no good. Glen and his twin were re-united, and he would not thank me for any attempt to split them apart once more.

The twinness was remarkably in evidence during that time. They were entirely one. Their every act was that of identical persons. Anything at all would set them off—a look, a word, an incident. Their eyes would meet, and they seemed to read each other's thoughts instantly. Laughter would come to them at the same moment—and they both laughed quite a lot. I could not understand this in Glen. He had suffered serious damage, met with real tragedy in the destruction of his best work—yet he could laugh lightheartedly with his sister as though nothing disturbed him in any way. If he recognized that he possessed a wife, I saw no evidence of it. It was as though Glynis had truly bewitched him. It was as though the lighter side of her had been freed from the broken alabaster and the black marble was in eclipse.

There were times when I ached with self-pity, wallowed in my new loneliness and the loss of Glen's affection. But there were other times, and they were increasing, when I was too angry to suffer. I remember the phrase Trent McIntyre had used when he called me a "victim." I did not like being a victim, and I meant to expose Glynis and the wicked trick she had played at my very first opportunity. I wanted most of all to save Glen, to find him as a separate person once more, whole in his own right. I would wait it out. My marriage was at stake, and so, in a way, was my integrity.

Once or twice I tried to talk to him in a quiet, reasonable way, but I could not reach him at all. Obviously he felt that I was trying to shunt off my guilt upon Glynis, and he would not listen. His coldness reminded me that, even in happier times, I had felt the Chandlers were winter people.

After the snowstorm we had days of warmer weather. Everywhere snow began to melt and run down sunny hillsides in rivulets. Where the hills stood in shade the snow stayed on, diminishing only a little day by day like that ice that Glen had laid on my heart. Often by night the temperature dropped so low that the surface water froze again and offered a good skating surface. But though I had learned to skate in New York, I had no heart for taking out my skates now.

As Christmas Eve approached, plans went ahead, as if nothing had happened, for the McIntyre bonfire party. Pandora had invited neighbors from along the roads that led to Gray Rocks for Christmas Eve by the lake. They were bringing in cords of wood, contributing food for outdoor winter cooking, as well as home-baked pies and Christmas cookies. Nomi was at her best, her cheeks a little flushed from the warm kitchen, her eyes bright as those of a child who anticipates a party. Now and then she would remember herself and prophesy doom and disaster, but the rest of the time she was as happy as I had ever seen her.

Both Glen and Glynis behaved as though his alabaster figure had never existed. I found this impossible to understand. Why wasn't Glen suffering as I was suffering? Sometimes at night I dreamed of that icy face he had created—a face that was mine and yet not mine. I yearned over the destruction of Glen's work, over the destruction of my marriage, my love. To Glen none of this appeared to matter. He and Glynis were one again, and that seemed enough for both. He'd obviously forgotten that he had ever spoken to me of escape from his sister's domination.

One thing in particular disturbed me about these two. They seemed to be plotting something against Pandora. Some scheme was afoot to discourage her development of a planned community on the other side of the lake. I caught meaningful looks exchanged between them when her project was mentioned, heard their whispering when no one but me was around. They seemed like prankish children—rather wicked children, against whom one must be constantly on guard because their behavior was not adult and rational.

Glynis had a new glitter about her that frightened me. She wore black a great deal—often trimmed with shiny jet, so that she caught the light as she moved, and it was a dark light that suited her—dark and cold, like a winter's night. I wondered if she wanted to remind Glen of the black marble head he had done of her—his real masterpiece.

The day before Christmas was bright, with a temperature just below freezing. The weather report promised a clear, bright night—not too cold. The Christmas tree was up in the drawing room and we were decorating it that afternoon when Colton returned. He came in laden with packages, cheerfully expansive, expecting nothing of disaster. But when he walked into the drawing room where we worked on the tree, the four of us looked at him in a sudden guilty silence that must have told him something had happened in his absence.

I glanced at Glen and realized how much he hated to have his father know what had happened to the alabaster head. His work had reinstated him in his father's eyes, and now he would dread to see this new respect diminished.

While we stared, Glynis broke the pause of silence by running to kiss her father and taking the packages from his arms, helping him off with his coat. This afternoon she wore tapered black velvet trousers, and a black crocheted pullover trimmed with black bugle beads. She had even tied a black silk scarf about her head to subdue her bright hair, and when Colton saw her he called her his ''dark angel.''

I would have chosen a different word.

Nomi had seen Glen's face, and she came down the ladder from where she had been hanging higher ornaments.

''Leave it to me,'' she whispered to him. ''Don't say anything till I've talked to your father.''

I kept in the background, sitting on the floor near the tree as I looped streamers of tinsel over low branches. When Colton had greeted Nomi and put an arm about each twin for a welcoming embrace, he came to draw me up from my place.

"You look like a small pink and silver ornament yourself in that sweater and gray skirt," he said. He did not kiss me as he had the twins, but held me at arm's length, studying my face gravely. "Something's wrong. I know faces. Something has broken you up inside."

"Leave Dina alone," Nomi said. "You'd better come and have a talk with me before you ask any questions."

Glynis smiled at him brightly, but Glen would not meet his eyes, and after he'd given me a light pat on the shoulder, Colton went with Nomi to her sitting room.

The moment he was out of the way Glen and Glynis behaved as though I were not there. They put their chestnut heads together and whispered in tones that were not low enough for me to miss.

"Don't worry," Glynis murmured. "When Pandora begins to see that the Lenape Indian name of the *Haunted Place* is the only right one for Gray Rocks, she'll give up her silly scheme."

"But how can you be sure—" Glen began.

Glynis tapped his arm gently and nodded toward me. "Little pitchers," she said, and they both burst into laughter.

Never had I felt so furious and alone and frustrated. When I tried to think of some plan, to see some clear road ahead, everything vanished in murk. My one hope still lay in Keith, and tonight he would be at Pandora's bonfire party. I must be alert enough to catch him off guard and get him to myself, so I could talk to him, make him understand. Perhaps Colton would help me. Surely, as the boy's grandfather—but I knew this would depend on what Nomi chose to tell him. If I knew Nomi, she would save him as much grief as possible.

They were not gone long, and when they returned Colton strode into the room ahead of her and went straight to Glen.

"Don't look like that, boy," he said. "Nomi's told me

162

about this miserable accident, and I know it seems tragic to all of us at the moment. But you mustn't brood over the loss. Don't you suppose I've had work destroyed before this? Once I had six portraits go down on an aircraft. And do you know what I did?''

''Yes, darling, we know,'' Glynis said, slyly teasing. ''You've told us a good many times. You started over. You did every one of those pictures over—at great cost of time, and all the trouble of getting the people concerned to sit for you again.''

He nodded at her triumphantly. ''And every one of those portraits came out better than it did the first time!''

Glynis smiled at him sweetly. ''This is different. I don't think Glen wants to do Dina a second time.''

''Of course he'll do her! He can't let something like this be lost. Glen—''

''No, Colton,'' Glen said, speaking up to his father as I'd seldom seen him do. ''I won't do Dina again. I have another plan. I'm going to do a head of Glynis—in wood this time. I'm going to use some rich dark wood that will give me the texture and patina I want. And it will be better than the alabaster head. Glynis has always been my best model.''

It was clear for all of us to see that he had kindled again. This was the way he had looked when he found me in the museum. This was the same sort of excitement that had lighted him while he worked on the alabaster head. I felt as completely shattered as the block of alabaster had been. Now I was truly bereft.

Glynis had kindled with excitement too. They were alike— dreadfully alike.

''At the same time that he uses me for a model, I'll use Glen!'' she cried. ''I can already see how I'll paint him. This will bring me out of my doldrums too!''

Colton was pleased with them both. In that remote fashion of the man to whom art alone matters, he had dismissed anything except getting his children to work again. He was not very pleased with me. He had tried. He had used the word ''accident'' about what I had done. But Nomi must

have told him much of what had happened, and he had chosen to blame me in the end. It was simpler that way.

If I had not wanted to find Keith, I would not have gone
to the bonfire party that night. But since Colton would not
save me, I had to go. I did not blame Nomi for not stressing
Glynis's part in the story. She could hardly throw that wild
tale of mine too strongly in Colton's face, when it was only
my word against his daughter's as to what had happened. So
I must go to the party, and I must talk to Keith. I must find
some way to defend myself.

It would be difficult for me to cope with any rival, but how
did one defeat a twin sister?

10

That afternoon when the tree was done, decorated by the twins in wild hilarity, they went to work upstairs in the attic, so eager to be at their double project that they could not wait until tomorrow. I offered to help Nomi with whatever further preparations she needed to make, but she swept me aside. She was too impatient with me at the moment. Colton was in his study writing letters, and even Jezebel had vanished outdoors into the bright sunshine of late afternoon.

Left to myself, I dressed for climbing, took Glen's pair of light binoculars with me and walked down to Gray Rocks. Again there was no sign of Keith, but the bonfire had already been lit. This time I sought the saddle at the place where the rock divided and climbed into it. These were twin pinnacles above me—his and hers, I thought dryly. Where one towered into the sky, I could see the stepway that led upward. The niches, some natural, some carved, fit easily to my hands and feet. I mounted step by step to a level space near the top and found that here the rock had been hollowed into a shallow cave. I sat down within its shelter, and stone walls pressed around me so that I was hidden from the world. No one would know I was here unless I chose to shout the fact above the lake.

Gathered in like a snail that had withdrawn into its shell, I thought about my predicament on this strangest of Christmas Eves. Nothing left like Christmas. All anticipation had died. Wistfully, I missed other times when there were city shop windows and hurrying shoppers, missed the Salvation Army Santa Clauses, even the mechanized blaring of Christmas carols. Brown winter woods, with hardly a trace of snow left, had nothing to do with Christmas. Nor had bonfire picnics.

I was a bride without a groom. But I had better not dwell on that. What had happened to Glen was temporary—it had to be. He would come back to loving me. I knew how he had felt about me. I could not lose something precious because a piece of alabaster that had been nothing a month ago, now lay shattered. I must fight down the sick doubt that welled in me. Vaguely I thought of Trent, wishing I could talk to him as a friend. Once he had comforted me, but I knew he would not now.

A sound of distant shouting reached me, and I crept from my snail's shell to stand up. Were they calling me? Was that Glen's voice? Or an echo?

Although there was only the rock wall of my crevice around me, and a bare face of rock opposite, I found that I could lean upon a chest-high barrier and see almost the entire lake. Up here I could hear amazingly well the sounds that came from a distance. No one was calling me.

The winter sun dipped toward the place where it would vanish beyond hills, and there were signs of a splendid winter sunset beginning to stain the sky. The bonfire across the lake was burning strongly now. I could smell woodsmoke from this high perch. In a little while it would be time for the Chandlers to go down to the lake, and I would not be with them. If they missed me, let them call. I would not answer. I was playing games—and knew it. But I was tired of their dares. I was separate now, and I would at least be myself.

I leaned cautiously out over my barricade and felt that strange sense of power which height can give. All the lake lay stretched beneath me. Halfway down the opposite shore I could see the McIntyre house, and on the level meadow below it the bonfire's mounting flames. In the darkening afternoon the fire bloomed a deeper scarlet from moment to moment. Small figures moved about the central mass—like the tiny *Walpurgisnacht* figures of Glynis Chandler's painting.

With the glasses to my eyes I could even make out individuals. None of the Chandlers were there, but I could see Pandora, small and plump in rather tight-fitting trousers and bulky sweater. Trent was there too, rounding the fire with spare, efficient movements. I did not know the guests and their children, but there was a busy air of anticipation over the scene. An anticipation I could not share.

I glanced over my shoulder and saw the spreading colors of the sunset—bars of crimson, gold, deep saffron—merging far up the sky into pale azure.

No one could possibly see me here in the shadow of my rock. I stepped from behind the parapet onto a high ledge from which I could have a still better view down the lake. My toe struck loose rock, and for an instant my heart was in my throat as a great slab of shale broke away and went crashing down the steep slope, striking the base at the bottom, then leaping outward in a thousand pieces to fall into the lake. But there was no one there to be harmed. In the circle of my glasses nothing moved, no one walked along the path.

I raised the binoculars and searched the far end of the lake, where Gray Rocks Inn faded slowly into the shadow of woods all around. There were lights in some of the windows, and I supposed that Pandora had been using the inn's kitchen and refrigerators for her picnic preparations. Somehow my eyes were drawn toward the small window of the office. When the glasses found it, my heart jumped again. The entire space burned a fiery red—alive with scarlet flames. This was how Glynis must have seen it in her picture.

But it was only the sunset, surely, touching one window after another to crimson. Light colored the face of the inn and fell across the lawn that sloped toward the water, while all else was lost in shadow. The sight was dramatic and beautiful.

As I watched, a human figure strode suddenly into view.

Keith had stepped out of the woods and was crossing the space that led around the inn to the entrance side. For once he carried no rifle, but he moved with almost furtive speed, as though he did not want to linger and be seen. In a moment he was out of sight. If he had been sent down there on some innocent errand by his grandmother, he would not move like that. I did not like the furtiveness, but there was nothing I could do from this distance.

The headlights of a car loomed along the road that curved above the opposite shore. I watched it pull up to a parking area near the McIntyre house. The door opened and Colton got out, went around to help Nomi out with her parcels. Together they walked toward the bonfire, but Glen and Glynis did not appear, and I wondered where the twins were. Was Glen looking for me? Had he given me a thought? Probably not, I told myself, and tasted bitterness in my mouth.

How they reached the party did not matter to me now, but what did matter was that Keith was at the far end of the lake alone. If I hurried down from this high place and followed the shore, I would still have light enough to show me to the inn. Once I reached it I would be between Keith and the bonfire to which he must, presumably, return.

Climbing down from the pinnacles of Gray Rocks was harder than going up. I slung the binoculars on their strap about my neck to leave my hands free and went down backwards, as I had seen Glen do, feeling cautiously behind me with each foot, a step at a time.

Once I was down I scrambled to the shore of the lake and found the path I had so often followed. It grew more difficult underfoot in the quick winter dusk. Already the sunset was no more than a faint memory of color in the darkening sky. Nevertheless, I walked as fast as I was able—yet walked carefully too, watchful for unfamiliar patches across the path, patches of leaves that might turn treacherously into a trap.

I was nearly opposite the bonfire now. I could hear its crackle and roar, see its sparks spitting high into the air. That section of the shore was clear, with no woods around to catch, and the ground was still wet from the snowstorm of last week, so it was safe again. Children ran about shouting and laughing, and adults were busy getting wieners ready to toast, parceling out buns. On ahead the inn was dark, and I wondered if I had only imagined lights in its windows. What I'd thought was electricity might have been merely the earlier gleam of the sunset.

But Keith was there—and I must hurry. I had not seen him come back along either shore, so he must be there.

Now I made such speed that I nearly ran into Glynis and Glen as they came down the hill from High Towers. I halted just in time and drew back behind the trunk of a big sycamore near the water's edge. Together they plunged down the hill, hand in hand, laughing. Glynis wore her burnt orange parka jacket, with the furry hood thrown back to leave her face white in the dusk, with her short hair making wisps of shadow about her head. Glen was bareheaded too, wearing his favorite quilted jacket and dark trousers.

When they reached the bank Glen sprang down to the ice and held up his hands to Glynis. She took them and went down like a dancer, vaulting lightly, gracefully. As I watched, they set off across the ice, sometimes sliding purposely, sometimes slipping and catching at each other, noisy and exuberant as two children. If ever tragedy had touched Gray Rocks Lake, they were not remembering it tonight.

They would not look back and see me—all their attention was on the goal of that soaring fire ahead. I left the shelter of my tree and hurried again, running now, trying not to stumble. I could no longer be sure whether Keith was still there. In the darkness he could have slipped away in any direction.

It took me another five minutes to reach the inn. Everything was quiet. The sunset had faded, leaving the windows blank and empty of light, except for one window at the far end which showed the leaping flames of the bonfire in its black depths. No boy stepped out of the shadows to confront me. No one answered when I called his name. I had missed him after all.

I might as well go on to the bonfire and see if he was there.

That was still the one thing that drove me—the need to talk to Keith, to persuade him to listen to me and understand the dreadful harm he had done. I knew I snatched at a futile straw, because the boy was so wholly and devotedly under Glynis's influence. He would probably laugh at me, or give me one of his surly looks and turn indifferently away. Yet I had to try. I had no other choice.

The walking was easier on this side of the lake, due to less brush and a more gently sloping shoreline. I could hear the laughter and the shouting and see the flames leaping high into the air, sending streamers of sparks out over the lake. The opaque surface of ice glowed pink in a semicircle around the fire, but there was little wind tonight and the flames burned tall as if they would reach to the stars. All around the area of intense light shadows hung black and impenetrable. Within the lighted area a score of figures moved about.

Glen saw me first and came toward me so quickly that for just a moment my heart leaped with hope. We met at some distance from the bonfire, but there was no loving greeting in his eyes or in his words.

"Where were you?" he said. "Nomi searched the house for you before she left with Colton. We all thought it would look better if you arrived with the family."

"I went for a walk," I said in a low voice. "I didn't think anyone would miss me."

Glynis was behind him, just at his shoulder. "She's feeling sorry for herself again. She's sulking because you won't listen to her lies about me. Why don't you tell her to go back to the house and leave us alone? We were having a lovely time until she came. Why don't you tell her?"

"Because I want her to stay," Glen said. "I want her to stay and put up a front for once. Let's see you smile, Dina. Let's see you pretend that you're an ecstatically happy bride."

I turned away from the bright mockery of his eyes. "How can I be happy when you won't listen to me?" I said helplessly.

Glynis was baiting too, and enjoying it. "There—you see! She's back to her old tune again—*listen-to-me-listen-to-me!*"

"Why did you come over if you're only going to be lugubrious and sorry for yourself?" Glen demanded.

I felt like an insect caught on a pin. No matter which way I twisted, they pricked at me again and again. I looked about a bit wildly, not for help because there would be none, but seeking for some avenue of escape. And I saw the boy. He stood a little way off, watching us with eyes wide in his shadowed face. Flame light played over him and his mouth was a wry twist of suspicion. He looked like a wild thing suddenly halted in his tracks because he had scented a predator. With all of his being he watched and listened.

"I came to see Keith!" I cried. "I want to talk to him. I want—"

But the boy faded away into the throng about the bonfire as I spoke, and Glynis took me by the arm and shook me roughly.

"You've been persecuting my son! He told me about the way you've been looking for him, wanting to pin him down— all because you've some notion that he might help you with your lies. But he won't, he won't!"

"How could he?" Glen snapped.

I'd had enough of the baiting and tormenting. I turned on him fiercely. "He could if he wanted to because he knows very well that his mother is to blame for what happened to the alabaster head. Once I can get near him, talk to him, when Glynis isn't there on guard over her young—"

Glen's slap came so suddenly and so hard across my cheek that I stumbled backward and nearly fell. Glynis put her hand on his arm at once.

"Hey—take it easy! This isn't the time for a public show. Why don't you leave, Dina? Leave for New York! Why don't you go back to the house right now and pack your things? You can't be looking forward to Christmas with us, and—"

I turned away from them both and ran without thought, without heeding my direction—anywhere, to be out of the sound of their hateful voices, out of sight of the twin malice in their faces. A clump of trees at the edge of the lake stopped me. I stepped gratefully into shadow and went through to the other side where the icy lake spread away at my feet and there was a big flat rock I could step out upon—a platform with ice crusting around its edges.

There in the starlight, with the bonfire only a flickering through the trees and the laughing shouts part of another world, I put my face in my hands and wept. I had no weapons to fight the evil that hemmed me in. I had no assuagement for the pain of lost love in my heart. There was in me only a great bewilderment and sorrow and pain. To weep was to release it a little, but the tears came on without stopping and deep sobs began to wrench me.

The hands that touched my shoulders were gentle. They were not Glen's hands. I turned to look up into Trent's face, shadowy in the starlight, though I knew the intense blue of his eyes. But this I could not bear either. Gentleness, tenderness, would undo me completely.

"Listen to me, Bernardina," he said. "Stop your sobbing and listen to me. Do you remember one afternoon a long time ago? A rainy afternoon in California when I found you lying on your face in wet grass, crying your heart out for another sorrow?"

I gulped myself into silence and listened, nodding.

"You thought you would die of grief that day. You thought you couldn't bear a life from which your father was gone. Do you remember that?"

Again I could only nod.

"Yet, you lived, and you found courage. Time passed and the pain eased, as it always does. Now you can think of him happily, lovingly, without the intense sorrow you felt then. It will be like that again. You'll face the mistake of your marriage—because it is a mistake, my dear—and you'll go on to better, happier things."

I wasn't capable of being comforted then. I could think only of the minute before me, the immediate happenings around me.

"Glen slapped me," I said.

"I know. I saw him. And I had to hold onto myself to keep from taking a hand and making everything worse. By this time you must know that you can't stay in the same house with Glynis. If there's still any chance for your marriage, it has to be away from Gray Rocks, away from Glynis."

I couldn't answer him. He didn't know it all. He didn't know what his own son had done in setting Glen against me. I could only raise my wet face to him, still lost in what was immediate, remembering that once he had comforted me long ago, aching for anything that would help me now and make the inner pain stop. Trent bent toward me. He cupped my face in his, and I think his kiss would have been gentle, reassuring. But Glynis's voice broke in upon us, striking through the darkness with its husky overtones.

"There!" she cried. "You see what I mean, Glen. Now isn't this a tender scene?"

Trent bent his head and kissed me roughly, angrily—then turned to face them. Glynis almost danced around us in her delight—because everything was going her way. Everything she had done to break up my marriage was bearing fruit, and she must have thought this the best thing of all. Tonight in her burnt orange jacket, she was like a flame herself, catching all reflected light—an exultant, triumphant flame.

Glen did not lift a hand, but his tone was cold, deadly. "Yes, I do see what you mean. Glynis has told me about you, Dina—about how you were in love with this man a few years ago, and how you've never got over loving him. What happened out there in California? What really happened between you two?"

Trent struck him then, and Glen went down under the blow, one hand to his jaw. Glynis would have flown at Trent, screeching with rage, but he pinned her arms to her sides and shook her until her head fell back and the screech died in her throat. She looked at him with frightened eyes and was still.

"There's a score to be evened between us for all the past damage you've done," Trent said. "Perhaps you'd better remember that. I've let you off so far, but unless you undo the lies you've told your brother, you'll have me to reckon with."

He flung her away from him against a tree and walked up the bank.

Glynis righted herself and then dropped to her knees to croon tenderly over her brother. Glen was not hurt—only dazed—and he was sitting up, shaking his head a bit dizzily from side to side. I could not bear to watch. I felt as dazed and confused as though I had taken Trent's blow myself. I stumbled back to the area of the bonfire, smoothing away the tears from my wet face, determined to govern myself—because I had not yet talked to Keith.

The rest of the evening went by in a strange, unreal blur. I managed to eat a little of what was handed to me, I tried with another part of me that seemed a stranger to join in with the gaiety and laughter. But when it came to the Christmas carols, I could not sing. Everything was too mockingly wrong. Songs about a Holy Night and a little town in Bethlehem did not fit into something that was unholy. Glynis had drawn Glen completely back into her unholy alliance and there was no place for me in Glen's life. Yet still, stubbornly, I had to try for the one thing I knew that I could do. I had to talk to Keith.

I saw him now and then flitting in and out of the crowd about the fire. He did not seem to mix with his contemporaries, and I had once more the impression of a wildness that permitted him at times to converse with humans, but was always ready to send him bolting to the safety of his own hiding places. There was no chance at all to talk to him.

Once during the evening Colton surprised everyone by announcing almost casually that he would sell Pandora the land she wanted on this side of the lake. Pandora was exuberant and they shook hands as though there had never been a rift between their families. Glen looked furious, but it was Glynis I watched, suspecting that this would make everything worse. Not even the crimson flames could brighten the look of dark jet in her eyes tonight, and I knew there were other tricks still to be played, and this time they might be fatal.

Glen had joined the circle again, returning to it with Glynis at his side, and the flickering light did not pick out the mottling bruise along his jaw. Trent stayed away from them both, and away from me, yet I had a sense of his watchfulness, and was grateful for it. I was not wholly alone in my fight against those two.

Glen did not come near me all evening until the time when everyone clasped hands and moved in a circle about the fire. This was the last ritual of the night, and this time I forced myself to sing with the others. Some remnant of courage and pride seeped back, and if Glen would take my hand for show, then I would put up a front too, and keep my misery to myself. I sang over the choking lump in my throat because the words of ''Auld Lang Syne'' had meaning for me. There were old acquaintances I missed tonight. Old loves long lost to me. My father. My mother—so remote and unreachable not only because of distance, but because she was old and ill. Trent, whom I'd lost long ago as a foolish young girl. And Glen—who was my husband. He clasped my right hand as we circled the fire, but his fingers were cold and I knew he held Glynis's hand on the other side.

Before the last cup of kindness was drunk, I had taken all I could bear. I broke out of the circling line and I think Glen scarcely noted my leaving because he was laughing with Glynis when I slipped away. But I did not know what cruel thing he might do if he caught me, so I ran off along the shoreline, to take the long way home around the lake. Out upon the ice I would be too conspicuous, too easily seen and followed.

I could not bear it that tonight was Christmas Eve and tomorrow Christmas Day. No matter how lonely I had been in the past, I had never been so bitterly unhappy, with no way to turn to assuage my pain, and seemingly no cure for it. Yet as I walked a saving anger began to return to me once more. I would not let myself down with endless self-pity. I had a right to be angry and sorrowful, if I wished, but I was not entirely beaten yet. What I was to do, I did not know, but I remembered Trent's words, and in this quieter moment they came back to me comfortingly. Sorrow did lessen with time. Better days did come. All I need do was live through what was happening to me now and find a course of action that would take me out of this morass of misery.

Ahead of me, as I neared the inn, something startling caught my eye. All the windows were not dark as they had been. From one narrow opening a streamer of scarlet licked the length of the frame and burst into fiery tongues. That was the room—the room in Glynis's picture! And this time it was truly aflame.

I was close to the inn and as I began to run smoke poured out the open window and the fiery tongues grew brighter, more eager and hungry. Once when I stopped to catch my breath, I tried to shout to those about the bonfire, to get their attention. But my feeble voice must have been lost in the sounds of singing and laughter. I ran on. The fire itself would summon them eventually.

When I reached the lawn I glanced up again and saw the lacing of flame inside the room, the thick smoke billowing. I fled across the lawn and around the end of the inn, stumbled up the steps—almost into Keith's arms as he came out through the main door.

I fastened onto him like a leech, and though he tried he could not shake me loose. I fastened both my hands onto his arms and shook him with all my might.

"Where is the water?" I shouted. "Where is the fire hose?"

He tried to peel me off, and when I saw he did not intend to help me, I let him go and rushed for the door. At once he came after me, and this time he was the stronger and held me back.

"You can't go in there! It's on fire. The inn's going to burn down. You can't go in!"

I stopped struggling and faced him. "So this is what you've done! You've set fire to your grandmother's property! You've done it because Glynis wanted you to. Oh, how could you be so stupid and blind?"

"It's none of your business!" he shouted at me. "You've done nothing but meddle ever since you came here."

"How could you be so wicked and so stupid?" I ran on. "Don't you see how she has used you from the start to get what she wants—leaving you to take the blame? You set up that alabaster head as Glynis told you to do—so I'd be sure and knock it over. Yet she would never be blamed because she didn't touch it herself. You've spoiled my marriage and turned my husband against me! Because I had to take the blame instead of your mother. It was all set up that way. But you aren't going to be so stupid a second time. This time we're going to stop what she has started. Come and show me where the hose is."

He had grown very still in the face of my rage. His grasp had dropped away from me. I could hear the flames crackling inside the inn. He turned abruptly and went back through the door and I went with him, right on his heels. He ran through the foyer, through the big dining room to the place were a hose was coiled on its wall rack.

"Turn it on!" he shouted to me as he snaked the hose from its holder.

Frantically, I turned the wheel of the faucet as he pulled the hose through the dining room and turned the nozzle upon billowing smoke and flame in the office. The fire hissed and spat, and steam rose furiously as he worked with unexpected enthusiasm, as though he were enjoying this phase of opposing the flames as much as he might have enjoyed setting them.

I could see now that the fire had been started in a plastic wastebasket, and had then run up the draperies beside the open window. One curtain still billowed flame into the outdoors, until Keith turned the hose on it with vigor and the remnants fell back into the room, a dripping black ruin.

There was nothing I could do except lose my temper further. "There—over by your grandmother's desk!" I cried. "Don't let it burn her records. What made you do such a wicked thing? Haven't you any will of your own? Haven't you any courage? Are you too much of a worm to tell Glen the truth about what happened and set me right with him?"

"The fire's just about out," he said quietly. "It didn't get

177

so far. I don't think it has spread any. So hush what you're saying now, or I'll turn the hose on you.''

I sputtered into silence, my fury dying as the fire died. Trent found us so, watching the wet, stinking mess in the office, almost shoulder to shoulder in our common misery.

11

"What's going on here?" Trent asked. "I saw the smoke, and—" He pushed past us and picked up the wastebasket, dripping with water and greasy ash, and dropped the whole thing out the window. Then he turned back to us. "What happened?"

Keith was turning off the water at the hose nozzle, and his look was sullen. His eyes avoided his father's.

I stumbled into words. For some reason I had to protect the boy. "Keith and I saw the smoke. We—we got here at about the same time, and he used the hose to put it out. Something in the wastebasket caught fire."

The relief in Trent's eyes made me feel utterly guilty. He laughed and clapped Keith on the shoulder.

"For a minute there I thought you might have started it."

"Why would he?" I rushed into words again. Keith had put the fire out—Keith could be reached. Unless his father spoiled everything with his anger now. "What a silly thing to say!" I ran on. "Blaming your own son for what was obviously an accident."

Keith threw me a look of scorn. "I did set it," he told his father, and then clamped his mouth shut and would not say another word.

The boy had no use for my defense, but I gave it anyway.

"Glynis put him up to it, but at least he stopped the fire from spreading. So perhaps no serious damage was done."

The scorn Trent turned on me was as great as his son's. He was no longer the tender, kindly man who had kissed me only a little while ago. "I think you'd better go home, Dina. You've had enough for one night. I'll take you back to High Towers."

"No," I said. "Stay with Keith. I'll find my way."

"You can't stumble through the woods after dark," he said. "Wait a moment and—"

"I'll go home with Colton," I told him, and turned away before he could stop me.

The blaze had been seen from down the lake and as I went outside I met Pandora hurrying toward the inn.

"The fire is out," I told her. "There's some damage, but not a great deal. Don't go in there now. Let Trent have some time with his son. And keep the others away."

Pandora was always quick and intuitive. She promptly took her stand on the steps, asking no questions, and I found the path back along the bank. On the way I informed any I met that the accidental fire was out. When I reached the dying bonfire, I noted that Glen and Glynis were still there, not in the least eager to visit the inn to find out what was happening.

We drove back to High Towers in Colton's car and the twins were keyed up and excited. Excited because of the gay evening, excited because Colton had said he would sell the land. Excited for other reasons that I knew about and Colton and Nomi didn't. Colton would allow no arguments on the subject of the land, and when the twins grew importunate, he simply told them to be quiet—and quiet they were. Now that Keith had failed in what he had attempted, I wondered what they would try next.

Back at the house I was glad that I had the bedroom to myself. To my surprise Jezebel was waiting for me. I picked her up in my arms and went to stand at the window where I could look out across the lake toward the stone house. Once more the light was on in Trent's room. I could see him through the window. The sharp staccato of typewriter keys came to me across the frozen plain of ice, and it seemed a companionable sound on this Christmas Eve. I was glad that his book was going well. My father had trusted him completely, and so did I.

I thought about Keith as well as I stood there, wondering whether I had reached him at all tonight. Wondering how Trent had handled him after I left. The boy had done a shocking thing, yet it seemed as though he had responded to me for a little while—as though I had, for a few minutes at least, got through to him. But was it enough to cause him to tell Glen the truth? This I doubted. What could be expected of him with a mother like Glynis, when she chose to influence him with her own particular wiles? Glynis was good at bewitching.

After I was in bed, Glen came into our room for the first time since he had moved to the room he'd had as a boy. He picked Jezebel up quite gently and put her out in the hall, where she whisked downstairs to a safer part of the house. Glen had no dislike for the cat, oddly enough, or she for him. Apparently he had this difference at least from Glynis.

I turned on my side and closed my eyes. I did not know why he had come and I had nothing to say to him. But he had something to say to me. Not an apology. There was no mention of the slap he had given me, or the blow he had taken from Trent, but it was about Trent that he wanted to talk.

"I never liked him," he told me, "even when he was married to my sister. I can imagine that he'd like to make trouble for us now, if he can. I'm willing to overlook that tender little scene on the bank of the lake tonight and give you the benefit of the doubt, Dina. But you must not see Trent alone again."

I was too angry to answer. I lay on my side with my back to him and said nothing until he came to sit on the bed beside me and bent over to tweak my braid with one finger. Then, rather methodically, he began to unbraid my hair, spread it out on my pillow as though it was something that interested him apart from me.

"Don't be angry with me," he said. "Let's forget what has happened as far as we can and start over again."

I wanted to tug my hair away from his touch, but I lay still. "There's never any starting over. Everything that has happened adds up and gets in the way."

"I never thought you'd be like this," he said, still gentle. "I used to think you were exciting when you were angry, but I didn't expect to find this unforgiving quality in you."

I rolled over abruptly and he let the strand of hair go. "Does that mean that you are forgiving *me*? Forgiving me for what happened to the alabaster head? Is that what you mean?"

He drew a little away from me as if he found my sudden vehemence distasteful. "It's not a matter of forgiveness. I want to go on to other things and put the past behind us. That alabaster head meant everything to me—everything!" There seemed a low, burning quality in his voice that was frightening to hear. "You owe me this, Dina. With your own hand you destroyed my work. Now you must give it back to me."

So that was it. He wanted something else of me now and he hadn't changed at all in his thinking about what Glynis had convinced him had happened to the head. I could only scowl at him.

He forced himself to relax a little, and reached out with one finger to smooth away the frown between my eyes. I tried to lie still beneath his touch and not resist him. Where had all my longing for his love gone that I should lie here in this stubborn, unresponsive state?

Once more he touched my hair. "Colton said I must get back to work—and he's right. I know what I'm going to do now. I'm going to use Glynis in the wood because she suits it—as you suited the alabaster. I'm going to use her face and being. It will work, I think. But I'll use your hair. Not golden in dark wood, of course, but the lightness, the fine, spun-silk quality. I can catch them in wood."

I sat straight up in bed and jerked my hair from his touch. "You'll do nothing of the kind! I won't pose for you again. Never, never!"

I burst disgracefully into tears, jumped out of bed and went to lock myself in the bathroom. There in the dark I sat down on the chenille rug and wept into my fingers, into my tangled hair. Which was, of course, a ridiculous state of affairs. I could not spend the night weeping in the bathroom. Yet I knew that something had outraged me far more than I had ever been outraged before. How could he ask me to be a part of such a plan? How could he imagine that I would allow him to use any part of me in a carving he was doing of Glynis?

After a time I got up, washed my face, rebraided my hair and went back to the bedroom. To my relief, Glen was gone. I lay down on the bed and stayed awake for a long time. I could hear, far away, belonging to another world, another life, typewriter keys chattering in the night.

Morning, once more, was that brighter, braver time. I was tired enough to sleep late, and when I got up I dressed in gray-blue wool and bound my hair in braids over each ear in the style that had suited my mother so well. It did not particularly suit me because it made me top-heavy, but at least there would be no strands afloat to remind Glen of last night's notions.

Nomi was up early and outdoing herself with a hearty Christmas morning breakfast. Glynis looked a sylph in pale yellow trousers and a psychedelic blouse, and she was playing the daughter of the house to the best of her histrionic ability. She knelt before the lighted Christmas tree, poked at her gifts delightedly, read names aloud, rattled each one of her packages, and was altogether entertaining and little-girlish for Colton's and Glen's amusement. I found that I was growing hourly older and more sour—as Nomi had said one might easily do in this house.

I think Nomi saw how it was with me because after breakfast when we gathered before the lighted tree for the ritual of gift-giving, she drew me aside.

"Don't mind the way Glynis reverts," she said. "It always happens on Christmas morning and we all know why. She still tries to go back to the day one week before her mother died and her world crashed in."

I could see then that this was what she was doing. She had become like the child she could never be again, happy and carefree, with no dreadful deed on her conscience. I could pity her a little, now that I understood, yet the result of her childish action had never seemed more dreadful.

Though Keith had not yet come, we did not wait for him, and took turns opening our presents. Colton was pleased with the book of Spanish castles I had bought for him—with Nomi's help. Nomi liked her sweater set. Even Glynis seemed to like the crepe blouse I had bought her—in a deep brandy shade that would accent her coloring. Glen exclaimed over the silk turtleneck I'd brought him from New York, and he put it on at once.

The most expensive gifts came from Colton to the twins. He gave them each duplicate jackets—soft brown suede on one side that could be reversed with leopard skin on the other. Each put on a jacket with the leopard fur out, and I had the uneasy feeling that there were two, only partially tamed, wild creatures in our midst that morning.

For me there was exotic perfume from Glynis—which I detested at the first sniff, and from Glen a large, cool aquamarine embedded in antique gold. The ring on my finger felt heavy, echoing the heaviness of my heart. Nomi's present was best. She had made a marvelous scarf for me on her loom—finely woven of soft brown wool, with zigzags of pink lightning striking through it. It was almost a serape length, meant to be worn like either a stole or a long scarf. I flung it about my shoulders, liking its dove-soft yet heavy warmth, and went to kiss her cheek—a gesture she tolerated without enthusiasm.

Colton's gift to me was a book called *A Year in the Country*, which told about season changes in northern New Jersey, and related the habits of the birds and animals who lived about the lake. I knew I would study it with pleasure and was grateful for his thought.

But the drama of our gift-opening lay in the final presents

Glen and Glynis had given each other. They were almost duplicate gifts, and Nomi told me that this had happened before. The twins thought alike, they had similar tastes, and probably a bit of extrasensory perception between them as well. This often resulted in similar choices in what they gave each other.

Glen opened his package first and found that Glynis had chosen a chain of gold links for him—its medallion a Greek profile that resembled Colton. In delight he shed his leopard skin and put the chain on over the turtleneck, urging Glynis to open her package. Hers, too, was a chain of gold links— more finely wrought than the male version, and also with a large medallion. Glynis laughed as she studied it, then held it up for us to see. The head on her medallion was one of a handsome, snarling leopard. She dropped the chain over her neck so that the leopard's head shone against the glitter of her blouse—and the gift could not have been more appropriate. They were too close, these two. There was no place for anyone else in their lives. Each might have made gestures of escape, but always they came together again—belonging to each other as no one else could ever belong. But how was I to accept this—live with it?

Keith arrived late, looking a bit sullen, almost defiant as he brought his gifts into a tissue-and-ribbon-strewn drawing room. He dumped them unceremoniously onto Glynis's yellow-clad knees, and stood back to await her verdict. Perhaps he expected blame because he had not succeeded in whatever she had set him to do last night—and had been caught at it besides. But Glynis seemed to have forgiven him readily, and I wondered if that was only because she wanted to use him again. It seemed likely.

Keith's gifts were surprisingly original, though all of a kind. He had whittled for each of us a small animal of wood, and when Colton held up his lion he gave the boy a look of approval.

"You're a Chandler after all," he said. "This is good work."

For Glynis there was the obvious leopard, crawling flat on

185

its belly as it stalked its prey. For Glen he had carved a unicorn. When I saw it I had to smile. The boy had more imagination than I'd have expected. A mythological creature was right for Glen, who was rather mythical himself. For Nomi there was a comfortable house cat, curled up and obviously purring, and for me a young doe, delicate and graceful, its ears pricked as if in alarm—which made me wonder.

When Keith had opened his own gifts of sweaters and skis, a new encyclopedia from Colton, and books from Nomi and me, I managed to find a moment alone with him. So far he had not met my eyes, and I knew he would avoid me if he could. But I came near him on the pretext of picking up wrappings strewn about his feet and asked him my question softly.

"Why the doe for me, Keith?"

He glanced at me briefly and then away. "Because you look like that sometimes," he said shortly and moved away from me.

Often that day I looked at the small, delicately carved creature and wondered about his words. I supposed they were surprisingly true and that much of the time I must seem too alert to alarm and impending danger. Perhaps he meant I was young too, and unformed, still seeking to know who and what I was.

Through all this time of gift-giving, one strange thing made itself felt again and again. Glynis was trying to make friends with me today, and Glen seemed to want her to do so. In small ways she made overtures. She no longer baited me, but threw the talk my way considerately when she could. I trusted none of this, and I saw Nomi watching her too, with equal mistrust. Perhaps Glynis was trying to please Glen? But that seemed hardly likely, since he was anything but pleased with me himself.

At any rate I was on guard, and when she suggested later in the morning that we go skating, I promptly refused—which seemed to upset Glen, so that he began to lecture me.

"It's time you were decent to Glynis," he told me sharply. "You can see she's knocking herself out this morning to

186

please you, and you've been nasty at every turn. Why not let her take you skating? I'm going to go on preparing the wood for my carving, and Keith wants to see how I go about it. So run along with Glynis and see if you can be decent for a change.''

What he said was all true. I had been nasty. I had been mistrustful. But all, I felt, with good reason after the things she had done to me. Yet when Glen put it this way I did not want to displease him further by refusing. I asked Nomi to come along, but she said skating was not for an arthritic knee. She was going for a walk instead. Colton was busy on some project of his own, and I decided to give in. Perhaps if some better relationship could be achieved between Glynis and me, this was the time to attempt it.

I dressed warmly in my navy blue jacket and slacks. I put Nomi's scarf of brown and pink over my head like a hood and looped it around my neck, with the long ends hanging down my back. Later I was to wonder what would have happened if I had not worn that scarf. Would everything have been totally different in its outcome? Could the mere wearing of a scarf change all our lives? I can't really believe that—and yet—

Glynis, of course, wore her new leopard-skin jacket, and it suited her magnificently. We climbed down to the shore path and walked along, swinging our skates, with Glynis chatting to me as cheerfully as though nothing unpleasant had ever happened between us. I felt less friendly. I wanted to fling in her face the charge that she had put Keith up to setting that fire in Pandora's office, but I managed to keep silent, to pretend that I was taken in by her cheery good humor. Yet I never really believed that the Christmas spirit had effected such a change in Glynis Chandler. The little girl reversion was over, and this performance was something new.

She was talking about roads as we walked along, and I made little sense of what she was saying in her soft, slightly husky voice.

''Sometimes the way gets so narrow there's not even room for a lay-by, as they say in England. There's no turnout space at all. You simply keep going until you reach your destination. There's no way ever to turn back.''

If there was some subtlety here, I did not want to think about what it meant.

"If we're going to skate," I said at last, "why don't we try it here? There isn't much choice in the ice, is there?''

"Oh, but there is,'' she told me. "The best place is around Gray Rocks. There's an area there that's the last to freeze and as a result it doesn't hold the snow. After a good freeze we always go there to skate. Come along and I'll show you.''

Was this the place where her mother had died? I wondered. But I need not go out on the ice unless I was sure of it—and wherever we skated, I would let Glynis go first. That was my thought. That was what I planned.

After we'd passed the base of the tall rocks, the shoreline cut in, forming a small, half-surrounded bay, and there the ice looked smooth and clean.

"It's a lovely place," Glynis said, and sat down on the bank to put on her skates. I joined her and got out of my shoes, laced up my skates.

She was out on the ice ahead of me, skating skillfully, executing fancy steps with complete grace and control. She did not seem doubtful about the cleared space, yet it seemed to me that she kept to the edges and avoided its center. Whatever she did, I would follow, and I would skate nowhere else because I did not trust her at all.

When I was ready, she came back for me, took my hands and skated with me until I gained some assurance. The ice seemed firm enough, though there were the usual surface cracks to be avoided, and my suspicion lessened a little. The one real obstacle was a massive tree stump that protruded somewhat to the right of center.

In a few moments we were warm, our cheeks stinging from the wind that always blew down the lake. Glynis began to show me a few simple figures, and I discovered that when she was in this pleasant, obliging mood she could be the best of company. I did not trust too much—but I began to relax a little.

When she skated opposite me and held out her hands, I took them in mine and she showed me the step I had seen in figure skating where one partner swings the other across in front of him, so that one skater vaults past the other in turn. She held my hands firmly, and swung me past, and then I swung her past me. We repeated the movement and the third time she suddenly let go of my hands, so that I went sailing toward the center of the cleared space. The moment I found myself flying free I slid my skates sideways, to brake, and in the same instant I felt treacherous movement beneath my feet.

Glynis was skating about me reassuringly. "It's all right. The ice is a little rubbery, but it will hold. Come along—do what I do."

She was laughing at me now, since I couldn't possibly do what she was doing. She made a spiral turn across the ice and went into a spin, came out of it and started to skate away—when something happened. The toe of her skate must have struck a crevice in the ice, catching her unaware. She went sprawling and her leopard jacket behaved like a sled, so that she hurtled across the ice past me to its very center. As I watched, the ice gave way and dark water spilled over the surface, engulfing Glynis, sucking her down by the very weight of her jacket.

Under my feet the ice was rubbery, but still solid. I managed to get as far as the thick tree stump that protruded from the ice. I held onto it with one hand and reached my other one out to Glynis where she floundered helplessly in the water, a look of utter shock and terror upon her face. But I could not reach her. The ice she grasped broke away at her touch and the space of dark water grew larger around her with every moment of struggle.

I shouted for help, but there was no one to hear. My fingers fumbled as I unwound Nomi's long scarf from about my neck. I wrapped an end of it around my wrist, held onto the stump and cast the scarf toward Glynis across churning water. She reached for it, caught it, lost it—then managed to snarl her fingers in the fringe.

"Hold on!" I shouted. "Hold on and I'll pull you in."

I braced myself against the stump, dug in the heels of my skates, and tried with all my strength to pull her out of the water and across the ice. But she came only a little way and then stuck.

"It's no use!" she cried weakly. "My clothes are caught on something under the water. I can't get free."

I could not waste my breath on talk. I tried once more to haul her over the ice. She did not move and I could see that I lacked the strength to pull her free of whatever held her.

Quickly I wound my end of the scarf around a deep split in the stump and knotted it firmly so that it would not pull loose.

"You'll have to hold on," I told her. "I'll get help as fast as I can. Just don't let go of this scarf."

"I can't hold on for long!" Her teeth were chattering, and mine began to chatter too, in sympathy and fear. "It's no use anyway. I'm going to drown. This is where my mother died. This is where—"

"Stop that!" I shouted to her, already climbing the bank, struggling out of my skates and into my shoes. "You've got to hold on until I can call Trent McIntyre. That's quicker than going back to the house."

Free of my skates, I ran along the shore path. I scrambled over the base of Gray Rocks and was within sight of the stone house across the lake. But though I shouted Trent's name, and Pandora's again and again, no one answered me. No one stirred anywhere either on this side or across the ice. Either the McIntyres were down at the inn, and out of calling distance, or they had gone off on some Christmas morning errand. There was nothing to do except get to High Towers as fast as I could.

But before I could run on, I heard Glynis's voice behind me once more, calling for help. Then, to my great relief a second voice shouted back to her. If help had come from another direction, then I need not go on. I might be of more use back there. I ran back to Gray Rocks and crossed the base to where I could look out toward the little bay. There was no one there but Glynis, and she lay deeper in the water.

I was going to be too late. Now I knew that no matter how fast I ran toward the house, how I punished my lungs in their gasping for air, I would be too late. I tried to cut through the woods, running uphill at a diagonal, but the going was rough. I fell more than once, always getting up to stumble on.

When the house loomed ahead of me, I had to stop briefly to catch my breath before I could shout. I could hear no sound anywhere except the wind in the pine trees. No feeble voice wailing for help—nothing. I banged my way through the front door, shouting as I ran up the stairs. My cries brought Colton to his bedroom door, and Glen down from the attic. Keith was no longer with him.

Gasping, I blurted out what had happened, and Colton and Glen flew into action. They snatched up coats as they ran out the front door, and I stumbled after them. I could not stay in the house and wait. I had to know. I had to be there.

The two of them took a short cut that went at a diagonal through the woods and I followed as best I could. We climbed behind Gray Rocks, and cut steeply downhill toward the lake. Glen and Colton were well ahead of me. They had made a chain between them by the time I reached the bay—a chain from the stump that anchored Colton to the black water where Glynis lay. Glen had more strength than I. He managed to pull her free from whatever had snagged her, and together they got her across the ice to land.

I stood by for a few moments while the two of them worked over her. Then Colton looked up at me, his face pale, his expression self-contained.

"Run back to the house, Dina. Find Nomi and have her call our doctor. Have her get a warm bed ready."

Once more I ran. But all the way there I knew that it was too late. Glynis had drowned in the very place where she had once seen her mother go through the ice. The very place in which she had tried to drown me.

Both thoughts were a heavy part of my awareness all the

way back to the house. Glynis had tried to drown me—and had drowned herself instead.

Fortunately Nomi had returned from her walk toward the other end of the lake. She was on the phone before I stopped talking. I listened to her, heard her words, did what she told me. And all the while I thought of how Glynis had looked with the stamp of terror on her face. And I could not bear it. I could not bear what this would do to Glen.

"I think she's dead," I told Nomi.

She was still Elizabeth's sister, even with her enemy defeated. "Good," she said harshly. "Now you'll be free. Glen will be free."

I flew after her about the house, trying to help with the bed in Glynis's room. "Oh, no! I don't want to be free that way! I don't—"

"What did she try to do to you?" Nomi demanded.

I couldn't tell her that. With Glynis dead, I couldn't tell anyone. I moved away from her, went to stand beside a window where I could watch for them to bring her home.

The black marble head looked at me accusingly from anguished eyes. I had not saved her. I had not been strong enough, or brave enough. Or willing enough? Was that the thing that frightened me?

Nomi watched me. "Stop it!" she cried. "None of what happened was your fault. It was hers—hers all the way, whatever she tried to do."

I did not ask her how she knew. I did not even think about asking. Glen was coming toward the front door carrying his twin in his arms. His face looked like death itself. I ran downstairs to help in any way I could, but Glen went past me as if I were a stranger, and carried Glynis up to her bed.

Colton shook his head at me wearily. "Let him go. There's nothing you can do for him now. Come get me a drink, Dina, there's a good girl."

I poured his Scotch and made it strong, carried it to him where he sat before the cold hearth in the drawing room. All around us were strewn the gay remnants of Christmas—red and silver, stars and bells. Brightly colored lights still winked from the tree, and I could not bear the look of them. When I had turned them out, I sat down opposite Colton—sat down heavily because my legs were trembling.

"She must have let go of my scarf," I said. "She must not have had the strength to hang on."

Colton lowered his glass. "What scarf? What are you talking about?"

I told him how I had thrown Nomi's strong, woven scarf to Glynis and tried to pull her in. How I had knotted it firmly to the stump and gone for help, leaving her clinging to it.

All the way through my account Colton shook his head. "There was no scarf there," he said when I finished. "There was no scarf there at all."

12

By New Year's Eve it was all over. And it was just the beginning.

The painful ritual of custom and ceremony had been observed. Glynis lay beside her mother in a small country cemetery a few miles from High Towers. By New Year's Eve the emotional shock had worn off to some extent so that we had begun to accept the fact that we would not hear her step on the stairs, would not hear her laugh again, need not fear her temper. Yet horror had only just begun.

By New Year's Eve snow was falling once more—large, soft flakes that were piling up outside, with no wind to blow them into drifts. We sat together—the four of us who had been five. We sat together, though not cozily, in the drawing room, and waited. Waited and watched each other—because of Nomi's gift to me, because of the woven scarf that had not saved Glynis from drowning. The fear that was to follow us had already commenced. It lay upon us all. Only Jezebel was free of fear. Eerily, she knew that the one she feared was gone forever and she moved freely about the house—willing now to enter every room but Glynis's.

Perhaps I ought not to have been so insistent about the scarf, and about the shouting I thought I had heard. When Colton told me no scarf had been found, I should have let the matter go. But with Glen looking at me with blame in his eyes, I had to make him understand—make them all understand—that I had tried to save her. No matter what she had tried to do to me, I would not willingly have let her drown. Nomi believed me, supported me. With Colton I was not sure. But in Glen I faced repugnance and a dislike that grew stronger as the days went by.

Once I went back to the place where Glynis and I had skated. I inched my way across ice to the stump of what had once been a great tree. Wedged tightly in the cracks of the wood were several pink strands of fringe from my scarf. I came home and told them all that the fringe was there, but my pleas persuaded no one to come with me and see for themselves. If what I said was true, they did not want to know, and when I went to check again a day or so later, the few strands were gone. I could only believe that someone had come secretly to remove them. Someone with a guilty conscience who wanted me to be blamed?

Colton canceled his January plans to leave. For the first time in his life he seemed a shattered man. I had known that Glynis was his brilliant, favored darling, but I had not expected anything outside his art to shake him to such an extent. He looked immeasurably older and his lion's mane of a head seemed more white than silver.

Nevertheless, there had been only one explosion of feeling on his part since the tragedy. It came two days after the funeral, when Nomi had gone determinedly into Glynis's room, meaning to put away her things, remove all reminders of her from our midst. She had summoned me to help and I had gone reluctantly to Glynis's room. Nomi's determination to wipe every trace of Glen's twin from the house seemed too extreme, and I was not sure why she felt so strongly.

Colton found us at our work and stopped us with a sudden fury that surprised me.

"Let everything be!" he told Nomi. "Where else is Glen to go when everything becomes too much for him to bear? Let him have his sister's things as solace for a while longer."

Nomi was never one to be intimidated and she had some

strong purpose of her own in clearing this room. She stood up to Colton sturdily enough.

"It's not solace—it's the self-indulgence of exaggerated grief. The sooner every trace of Glynis is gone from this house, the better for us all. It's unwise to let this room stay as it was. Glen is clinging to illusion and it's unhealthy."

This was the first time I had realized that when Glen disappeared, as he often had in the last few days, he went to his sister's room. He would be gone for an hour or more, and when he returned his face was blank of emotion, as though something had washed all ability to feel out of him. Intense pain might do that—the pain he would suffer among his sister's possessions, letting it mount to a peak until he could feel no more. Nomi was right and I wanted to support her, but I dared not interfere when Colton gave the orders.

"Leave the room as it is," he said flatly, and turned away.

I had not known that Glen was upstairs in his own small room until he heard our voices and came to the door. A glance told him what Nomi was up to and he strode in and took the box she was packing from her hands. He did not look at Colton, or at me.

"Don't touch anything! I want it left exactly as it is. I'm moving into this room today. All Glynis's things belong to me now. That is the way she would have wanted it."

I think not even Colton wished this, but there could be no opposing Glen in a mood that was almost as stormy as those his sister used to indulge. Colton turned away, his face tight with strain as he held back any remonstrance. This room carried too many memories for him.

Glen stopped him. "Father—you might as well know that I've countermanded the order you gave for an inscription on the headstone for the grave. I'm going to carve it myself. No one else is going to do that last thing for her."

Colton nodded stiffly and went out of the room.

Nomi made a little dusting motion with her two hands as if she dismissed all notions she'd had of dismantling the room, even though she was obviously not pleased with Glen. Then she had gone, too, leaving me to face him, to speak any sensible plea that might be offered. I did not want to stay. I had no confidence in my ability to change his mind. Yet what he was doing was wrong—the worst possible thing he could do, so I had to try.

"You'll only make yourself increasingly miserable," I said. "Isn't Nomi's way better—to put Glynis aside for a while until everything eases a little?"

All his new dislike for me looked out of his eyes. "What do you know of what's good or bad—for me? What has happened is your fault. It was your fault from the beginning when you shattered the alabaster head. And now you've brought about Glynis's death. What bad luck it was when I walked into the museum that day. Go away, will you, and leave me alone."

The shock of his words left me shaken, and I made no further attempt to change his mind. To get away from the house and all it hid, I dressed warmly and went outside. I suppose that I must still love Glen, but I did not really know. Did love which blossomed so quickly die with equal speed? Or was it just that I had grown numb and unfeeling? Perhaps after a time all my deadened wounds would begin to throb and torment me. Then I would come to life and long for a love that was lost and over. But even while I walked down the hillside toward the lake, this seemed an irrational thing. I did not want Glen any more, yet I might still be in love with the gay, exuberant, demanding man who had swept me off my feet in New York. A man who did not exist. As his sister had died, so had Glen.

Halfway down through the woods I met Trent coming up the hill. His smile warmed me. I had not known how cold I was until he smiled at me.

"I was coming to see you," he said.

I could only shake my head helplessly. "Don't come now. We—everyone—is so upset. And—and Glen—" I broke off because there was nothing I could tell him. Indeed, I had the horrid unreasoning feeling that if Trent knew about the scarf and that I had gone off and left Glynis without pulling her in, he might blame me too. I could not bear any more blame.

"I won't come to the house if you'd rather I didn't," he said quietly. "I only wanted to thank you for what you did for Keith the night of the fire in the inn."

I could only stare at him. "But I thought you were angry with me for trying to protect him. You were both angry with me."

"What you wanted to do was foolish," he said. "But it was because of you that he stood up like a man and faced what had to be faced. We had a long talk that night, and perhaps I got through to him a little. Certainly *you* did. Whatever you said to him earlier made him stop and think. Not that he feels any differently about his mother, except that for a time he was furiously angry with her. You stirred him to that, at least. I think he's aware of the monstrous thing Glynis prompted him to do by using that picture she had painted—getting him to destroy his grandmother's property. So perhaps he will behave differently from now on. Pandora doesn't know. She may guess, but I'm not going to tell her. It isn't necessary now."

Trent still did not know what Keith had done in obeying Glynis about the alabaster head, but this I still could not tell him. Perhaps Keith had been angry with his mother on that score too—I could only hope so.

"I'm glad you reached him," I said. "I was afraid of what you might do while you were angry."

"I know. I saw the fear in your face. That's what sobered me and brought me up short in what I said to him. So thank you, young Bernardina."

"Young?" I repeated wryly. "Oh, no. Not any more. I feel older than Nomi now. Older than anyone."

He shook his head. "You're very young and you'll be happy again." He came close to me and put his hand beneath my chin, tilted my head and kissed my mouth—lightly, swiftly. "I keep wanting to do that," he said. "I can't think of you as Glen's wife."

I wasn't Glen's wife—not any more—and for an instant I

yearned toward him, wanted to go into his arms and be comforted. But he could not be my love, and I stepped away.

"I've brought you your Christmas present," he said. "I meant to give it to you Christmas Day, but after what happened there was no chance." He pulled a flat, narrow box from his lumber jacket pocket and gave it to me. The bright wrapping and gift ribbon looked incongruous now—our Christmas had been so very far from merry—but I was touched that he should have thought of me and I found that tears had come into my eyes.

"Don't open it now," he said quickly. "Take it to your room and open it when you're alone." He started away from me, and then stopped, turning back. "Are you all right, Bernardina?"

"I'm all right," I said. "I'm all right now."

"You've only to call if you want me," he said.

I already knew that and the assurance was comforting to me. I turned away and climbed the hill toward the house, carrying my package. Once when I stopped and looked back I found him still standing there, watching me go. I waved to him, comforted and just a little braver because Trent McIntyre cared what happened to me.

In the house I ran quickly upstairs and shut the door of my room. Then I untied the ribbon, opened my gift. Inside the box was a packet of letters and a note from Trent: "—because I thought these would mean even more to you than they do to me."

Folded inside were all the letters my father had written to Trent over the years, from the time when he had been a young man just out of college, until he had come to our house before my father's death. There were not a great many, but Trent had kept every one, and I sat down then and there to read them.

It was a warmly moving experience. Not only did my father come into the room and sit beside me, but Trent came more alive for me too. I could know him better through these letters than I ever had. By what my father wrote to him I could tell how much he valued him, trusted him, and wanted great things for his future. There were bits about my mother and me too in these letters, and all our warm, satisfying family life came back to me as it had not for a long while. Now the bits of philosophy with which my father had so often flavored his talk had meaning for me as never before. It was almost as if he broke the long silence of death because I needed him so very much. This was why Trent had given me the letters.

There was one simple statement that struck home to me especially. John Blake had been an essentially simple man. He had never made much out of little. "Courage," he had written Trent, "is often no more than the ability to keep going ahead. Those who don't have it turn aside, or quit altogether."

To keep going ahead. That was the advice I needed now. To keep going from one day to the next, no matter how hard life at High Towers became for me, no matter how darkly Glen looked at me. There had to be an end. I must keep going and know there was daylight somewhere, on there ahead.

Nevertheless, on New Year's Eve, when we all sat together in the drawing room, I wondered how I could endure the waiting for a new year to begin. Once I had looked forward eagerly to this time. Until a week ago I had been ready to greet the new year with hope, no matter what Glynis said or did. I had not yet come to the place where the relationship between Glen and me seemed hopeless and over, as it seemed now. Even in death Glynis had defeated me and the courage prompted by my father's letters began to waver at times, like the uncertain flame of a candle. I was coming to the conclusion that for me courage might well lie in getting away from High Towers, not in staying here.

At least all the frivolous Christmas decorations were gone from the house, and the Christmas tree had been taken down, so that outward reminders of Christmas morning were few. Yet the reminders were still there. When I closed my eyes I could see Glynis exclaiming over the golden medallion with its leopard's head that Glen had given her. In fact, I hardly needed to close my eyes because tonight, on New Year's Eve, Glen wore the chain she had given him—though he had put away my gift of the silk sweater. If anything, the resemblance between him and his twin was more marked than ever. It was as though, in his grief, Glen had taken on the very stamp of Glynis's expression. Now one saw for the first time that his face resembled her black marble image.

With the snow blowing outside and the gilt clock on the mantel ticking relentlessly on toward another year, Nomi sat close to the fire, knitting quietly, calmly. Sometimes I watched her fingers in fascination. Only a little while ago they had been weaving a streak of pink lightning into a scarf for me. Now they knitted a sweater for Glen—a heavy winter sweater with an intricate Norwegian design. I sensed that she worked at this because she had to; because if her fingers were busy her thoughts would let her be for a time.

But in spite of our silence, there was no real quiet among us on this New Year's Eve, and I, perhaps, was the most restless one of all. For the third time I jumped up and stood at one of the French windows watching snow falling softly over the drive. It was not deep yet. A car with snow tires could easily get down the hill.

I wished that I could take Glen's car and drive away. Away anywhere. Away at least as far as the McIntyres' across the lake. How would they be awaiting the New Year tonight? Tragedy had touched them too. Glynis had once been Trent's wife. She was Keith's mother—and Keith had worshiped her with a sort of love that was doomed to eventual disillusionment. Perhaps that disillusionment had already begun before her death. Perhaps, though he could not realize this now, her sudden dying was a boon to Keith. Now his suffering would be sharp and clean. His love would not linger on into disintegration, as he found that what he loved was not worth his suffering. As it was with me? As my love had disintegrated so swiftly? The skyrocket plummeting to earth!

The porch light was on, and snowflakes danced toward earth, each feathery and clearly defined in the glow of yellow light. I could see some distance along the drive. Once I thought something moved far along in the shadows. I stood very still, watching.

Behind me Colton spoke to his son. "When are you going to get back to work, Glen?"

"Work?" Glen echoed the word as if he did not know what it meant.

"Of course. You must throw yourself into something new—that's the only cure for pain. I had to learn that when your mother died."

"Throw myself into what?" Glen asked bitterly.

"You used Dina before," Colton said. "Do her again. She's here—available. Put her into wood this time."

"But I don't feel—" Glen broke off, perhaps because I stood at the window and he was not yet utterly callous.

"You don't have to feel anything to get started," Colton assured him. "Every creative worker must learn that. If the feeling is lacking you nevertheless begin. Give it time, let your interest catch at something in your work, and you're on your way. Why not start with her hair? You've always been intrigued by the mystery of her hair. Capture it now in the wood. Get it out of those spinsterish rounds over her ears and let it float on her shoulders. Wood can be airier than stone."

The last thing I wanted now was to pose for Glen. Yet if it would help him, if it would cause him to look at me with less hatred in his eyes . . . I turned from the window.

"I don't want to try!" His cry was almost violent.

Nomi put aside her knitting in the chair beside her with an air of joining the fray. "Yes, Glen. This is the answer. Begin and let it come. Your father is right."

I was looking out the window again, unwilling to offer my help. It was fine with me if I never had to pose for Glen again.

Out on the drive a tall figure climbed the hill approaching the house. The figure of a boy—Keith. He seemed to be burdened with a load that he was carrying.

"Here comes Keith," I said. "He's bringing something up to the house."

Nomi rose and went to the door. We could hear her speaking to Keith, inviting him in, telling him to put his load down in the hall. Then she brought him to the door of the drawing room.

"Keith wants to speak to you, Colton," she said.

Colton did not move from his comfortable chair. "Come in, boy, come in! What has brought you out on New Year's Eve? Anything wrong over at your place?"

Keith shook his head. "I walked out," he said. "I left. I want to stay here, Grandfather."

We looked at the boy in astonishment. For one thing, in spite of being Glynis's son, he was not, strictly speaking, one of the Chandlers. For another, he had never, within my hearing, called his grandfather by that name. Colton disliked being called "father" or "grandfather," and Glynis had followed the same pattern with Keith, not allowing him to call her "Mother." But while he called his mother "Glynis" readily enough, Keith avoided calling Colton by that name. Now he had used "grandfather" boldly, placing himself among us, perhaps reminding Colton of his responsibility.

"Come in, Keith," Nomi said. "Take off your wet jacket. Here, let me have your things."

He got awkwardly out of his jacket, gave it to her with his cap, and ambled uncertainly into the room to the straight chair she offered him.

Colton had recovered from his first surprise. "What's wrong, Keith? You'd better tell us. We can't take you in against your father's wishes unless we know what's wrong."

The boy threw me a quick, hostile look that I did not understand, and left his chair to approach his grandfather. "I don't want to talk about it. They don't care what happens to me at home. They hated Glynis. I can't stay there any more. If you'll let me come here, I'll work around the place. I'll help Aunt Nomi. And I'll be going back to school day after tomorrow, so I won't be much in the way. I can sleep any place—I don't have to have a room. A cot in the attic—or anything."

Colton seemed more at a loss than I'd ever seen him. He

had not been strongly himself since his daughter's death. "Have you told your father and grandmother you were coming here?"

Keith shook his head. "I just packed up some things and walked out. They probably know where I'd come."

"Let him stay," Glen said. "He's Glynis's son and he's better off raised as a Chandler than over there. He's more one of us than he is one of them."

"Feuds!" Nomi said scornfully. "Don't talk like that, Glen."

It was still Colton's decision to make, but before he came to a conclusion the telephone rang, and Nomi went into the hall to answer it. In a few moments she was back.

"That was Trent. He wanted to know if the boy had come here. He wants to talk to us, Colton. I told him to come."

Colton set his book of Spanish castles aside. "We'll have to see him, of course. Do you want to stay and listen to what he says, Keith?"

"No, sir. I know what he'll say." Again the hostile look was flung my way, leaving me puzzled and troubled.

"Then you'd better go upstairs with Nomi," Colton told him. "A cot in the attic will do for the moment."

"Come along," Nomi said. "Bring your suitcase, Keith, and that dreadful picture you've toted over here. There's already a cot up there, and you can help me fix up a corner for yourself."

No one was paying any attention to me, and I went out of the room and slipped upstairs. There I put on my coat and came quietly down, so no one would hear me. I opened the front door and stepped out onto the snowy veranda. The night seemed utterly quiet. There was no wind and the trees stood straight and stark under their rimming of white. Even without a moon or stars the night seemed bright, and the snow came down softly, thickly, without dancing in the air as it fell.

I could see Trent's headlights from afar. As he turned up the drive a tree flashed brightly into view, then turned dark again as he passed. When he was almost opposite the house,

I went down the steps through soft wet snow and walked toward the car.

He saw me coming and braked near the house, swung open the car door.

"I have to talk to you," I said and slid into the seat beside him. "Thank you for giving me my father's letters. I couldn't have had a finer present."

He took my cold hands and held them. "What has happened now? Something's very wrong, isn't it?"

"Yes!" When I nodded flecks of snow flew from my hair. "Everything is over for me at the Chandlers'. I must go away soon. Glen doesn't want me there now."

Trent's hands tightened about mine. "I'd like to tell him—but never mind. You can come and stay with us, if you like."

"No. Thank you, but I need to get a long way off from Gray Rocks Lake. I—I have some things to—to figure out. I can't think here. I don't know what to think, or how I feel with *them* around me. But I can't leave yet."

"Why not?" he said.

I drew my hands gently away. "Because of the scarf that I tied to the stump of a tree out in the lake. I gave Glynis the end of it to hold onto."

I told him then—everything. About how Colton said there was no scarf there. About the voice I had heard shouting to Glynis. Someone had been there. Someone had unknotted the scarf and pulled it from her hands, left her to drown. I had to know who. I had to know before I left. The only thing I did not tell him was what Glynis had intended. There was no use in talking about that now.

Trent heard me out. "I suppose you've told them about this?"

"Yes, of course. But no one has admitted to seeing the scarf. They don't believe me. Except Nomi, perhaps."

"You couldn't recognize the voice you heard?"

"No—not really. The cry was shouted and distorted with echoes besides. I couldn't place it. It might have been a man or a woman. And how can you remember a shout when it has stopped sounding? It's not like remembering a face."

"I don't like this," Trent said. "I don't like the smell of it. Whoever called to Glynis, whoever took away the scarf, may be worrying that you will remember and come to a conclusion about him."

"I know," I said. "I've thought of that. But whoever it was is safe enough because I haven't the faintest notion of who it might be. Anyone could have gone along the high path while I was traveling the shore. They all move faster than I do outdoors, and the woods are thick there. We would never have seen each other. But how can I go away, leaving the others to blame me, to think I'm responsible for Glynis's death? If the removal of the scarf was deliberate, then we're talking about—murder."

"You and Keith," Trent said dryly.

"What do you mean? What has Keith to do with this?"

"Nothing, except that he has asked a question that's hard to answer. Glynis knew that springs feed that part of the lake. It's the first place to thaw and the last to freeze. She knew that her mother drowned there. So why would she go there to skate? She must have known it wasn't safe after the warmer weather we'd had. The swamp area thaws and so does the stream, so that water flows under the ice to start melting it from beneath. When this is helped along by the springs in that section, you get ice that isn't safe for skating, even though it looks firm enough on the surface. Even if she took you there, she would never have gone near the center herself. So Keith has asked the question of why she went out there, how she happened to fall through."

I stared at him in the light from the dash. "Do you mean he blames me? Does he think?—"

"He thinks you might have acted on impulse. He thinks there wasn't any scarf."

"But that's dreadful," I said. "And you? Do you believe—?"

He answered me roughly. "Don't be an idiot! I know Glynis. I can guess why she took you there, even though you've made no accusation yourself."

206

There was relief in my sigh. Trent knew. I could talk to Trent.

"Yes," I said. "She wanted me to go through the ice. But she trapped herself instead. Only I can't tell them that—even if it would do any good."

"Then you must go away soon. You can't stay in that house with someone feeling edgy about what you know."

From the veranda Glen's voice called to me. "Dina? Where are you, Dina?"

"I'll have to go in," I said. "Come with me."

Trent came to open my door and helped me out into the snow. We went up to the house together.

Glen spoke curtly to Trent. "Colton's waiting for you. He'd like to talk to you alone."

The moment Trent had gone into the drawing room, Glen whirled on me. "Why were you out there with him? What do you have to talk to him about?"

I answered quietly. "That's nothing I want to discuss," I said, and started past him up the stairs.

He came after me at once. "Dina—don't make an enemy of me. I want to believe in you. I want to love you—just as I did in New York."

I paused on the stairs and faced him. He stood one step below me, and I remembered the look of his bright chestnut hair as it swept back from his forehead, just as I had first seen it that day in the museum—and as I had seen hair like it so recently—wet and floating from Glynis's head as she lay in the water and broken ice.

"What is it you don't believe about me?" I asked.

He flinched from the direct question. I could credit him with that at least. He did not want to believe the worst of me.

"Never mind. I want you to have nothing to do with Trent McIntyre. I don't trust him."

"*I* trust him," I said. "I trust him more than I do anyone at High Towers. And that includes my husband."

Something darkened in Glen's eyes as he came up the stairs with me. But on the upper floor he began to plead again.

"Dina—I need you to help me. I'm going to try what

Colton suggests. Will you pose for me again? Will you let me do you in wood?''

So this was why he wanted to love me, trust me—for the sake of his art. So that he could use me to save himself, as he had used me before. Posing for him was the last thing I wanted to do, yet I could not refuse. I did not want him to touch me, or make love to me. I did not want him to pretend liking for me, when I knew there was none. But I could not refuse to help him in his work.

"All right," I said wearily. "I'll pose for you tomorrow."

"Not tomorrow—tonight! Tonight while it's still the old year. I want to be working when the new year comes in. Don't you see, Dina—if I can begin again, then—"

He did not go on because he had seen by my face that I would do as he wished. There was no need for persuasion that went against the grain. He caught my hand and drew me quickly into the bedroom, began to take the pins from my hair as the old excitement kindled in him. I stood very still under his hands and let him do what he wished. With all my heart I tried not to remember. The man I remembered was gone. I must not think of him again. I must not recall that day in the museum. One did not suffer heartbreak over what was purely imaginary.

As he pulled the last strand from its restraining braid, he took a handful of pins to cast them toward the bed, but in the act of flinging them down he stopped and stared.

"Look!" he cried. "Look—there by your pillow!"

I looked and saw the gleaming yellow ball resting on my bed—another witch ball.

Glen caught me by the wrist. "Why did you put it there? What are you trying to do?"

"I didn't put it there," I told him.

He flung my hand from him and went to the bed, picked up the ball and held it up to the light—as though he would look into it and see something I could not see, wrench from it some secret it had to tell.

"She used to say that sometimes she could see what was going to happen when she looked into one of her witch balls," he said. "If only she would come back to help me now. If only she would get me through this time of missing her! She had more magic in her than I ever did. I wonder if she could—"

"Don't talk like that!" I cried. "The dead don't come back to guide the living."

"Not even when they die by violence and leave something unfinished?" he said, staring at me.

Here it was again—the same thing Keith thought, and the others might be thinking. Except for one—the one who *knew*.

"If there was violence, I didn't intend it," I said. "I've told you the truth—that I tried to save her."

He held the glass ball wonderingly up to the light and turned it so that it winked its great yellow eye at him, while iridescent lights flashed across the surface.

"Perhaps it's a sign," he said. "Perhaps—"

I held out my hand. "Give it to me. I'll put it back in her room." I did not like to think of which one of them had brought it here—to upset Glen, or perhaps solely to upset me.

He snatched it out of my reach. "No! Its being here in this room means something. I don't know what, as yet. But it points to something I need to know. So let it watch me while I work. Perhaps it will help me to begin again."

I have never known a more dreadful New Year's Eve. We went up to the attic and Glen carried the yellow witch ball with him and set it upon a shelf. Nomi was there, helping to fix a comfortable place for Keith to sleep. The cot had been set up in Glynis's studio space and Nomi had found a chair and an old stand that he could use as a bureau for his things. Keith was doing as she directed, but rather in a daze, as though he had moved too fast to catch up with what he was about. He had already placed the framed picture of the burning inn upon his mother's easel.

Glen paid no attention to them, and when Nomi left the attic she went past us softly in order not to distract Glen from what he was doing, though she raised an eyebrow in surprise to find me willing to pose again. When she had gone, Keith sat on his cot, his hands hanging limply between his knees, watching us with a fixed, entranced look that made me uneasy. I must find a chance to talk to the boy soon. I must try to persuade him out of his unhappy notion.

Glen had uncovered the block of reddish wood that now occupied his turntable. I saw that when he had worked with Glynis, he had done much of the preparatory work of cutting away superfluous wood with saw and ax, and was ready to get down to the shaping of the head. He faced me as he wished, walked around me several times, tipping my chin, bowing my head—then decided.

"I want you to look up and out," he said. "Up at something far above you—high on the top of Gray Rocks. Then your hair will float back on whatever breeze is blowing. Perhaps I'll use an electric fan so I can get the effect of hair blowing backwards on a wind."

But when he returned to the wood he was clearly dissatisfied. "Your hair is too pale," he said. "Glynis's hair was exactly the right shade for this wood—a rich mahogany shade. But no matter. I'll try for texture and get my lights into it by the use of planes and angles."

He went to work with what seemed to be new assurance and I sat very still, watching him work. He did not seem to mind my watching him now. Indeed, I sometimes felt as though I were not really there as a person, and that he saw my hair as an abstract element suspended before him, independent of the girl who wore it.

Because he had often talked to me before, while he was working on the alabaster head, I knew something of what he would do this time. Wood carving—while the texture and the dangers of splitting wood were different—was sculpture, like any other. Glen was modern in the way he worked. He would not put every fold in a piece of drapery, or every lock in a woman's hair. But as he had told me, a sculptor had to know what was there before he could leave anything out. Now he was working quickly, expertly with mallet and chisel and gouge, trying for the planes that would give him highlights, for the suggestion of something that was silky and airy, yet without the use of intricate detail.

It was not going well. I could tell by his face, by the way he struck mallet on chisel, almost resentfully. I understood this too. The vision in the artist's mind could be a shining dream, and when reality would not match the vision, the artist suffered.

I grew stiff and tired in my chair, and my throat muscles ached. Once, to rest myself, I turned my head to find Keith staring at me fixedly. He still sat on the edge of the cot, his hands hanging limply, and stared at something he obviously did not like. I tried to smile at him, but he glowered back and his fixed look did not waver. When I turned my eyes from him, I saw the yellow witch ball staring as steadily as he from the shelf where Glen had placed it.

"Stop fidgeting," Glen said. "Get up and move about, if you must. It doesn't matter. I'm not getting what I want. I'm forcing it without really caring. It's the wrong face beneath the hair."

He said it callously, but I was not hurt. I did not care that it was not my face he longed to see. I stood up and stretched. Across the attic a clock ticked loudly, and I wondered what time it was. Would there by any whistles and bells to be heard here in the country? And even if there were, would we hear them up here in the attic?

"Is it the New Year yet?" I asked Keith.

He growled something and looked at the watch on his wrist.

"Not yet!" Glen cried. "It mustn't be. I'm not ready for it yet. I haven't caught what I want in the wood. Get back into place, Dina. I've got to go on. If I can catch something before twelve o'clock, I'll be all right. If I can't, I'm done for."

He glanced up at the yellow glass sphere on the shelf and returned to work. This time he turned me away from him, in profile, and I could not see what he was doing. But at least I knew that he was working eagerly now, though what he carved escaped me.

When it was midnight, Nomi and Colton climbed the stairs, bringing us drinks to toast the coming year. The moment he heard them Glen flung down his tools and snatched up a cloth to fling over the block of wood.

"It's coming!" he told Colton triumphantly. "I've left off struggling with the hair. I've caught a suggestion of it, I think, but I'd rather work on the face. Faces always mean more to me—and I'm catching it this time—catching something better than I ever did in stone."

Colton was curious, but he would allow Glen his privacy until the work had advanced far enough so that a "showing" could be permitted. He was pleased, hopeful. There was, after all, something to toast for the New Year, and we all joined in, touching our glasses at the rims, toasting the same thing—the only thing we could toast—the success of Glen's new work.

Keith watched us moodily, drinking the hot chocolate Nomi had made for him, and undoubtedly hating the fact that he was still suspended between the state of being half boy and half adult.

The occasion was hardly festive, and we did not stay up long after we had finished our drinks. Colton and Nomi went downstairs first, and Glen followed, calling to me to come along. But before I left the attic, Keith dived from his cot and caught me by the arm. For just a moment I was afraid of him. He had moved so suddenly, and he looked so wild and lost and miserable. But he was still a boy who needed help, no matter what he thought of me, and I stayed on in the darkened attic.

"You'd better look at Glen's work!" he whispered to me. "I can see what he's begun to do. You'd better look at it and watch out."

I did not know what he meant, and I would not look. If Glen was working well, I would not interfere or pry. Even if he put Glynis's face into this carving, I would not care. Let him do as he pleased. For me it did not matter. I wished him well, but he could no longer touch me.

I wonder if it would have made any difference if I had

looked? I'm not sure that I would have recognized the dreadful thing that had begun to happen inside Glen, even if I had removed the covering from that mahogany head. I would not have believed it then. I would have been shocked, but not frightened.

13

Glen's work progressed from day to day and I had a sense of history repeating itself. But it was an eerie feeling that did not bode well for the future. He drove himself for long hours, and when he worked I must be there—though I hardly knew why. Often he would not look at me twice in an hour, though I sat as he posed me, always facing away from the head he was carving, so that I could not see it. I could glimpse Glen's face in the mirror sometimes, but I could not see his work.

Sometimes he talked as his hands moved, but more to himself than to me, and often the words were not reassuring because he spoke about the alabaster head and all it had meant to him—all that had been destroyed with its shattering. There seemed to be a growing, continuing resentment in him that he had to release in words that he wanted me to hear. This posing was not a happy time for me.

He took so long that I felt he must have finished the head many times over—yet still he worked, refining, improving, while the pile of shavings grew about him and I wondered if there was anything left of the wood. One could cut too deeply into stone or wood—one could destroy.

The weather grew bitterly cold, dropping below zero. Occasionally there was snow, snow that lasted, with no thaws to melt it away. It was no longer the soft snow of the cities, easily walked through. Instead, it froze to a hard slippery crust that offered no purchase to the feet and made any walking off the cleared driveway a hazard.

Keith had gone back to school after the holidays and we saw him only in the late afternoon and early evening. He lived his own secret life, never truly fitting in with his relatives. His grandfather made a few desultory gestures in the boy's direction, but his heart was not in it. This boy did not bear his name. Colton was, I felt, marking time. Now that Glen was creatively busy, he wanted to stay long enough to view his son's new work. Then he would be on his way. His lecture tour through Britain had been postponed till February and he would be off again early next month. One thing he wanted to accomplish before he left was the sale of the land on the other side of the lake to Pandora McIntyre. Glynis, apparently, had been the chief obstacle to his selling of the land, and now that she was gone, Glen did not seem to care what happened to Gray Rocks Lake. I suspected that he would leave High Towers himself as soon as his present work was done. What would happen to me then, I did not know. There had to be some ending between us, since no beginning again would ever be possible. But I put off leaving, put off speaking the words that would cause our final sundering until Glen's work was safely finished. Mostly I existed numbly in a vacuum. I did not want to think of Trent.

Periodically one of Glynis's witch balls would appear somewhere in my room—but no one in the house would ever confess to moving them about. Each time I took the glass object back to Glynis's room and put it with its sisters in the basket which held them. This was an annoying trick, an attempt to disturb me, but nothing more. Who was behind it, I did not know.

Once when Nomi and I drove to the cemetery we found Colton standing in the bitter cold, looking down at the snow-covered mound with a new marble headstone, beside the grave of Elizabeth Chandler. When I saw Colton ahead of us there, I tried to persuade Nomi to turn back, but she was never a retreating sort of person, and we made our way through snowy aisles and stood in silence beside him. He gave us a single blind look, and then turned away, his feelings hidden as always.

Nomi laid the holly wreath she had brought upon the grave. A wreath of green leaves, with the red berries carefully clipped away. Because there was now no color in Glynis's world, Nomi said, and we must not mock her.

We stood in silence for a few moments before the headstone Glen had carved so lovingly with the single inscription: *GLYNIS*, but if we prayed, I think it was not for the woman who lay there.

I had been surprised that Nomi had wanted to visit the grave, since she had refused to mourn for the girl she had disliked so intensely. But something she said while we stood there after Colton had gone, gave me a startling clue.

"I just want to make sure," Nomi said. "I wanted to make sure she was here."

"Here—but where else would she be?"

Nomi seemed not to hear me. "I can sense that she's here. But of course we can never be entirely certain. Not unless she was buried with a stake through her heart."

"Oh, Nomi!" I wailed. "Don't *you* go down some weird road too! Nomi—is it you who keeps moving those witch balls into my room?"

She stood beside Glynis's grave and looked at me with wide, tragic eyes. "Don't you know who does that?" She gestured. "She's the one. Glen has seen her about, you know. He's told me so, and I believe him. He thinks she will keep on coming until something is done about the person who caused her death. That's why I had to come here. But it's all right now. She's here—asleep. It's when she gets restless that we're all in danger."

I put my hand none too gently on her arm and drew her away from the grave and back toward our car. "I have never heard such dreadful nonsense in all my life! And from you! I expected more of you, Nomi. You're the one with the level head. You're the one who isn't a Chandler."

She seemed to wake up with a shivery laugh which did not reassure me. I could hardly wait now for Glen to finish his work and let me go. Escape was in my mind day and night. Escape to sanity and safety.

My one sense of solace at this time was the knowledge that Trent McIntyre was across the lake. Sometimes I saw him from a distance. Sometimes he came to the house to see how Keith was getting along, and I found myself looking forward to these visits. His was a quiet, sane, blunt-spoken presence. I could imagine what he would say to Nomi if he knew about her weird remarks in the cemetery. Now and then, weighing these remarks, I wondered if she had been merely trying to frighten me—if she too wanted me gone.

Unfortunately, I had no real chance to talk to Trent at this time. There were brief moments when our eyes met and he told me more than he could speak. I was glad he existed in time and in space at the same moment as I. But that small comfort was all I had the right to as long as I stayed in this house.

The house *was* haunted. I knew that well enough now. It was haunted, not by the spirit of Glynis Chandler, but by the guilt of whoever it was who had taken my scarf away and left her to die. Not Colton. He had been too proud of his daughter to do her harm, whether he cherished her or not. His clan feeling was paramount. Not Glen, who loved his twin as though she were a part of himself. Not Nomi, who would not stoop to murder, however much she hated. There was no one else. If I went further afield—Keith had loved his mother desperately. Trent was no murderer. And Pandora was not involved—except in the past, through her son, and possibly through the land she wanted. But Colton meant to sell her the land anyway. So there was no one who could logically have taken away the scarf I had left securely tied to that tree stump in the lake. Yet one of these was guilty—and guilt itself walked the hallways of High Towers, sat beside our fires, loomed solemnly at every meal we ate.

The awful thing was that some of these people, including Glen, still believed that it was I who had caused Glynis's death. If I had any purpose during those days it was to prove undeniably that I had done what I said I had done. How could

I run cravenly from High Towers while this ugly shadow of guilt hung over my own head? There was another reason to stay, but I had not seen it then.

The following Saturday morning as I sat for Glen I found him in a strange mood. Strange because he was being rather kind to me. I think he was pleased with his work, confident that it was turning out well, so that perhaps he could afford to be kind. Yet the change made me uneasy. He was nearly through now, and he had turned to sandpapering and polishing to bring out the gleam of the natural grain.

"I'm grateful to you, Dina," he said almost lightly. "I couldn't have done this without you. I had to have you there every minute, or I could never have succeeded."

"When am I to see it?" I asked.

His eyes were darkly bright—eyes that reminded me of his sister's—as he looked at me over the work he would not let me see. I could catch his face in the mirror, but nothing else.

"Soon, soon, my dear," he told me, but somehow I did not find either the promise or his gentleness reassuring. It was as if he promised me something more than a viewing of his work.

"Tell me again, Dina," he went on as he worked, his tone deceptively gentle. "Tell me what happened that day when Glynis fell through the ice."

So this was where his coaxing manner led!

"I've told you," I said wearily. "I've told you so many times."

"Then tell me another time," he urged, his voice very soft, very gentle with me. "Tell me, because I've never really understood."

I knew suddenly that I was afraid of him. He blamed me for Glynis's death and now time was running out on the head he was finishing. When it was done, he would not need me any more.

Suddenly I saw him move in the mirror, saw him snatch up the cloth and fling it over the head to conceal it from view. Then he came to take me lightly by the wrist.

"We're going there now," he said. "Come with me, Dina.

Make me understand what happened. Make me understand all of it.''

I tried to object, but he was once more a driven man, and when he was in this mood he would take no opposition.

"We'll go now," he said. "So get into your coat and boots. The sun is out and perhaps there'll be enough thawing of the snow crust so we can get through the woods. Hurry now.''

I tried to find some way to object, to at least postpone what he wanted to do. "But Colton was speaking earlier of seeing Pandora today, working out the business of the land. He said you were to go with him.''

"I haven't forgotten," Glen said. "I'll meet him there later. First, however, you and I are going out on the ice to the place where Glynis fell through, and you're going to make me see everything just as it happened.''

I needn't be afraid, I told myself. The ice was solid enough now. Even the place where the springs fed from underneath would not weaken the danger spot today. I had better do as he asked. Perhaps this was one way to make what had happened vivid enough to him so that he would really understand. If only those few strands of wool had been left in the crevice, I could have shown them to him to help support my story.

When we went out we found it slippery enough underfoot, but Glen had brought along a couple of walking sticks for us to use as alpine staffs, and by stamping firmly with every step we were able to make the downhill path. Along the shore where the sun shone the going was easier and here we could walk lightly on the crust without slipping. We made quick enough time in the clear bright morning on the way to Gray Rocks.

I could see the pointed towers reaching upward from the shores of the lake, and I remembered when I had thought of them as "his and hers." Now there was only one twin left. One twin, bereft of his right hand. Yet the twin towers of rock still stood. When I saw them ahead I had no sense of the ominous about them. All my uncertainties, all my sense of the ominous rested in the man who hurried along the trail ahead of me. I had forgotten about that other one because there were enough things to frighten me about Glen. There was the heavy stick he carried, for instance. And there was that coaxing gentleness that I did not trust. But I gave no real thought to the towers ahead.

More than once I glanced across the lake toward the McIntyres, but no one was in sight. I was not even sure Trent was home. Sometimes he made the drive into New York to see his editor. And often he took long hikes through the hills while he waited for ideas to jell before writing.

When we reached the base of Gray Rocks, Glen stopped ahead of me, looking upward. For a horrid moment I was afraid that he might actually call out to Glynis, to see if she was there. But he only smiled at me over his shoulder and went on. There was something so twisted and sly about his smile that I hesitated as he started across the base of the rocks, wondering if I should go on. Thus I was able to look up at the first sound of something sliding from high above. I saw the small knot of pebbles spring free and separate themselves from the mass as they came bouncing down, to be followed by a great loosening slab of rock that plunged furiously down the wall. I sprang back and screamed a warning to Glen just as the huge slab crashed to the base, landing squarely between us, shattering itself over the ice.

For a moment we stared at each other, in frozen, shared fear. Then I looked upward in time to see something move up there, hear some soft grating sound as whoever had flung the rock over tried to make his way as quietly as possible down the far side, well out of our sight.

I called out to Glen. "There's someone up there! Someone deliberately threw down that slab of rock. It might have killed either of us."

To my further horror, Glen looked exhilarated, exuberant. "Of course she's up there, Dina! She's still after you, isn't she?" He flung back his head and shouted so that the echoes went roaring down the lake. "Glynis! Glynis! Stop your pranks now! We know you're there."

I heard the sliding, slipping sounds of someone climbing

down the rock, making away through the icy woods far above us, well hidden behind the thick growth of spruce and cedar.

I felt as appalled by Glen's shouting as I had by the crash of rock. "Wake up!" I called to him. "That wasn't Glynis. Don't *you* play games!"

He was staring at me from the far side of the base, and suddenly his face seemed to crumple into grieving desperation. He turned away from me and went stumbling on along the shore road alone. I had no wish to go with him now, or try to bring him back. I had my own desperation to drive me, and I began to stumble back in the direction from which I'd come. I leaped from grass tuft to grass tuft, broke ice with my stick when I had to, slipped and slid my way along the path through the woods. Only once did I stop for breath, stop to listen, but whoever had climbed Gray Rocks must have followed the upper path more quickly than I, and was already out of range, so that I heard nothing. The woods were quiet, the lake gave out no echoes, and only fear clattered and crashed through my own mind.

That slab of rock had not been meant for Glen. My enemy had been up there. Someone had known that I was coming that way and had waited for me. Someone who wanted to save himself at my expense. The same someone who had spoken to Glynis while she floundered in the water, and taken away the scarf I'd left for her to cling to. I wanted to shout to the woods that I did not know his name—that he was safe enough from me. But that was Glen's mad road. There was only one thing to do, and I knew it very well now. For my own safety, I must get away from High Towers.

When I reached the house, panting and breathless, terribly warm from my struggle uphill, I found Colton and Nomi talking together in the lower hall. How long they had been there I could not tell. They looked at me in astonishment when I burst into the house.

"There was someone up on top of Gray Rocks!" I cried. "Someone flung over a huge slab of rock that might have crushed either Glen or me. It's only luck that we escaped."

"My dear," Colton said, and began to help me off with my coat.

Nomi threw him a quick look. "Where is Glen now?"

"He went on," I told her. "I—I was with him because he wanted to look at the place where Glynis died. He wanted me to show him just what had happened. But—but after the rocks came down, he went off toward the far end of the lake."

"He'll come back." Colton was reassuring Nomi. "He knows I want him to be at Pandora's to talk over this sale of land. If he comes here, Naomi, send him over at once."

"I'll go look for him myself," she said—but before she could move away he touched her arm and spoke more sharply.

"Let him alone. You coddle him too much. You've got to let him work things out in his own way. I'll see you later. That is, if you're still sure you won't come along while I talk to Pandora."

"I'm sure," she said, and went down the hall to her own sitting room. When she opened the door Jezebel slipped quietly into the hall and sped like a striped shadow to the front door—to slip out when Colton opened it.

I flung my coat over the stair rail and ran up to the attic. I knew what I must do. Before I left this house there was something I had to know. Once I knew, I would leave. I would pack my things and get away before Glen returned.

My boots clattered on the stairs and I burst a bit wildly into the empty attic. I went at once to Glen's studio and stopped before the covered head on the turntable. I pulled off the mittens, loosened my furry hat and jerked it from my head, tossed it aside. I needed to be unhampered in what I meant to do.

I took a step nearer the pedestal and put my hand on the cloth that hid the carving from view. For just an instant it seemed as though something lived and breathed beneath my hand. I stiffened myself to pull off the cloth.

The face was turned away from me. Bright chestnut hair that caught morning light from the sky window flowed over and down the tipped-back head, giving the locks a chance to

222

lift free in an apparent breeze. Without intricate detail the hair had been made to seem alive and real. It was not Glynis's hair, except for its color; it was mine—and it was far more alive than Glen had ever caught it in stone.

Then I saw something that sent a creeping of horror up the back of my neck. Set high on either side of the head, and visible through strands of hair, were angry, laid-back ears— the pointed animal ears of the monstrous thing Glen had created. I walked about the clamped stand. Wild, animal eyes looked into mine, glowing and predatory in the gleam of shining wood. I could see the blunted nose, the snarl of fangs, the lips drawn back in the evil grimace of a leopard about to pounce. No—not pounce—bound! Bound high into the air toward Gray Rocks, on which that gleaming, distant gaze was fixed.

I felt sickened, betrayed. Why had he needed me to pose all these long weeks while he created something that had nothing to do with me—something that was all Glynis, the very essence of Glynis?

What happened next came so quickly that I had no chance to escape. Soft folds dropped over my head so gently that my frozen stare was hardly interrupted. They dropped softly and thickly about my neck like a cowl collar—and then began to draw chokingly tight. I gasped and tried to tear the thing from my throat, only to have it pulled more tightly, so that I was held in a vise that would not let me turn to see my tormentor. I stood rigid against this new terror, trying to lean backward into the pull that choked me.

The boy behind me laughed—and the noose was loosened. As I whirled to face Keith McIntyre I still gasped for breath, unable to speak. I saw the vivid blue excitement in his eyes, saw the smile of triumph on his thin young face.

"How easy it would be!" he said. "How easy to hold this tight so you wouldn't be standing there now. I scared you, didn't I? Just as that leopard carving scared you. It's awfully good. Better than the alabaster—because he was thinking of Glynis while he worked. And it's like her—terribly like. I know because I'm her son. I told you in the beginning to look at it. You needed to see it before it was too late, because *you're* the victim. You know that, don't you? You're the victim she's going to pounce upon." He moved close to me with the noose of the scarf tantalizing me.

I put my hand to my throat, still trying to catch my breath and ease the hurt, and the boy moved about me—and about that dreadful leopard's head with the human hair. He moved lithely, as he did in the woods, with the grace of a dancer, a bullfighter, a dueler! And he dangled the long scarf before me as if it were the weapon he would use to skewer me with.

I found my voice. "Where did you get that scarf?" I asked.

He held it up before his own eyes as if he were really seeing it for the first time. "Back there," he said, waving a hand vaguely in the direction of Colton's end of the attic. "What difference does it make where I found it! Aren't you grateful that I let you go? Aren't you afraid of me?"

I was too angry to do anything but explode. I flung out at him with both hands. With one I snatched the scarf into my own keeping, and with the other I slapped him hard across one cheek. He fell back from me with a gasp of angry astonishment, and I gave my attention to the long strip of cloth I held in my hands. It was dark brown with streaks of pink lightning woven the length of the pattern.

"If you weren't so stupid," I said, "you'd recognize this as the scarf Nomi gave me for Christmas. I was wearing it that day when Glynis and I went skating. It's the scarf I threw to her to keep her afloat and that I tied to a slit in that tree stump in the lake. Look—you can see how it's shrunk, and how the colors have run. Here's where bits of fringe were torn loose."

He had put one hand to his cheek, and he was staring at me with a wide, angry look that was nevertheless a little frightened. I advanced upon him, waving the scarf.

"Show me exactly where you found it! I won't be bullied by you or by anyone else. If you found it among Colton's things, then I want to know where."

The grace had gone out of him. He shuffled his feet as he walked, leading me back to Colton's studio. I had never stepped into this section of the attic before, since the rules said it was off bounds for anyone but Colton, unless one was especially invited.

Keith lifted the lid of what looked like an old sea chest and poked in among a miscellany of discarded articles.

"It was down there, squeezed into one corner," he said.

"And how did you happen to find it?"

He hesitated before answering. "I was just poking around. I wanted to see if my grandfather had any old carving tools I could borrow. I mean, that he wouldn't miss. And I found that."

"All right," I said. "I'm glad you did. It's time for you to face the real world and not the make-believe one you've been living in. I know all about dream worlds. I've lived there too. It's a dangerous country because when you stay there too long it's like being under the influence of a drug. After a while you can't tell what is real and what isn't. Your actions stop matching the real world, and what you do can blow the dream world and your life all to pieces. Now we're going to face what's real together. We're going across the lake to show this scarf to your grandfather. We're going to clear this up right now. If someone hid it among his things, he'd better know."

"Maybe *she* hid it there!" His voice went a little shrill. "Glynis, I mean. Maybe she's still trying to make me do things I don't want to! But if she's not quiet yet, what am I to—"

"I'll take that scarf, if you please," Nomi said.

She must have climbed the stairs so quietly that we did not hear her until she spoke behind us.

She came toward us with her hand extended, moving erectly, her gesture commanding. I put the scarf behind my back.

"I think Colton must know about this," I told her.

"No!" The word had a flat and final ring. "I won't have him disturbed any further. Or Glen either. I'm beginning to think that you are a completely disrupting influence here,

225

Dina. For the time being I'll take charge of the scarf. Let the wounding heal a little before it's all ripped open again.''

"What about me?" I said. "What about the fact that everyone is blaming me for Glynis's death, when all I did was try to save her? Even Keith thinks I'm to blame. He tried to choke me just now. He put this scarf around my neck and—"

"I wouldn't have choked you," Keith said sullenly. "I only wanted to scare you. You didn't do it. I—I know you didn't."

"Why?" I said. "Why do you like to frighten people?"

His blue eyes that were so much like his father's, and so unlike—blazed in his thin face. "Because you're nothing but trouble and you ought to go away. My mother hated you. She didn't want you to be Glen's wife. She didn't want you here and she's still trying to get at you."

His face was sickly pale and I turned from him in disgust and spoke to Nomi. "Come and see what Glen has been doing. I think you'd better know."

"I do know," she said. "Do you think I haven't watched it all along? And it's a good thing he has done. I don't mean just artistically. I mean that it's therapy of a sort. Better that he put his feelings into the carving than—than into—"

There was a sound of a door slam from downstairs and she broke off to listen.

"That's Glen now. And Keith is right, Dina. You'd better go away. Stop interfering and go at once. He'll never miss you if you leave, and if you stay you may be harmed. Go back to New York. Leave us to our tragedies. They aren't yours."

I said nothing to either one. I gave her the scarf and went slowly down the stairs, and as I moved I could hear Glen coming up from the front door—so that we met in the hallway below at the halfway point. He looked more ravaged and more desperate than I had ever seen him. Nomi had run down the stairs behind me and she spoke to him in alarm, but he did not answer. He walked straight past us both and went into his room—into Glynis's room.

Nomi would have followed him, but I caught her by the arm and held her back. "I'm his wife," I said. "This is for me to do."

She gave me a look and let me go. I knew now that I could not run away behind Glen's back without talking to him first. No matter whether he would miss me or not, I had to tell him what I meant to do. He had closed the door behind him, but I did not knock lest he lock it in my face. I turned the knob and walked in. He had gone straight to the spotlight that illumined the black marble head and turned it on. He stood before the head and when I saw what he was doing the creeping terror washed over me again.

Very delicately and thoughtfully, as he stared at the head, he was running the fingernail of his left thumb over his own eyebrow. Over and over again in a gesture that was Glynis's only—a gesture I had never seen him use before.

14

I went to him and drew him away from the black marble head. "I have to talk to you, Glen. Come and sit down, please. I've seen what you did with the wood carving up-stairs. Why, Glen—can you tell me why?"

He let me push him gently into a chair and draw up another chair so I could sit before him, waiting for an answer that did not come. From the basket by the window colored witch balls winked at me wickedly.

"Tell me why you needed me while you worked, Glen. I want to understand. I know the work is good. But the motive behind such a result seems evil. So what had I to do with it?"

For the first time his eyes seemed to focus on my face, and he flashed a shadow of his old smile at me.

"I needed you there! I had to look at you constantly be-cause I had to see you with her eyes. I had to see you so that I could build the way she felt about you into her leopard face."

I recoiled a little. I wanted to jump up and run out of the room—run from the house for good and never come back, but I sat where I was because something in Glen's face would not let me go.

"And now that you've finished with the head?" I said.

He raised his shoulders in a helpless shrug. "I don't know.

I feel empty, drained. There doesn't seem to be anything left.''

"You'll work again," I said. "Doesn't every creative worker feel drained when one piece is done and he isn't possessed by the next one yet?''

He looked up at me strangely. "Possessed! What a good word for you to use. Because that's how I feel—empty and waiting. As though something must move into the emptiness—and possess me.''

"As it will," I said. "Wait for it and it will. But in the meantime, Glen, I'm going away. There isn't anything left for us, now that your leopard woman is done. This was a wrong marriage for both of us. I fooled myself with a mirage, and so did you. There's nothing right about it now—or ever will be.''

"You're going to Trent!" he said sharply.

"No. I'm not going to anyone. I'm going to return to being myself. To finding out what myself is. I'm not sure I know any more.''

"No!" he cried. "No—you can't leave me! I won't let you go away!''

I could only stare at him in astonishment. "But you have no need for me, Glen. And love isn't something that can be revived once it's over—if we ever did love each other. I think what each one loved was only that mirage I've mentioned. Nothing real.''

He did a surprising thing. He left his chair and came suddenly to kneel before me. He gathered me to him in both arms, and put his head against my breast.

"You can't leave me. You're all I've got to fill the emptiness. If you don't fill it, something else will. Something that's waiting for its chance—to move in and possess me. Something I'm afraid of. I can feel it standing there in the shadows, waiting and watching. I'm terrified, Dina. And you're wrong about me. I've never loved any woman as I've loved you. Stay with me, darling—don't leave me.''

When the rap came on the door he did not move and I had

to disengage myself gently and go to the door. Keith was there, looking hangdog and embarrassed.

"My father wants to talk to you," he said gruffly. "My grandfather and Gran are going over the contract details, and he's come away. He's downstairs now. Will you see him?"

Glen rose to his feet and turned away from me. He had heard Keith's words, but he would not turn to me again. He went to stand at a window and look out at the icy winter world.

"I'll come," I said.

The feeling of wings began to beat through me as I ran downstairs. Wings that led to freedom, to happiness. Oh, it had to be—it had to be!

Trent waited in Nomi's sitting room, and Nomi was there too. He said she need not go away. He wanted her to hear what he had to say to me. When I walked into the room he came and put his hands on my arms, held me off so that he could look into my face.

"You've had enough," he said. "Keith has told me about that carving of Glen's. I won't have you submitted to this sort of thing any longer."

The wings were still beating, but more weakly.

"Won't have?" said Nomi sharply, on guard for Glen's rights, as always.

"Won't have," Trent repeated. "Bernardina belongs to me, Nomi."

My eyes were swimming with tears, and I wanted with all my heart to go into his arms for good. This was real. It always had been. I was awake now.

"I'm going to take you away, darling," he said. "You're going to stay with my mother for a time—or go back to New York if you wish. But the thing you're not to do is spend another night in this house. I'm going to talk to Glen myself." He let me go and went toward the door.

I said, "Wait!" in a voice I hardly knew as my own. There were no more beating wings. He turned back to me, questioning for the first time. I went on. "I can't go with you, Trent. Not because I don't love you. I suppose I

230

always have and always will. But I can't go with you, because of Glen.''

"What are you talking about?'' he said roughly.

I stood my ground, my fingers wound tightly together so that my hands would not do foolish things. I knew very well now what I had to do and I needed to find the strength to do it. Glen was real too. Not my love for him, but his desperate need, to which I was bound. To stay—this was what my father meant by courage.

"I've been living make-believe,'' I told him. "But now I'm out of it. Glen needs me, and I can't walk out on him now.''

Trent's impatience grew. "That's absurd. If you think—''

"Listen to me, please,'' I said. "I got myself into the situation I'm in. If I acted foolishly and impetuously, it's my fault. But it's done. Now I've got to stay and see this through. Please don't make it any harder for me than you have to.''

"Bravo!'' said Nomi softly, and Trent threw her an angry look.

"We're not through with this discussion,'' he told me, "but I'll let you go for now. I'll give you time to come to your senses. And I won't be far away, whatever happens.''

"My senses don't have anything to do with this,'' I said. "My senses tell me how much I love you. But only a little while ago they were telling me how much I loved Glen. So I'm not much inclined to believe in them any more. I have to believe in what needs to be done.''

I went past him and out the door. I climbed the stairs and went back to Glynis's room. Glen stood by the window where I had left him.

"I'm going to stay,'' I said. "But if I do, we can't remain in separate rooms. You need a chance to recover from your suffering over Glynis, and you won't if you stay here. It's not good for either of us that you should.''

He turned from the window and stared at me. His left thumbnail was stroking the curve of his eyebrow thoughtfully. I went to him and drew his hand from his face.

"That's a gesture that belongs to Glynis," I said. "We've got to put Glynis behind us—somehow."

He swept me into his arms and held me close, buried his face in my hair. I let him hold me. I tried to hold him too, tried to feel what I used to feel. But I did not feel anything—for anyone. I was quite numb and without emotion, yet that did not seem to matter very much. Responsibility was a word I had never faced seriously before, and I found it an unemotional word. Actions have consequences. Certain things had to be done if I was to live with myself. I was my father's daughter. I would find the strength to do them.

Glen let me go at last, his own facile enthusiasm rising to the fore.

"I'll accept your terms, Dina. You give me something to live for again. I know that you and Nomi are right. Glynis's room must be dismantled. Every trace of her must be put away, hidden from sight. It's the only way to quiet her."

I did not like that phrase "quiet her," but I agreed before he should change his mind. Together we summoned Nomi, and since Keith was hanging about uneasily, with no school on Saturday, we commandeered him too. Perhaps he too had a ghost to lay.

All of us went to work in Glynis's room. Glen might not have faced the task alone, but with all of us moving as a team, he joined in with a will. He and Keith brought down empty boxes from the attic, and Glynis's clothes were packed away. I packed her dresses myself, so that Glen would not have to touch them. With a certain sadness I put away these outward markings of the gay, sophisticated, rather brittle and self-serving life she had led. It always seems strange to those who are left that mere silk and cotton and wool should outlive the bodies they have served.

Glen placed her jewelry in a velvet-lined box. Her hosiery and lingerie Nomi laid between tissue paper. Later some of these things would be given to local charities. But they would be kept in the attic until something could be arranged.

Of the four of us, strangely enough, Keith was the most emotionally involved. His expression, when I caught him off guard, was one of bewilderment—as if he could not yet believe his mother gone. More than once, he lingered by the great basket of witch balls, and when Glen and Nomi had carried a load up to the attic, he picked one of them up and held it in his hands. He spoke to me over his shoulder, his face hidden.

"Do you think Glen would mind if I kept one of these?"

I felt sorry for the boy, no matter how badly he had behaved. "I don't think he'll mind. But why do you want it?"

He held the purple sphere up to the light from a window. "Because she read my fortune in this once. She looked into it and told me what she saw."

I did not stop what I was doing, but asked my question casually. "What did she see?"

He stared into the ball as though he might recreate the vision he had glimpsed through his mother's eyes. "She saw me standing in a high place with a rifle to my shoulder." He shuddered faintly. "When she told me she dropped her voice very low and husky, the way she could sometimes, and she said, 'Be sure you shoot to kill!' But what happened after that she never told me. She said the mist came in and she couldn't see any more."

Impatiently, I left the box of dresses I was packing. "You're too much concerned with killing, with frightening, and with injuring, Keith. Why? What satisfaction do you get from that sort of thing? And don't tell me you want to play God."

He did not answer me directly, but set down the purple ball among its fellows and turned to pack a box of Glynis's shoes. "It's good we're putting all this away. I wish everything of hers could be put into locked trunks, and the attic locked besides. Then maybe she couldn't get out."

His vehemence startled me. "Oh, come now!" I cried "You're not letting Nomi's nonsense take hold of you, too! All that about Glynis not resting in the cemetery!"

"Are you sure it's nonsense?" His blue eyes looked darker than I'd ever seen them and I remembered that there was both Irish and Scottish blood in the boy—a mixture that might

233

lead to curious notions. "Don't you think if we put all her things away and lock them up it will be harder for her to get to us?" he questioned. "I think she needs to touch something of hers before she can make an entry."

"Entry!" I repeated, appalled. "Whatever are you talking about?"

"Don't you ever feel her around?" he asked. "Don't you ever feel her beating at you as if she was trying to get in? Glen says she'll get in wherever she finds a chink."

"She doesn't beat at me," I said dryly. "I think you walk around in the woods too much alone. Why don't you talk these things over with your father?"

"My father!" Keith was scornful. "I know what he'd say and how he'd laugh at me."

"You underestimate your father," I said. "I've known him for a long time. I knew him when I was your age, when my own father died. I was ready to die of grief then myself, and it was your father who coaxed me back into wanting to live. He made me know that I really could get along without my father and go on to other things. Maybe you haven't given your father a chance."

He scarcely attended my words. His young eyes were dark with an unhappy, inward-turning vision that the purple sphere had raised in his eyes.

"Glynis not only tries to get in—sometimes she does," he said. "That's what happened upstairs in the attic when I took that scarf and tried to frighten you. It's what *she* wanted. But I think it's not me she means to use—I think it's Glen she wants to get at. And she reaches him sometimes. I know she does. Haven't you seen her look out of his eyes?"

Reluctantly I remembered the gesture of thumbnail to eyebrow. "I think you mustn't indulge such notions, Keith. They're not real, though perhaps you find them exciting."

He turned to me suddenly. "I'm sorry I tried to scare you up in the attic. I don't blame you for slapping me. It helped me because it frightened her off."

The others came back, and there was nothing more I could

say—or wanted to say. The boy alarmed me, but I put these thoughts away as something I must talk about with his father.

Glen went to strip the bed, take off the quilt that was Glynis's favorite, pull off the tinted sheets that no one else in the house used. Keith watched him for a moment, watched the vigor with which Glen went to work, as if he would rip Glynis out of his mind and his heart. Then, moving quickly and without warning, Keith sprang to a window, flung it open, picked up the basket of witch balls and dumped the whole thing out the window. The balls clattered into a snowbank outside, crashing into one another, shattering and splintering with a great ringing of sound.

Glen turned to stare at Keith in astonishment.

Nomi said, "A fine mess you've made, boy. Now you can get down there with a shovel and clean up all that glass."

Keith moved exuberantly, as though released from a spell. "Sure, I'll clean it up!" he shouted and went clattering off down the stairs.

Glen went to look out the window. "There's not one left whole," he said. "Now she'll have to stop putting them about."

I'd had enough of such talk. With a sense of revulsion I laid aside a sweater of Glynis's which still bore her scent and went out of the room. I wanted to be free of Chandlers for a time, but there was nowhere to go, and I rejected the thought of running to talk to Trent about his son. This I must not do. I was suspicious of my own motives by this time.

The day was a long one to endure. I went for a walk, though I did not wander far from the house. I joined Nomi in her sitting room and was reminded that here I could be safe from Glynis. Because of Jezebel. Only the tiger cat seemed to have no fear of the house being haunted—and that was reassuring to me. Jezebel wandered about freely, even in to Glynis's room, now that it was an empty, impersonal place.

And all the while I knew that night was coming and that I was a wife again. During the evening it began to snow gently—big soft flakes that piled up, shutting us in. None of us wanted to stay up except Colton. There was a late show he wanted to catch on the television screen in his den and we left him to it and went up to bed.

It was Glen who slept on my shoulder that night. I lay awake into the early hours, my arm stiffening under his head, my mind full of lost, lonely thoughts. And there was no courage in me. I had only to give up, to abandon Glen—and Trent would be waiting for me. For a time he would be waiting for me. Yet I could not go to him, and neither could I make myself accept wholeheartedly the life that awaited me here. I was neither fish nor fowl and I did not know how to order my life.

When Glen finally turned away in his sleep, I was able to withdraw my arm, and I too fell asleep. When I wakened to a snowy morning, Glen was gone from the bed. I peered from beneath warm covers into pale, rose-tinted daylight, and saw that he was up and dressed. He had lighted a fire, and was sitting on a hassock pulled up before it. When the bed creaked, he turned to look at me.

"Good morning, Dina." He was smiling at me with the old loving expression, and I ached a little for a loving I could not return.

The thought of Keith and what the boy had done yesterday returned to me. With Glen in a good mood, perhaps I could talk to him and through the subject of Keith lead into something more urgent—our leaving High Towers.

"There's something I need to tell you," I said. "About Keith."

His mood remained amiable and he spoke to me over his shoulder, holding out his hands to the fire. "Talk ahead."

"I don't think you should put the idea into the boy's mind that Glynis is trying to reach us. You've given him a notion that he is being—oh, it's such a silly word!—*possessed* by her. We've got to undo this somehow. He half throttled me yesterday—as a sort of prank that he feels was inspired by Glynis."

If I had hoped for an amused reaction, I was wrong. Glen turned his head and looked at me gravely, searchingly.

236

"But I've felt the same thing myself," he said. "That's why I warned the boy. That's what I intended it to be—a warning. So that he would be careful not to open any cranny that would let her in."

So here it was again—and worse to deal with in Glen.

"We've got to get away from this place," I told him. "We could go to New York, or abroad, if you prefer. We need to escape High Towers for a time. If Glynis's spirit is wandering, let her rest. Perhaps she can't with us here. I don't see how you can stand to stay here anyway, knowing that she was—murdered. Haven't you faced that, Glen? If you haven't, you must."

"I suppose you mean because of the scarf?"

"Of course. Who could have taken it away except Colton or Nomi? You've got to stop living in an imaginary world and face what's real. That's what I am trying to do. I don't want to believe it of either of them, but who else is there?"

Glen rose from his hassock and came toward the bed. "There seems to be one person left whom you haven't thought of—the one person who really hated her—Trent McIntyre."

I sat up indignantly and reached for my gown. "That's absurd! Trent's not the sort to turn to violence."

"Not even when he thinks his precious son is threatened? Not even when he knew Glynis might try to interfere with Pandora's plans? There's where your motive lies! Not with Colton, who loved her. And not with Nomi, who has borne her old hates for a long time and would never do anything about them."

I sat on the edge of the bed shaking my head, until Glen put his hands on my shoulders.

"It's time for *you* to face reality!" he cried. "Just how much does Trent mean to you? Just how fickle and false are you? Once I thought you were the one woman I could trust. I don't think that any more. I knew the truth when I held you in my arms last night."

My shoulders went limp beneath his hands. "I've tried,

237

Glen. If you needed me, I meant to stay. But you make it too hard. I don't know what to do—or how to live with you.''

His eyes were bright and dark—the old look of jet that made him seem like Glynis. ''What if I can prove to you that Trent is the one who took the scarf away? What if I know how to prove it?''

''You can't,'' I said. ''You can't because it isn't so.''

''Get dressed,'' he said curtly. ''Get dressed and I'll show you. I'll prove what happened so you'll never doubt it again.''

I had to go with him, if only to disprove this new wild notion that drove him. It took me only moments to put on warm outdoor things and pull on my boots. Glen wore his leopard jacket as we went downstairs together in the early morning light.

I heard others moving about in the house, but only Jezebel came into the lower hall as we came downstairs. Ordinarily Glen paid little attention to the cat, but now he paused and looked down at her, with one hand on the rail. Jezebel did a strange thing. She laid back her ears and bared her teeth, her fur rose all over her body and she stood on her claw tips, hissing.

Glen laughed and vaulted the rail, landing lightly beside her. The cat yowled in terror and fled for the open door of Nomi's sitting room, while Glen stood laughing up at my shocked expression.

''You see? Jezebel knows! Jezebel has more sense than you have, darling. Come down here to me.''

He was like the vital, exuberant man I had first known, yet with an uncanny difference. As I came down to his level, he swung me into his arms and grazed my cheek with his man's rough face.

''Do you see, Dina—we're twins now, Glynis and I. Twins as we never could be before.''

As I pulled away in horror he caught my hand and drew me out the front door before I could protest.

''Enough of such nonsense,'' he said and I saw that he

was himself again. "It won't take long to show you the truth, my darling. We'll take the upper path this time. It's faster. There's snow over the ice, but it's not too deep. Come along, Dina, and I'll prove the truth about Trent."

I went with him across snow that was gold-tinted in this early hour of sunrise.

15

The snowfall had not been deep and walking was easy enough. Now and then my foot pressed through snow and slipped on the icy crust beneath, but this did not happen often. The higher path was easier to follow than the shore path, where the snow drifts were high. Glen moved with consideration, holding back snow-laden branches so they would not slap me, assisting me when the going was rough. Long shadows lay across our path like gray bars upon the snow.

Once when he went ahead I called to Glen to know where we were going, but he seemed not to hear me. When we reached the twin pinnacles of Gray Rocks, he started down through the woods toward the saddle between, and only then did he turn back to answer my question.

"We needn't go all the way to the lake," he said. "From Gray Rocks we can see everything. And I can show you what must have happened."

I still did not believe he knew what had happened, or that Trent had any part in it, but I had to hear his accusation before I could refute it. If what Glen believed was serious, then Trent must know so that he could answer it.

Glen climbed up into the saddle, from which most of the snow had blown away, and reached out to help me across. Over the lake the sun was rising above dark hills, etching green reflections of spruce trees where snow had drifted away from the ice-covered lake.

"Come along," Glen said. "We're going to the top."

It was sharply chill and I had no desire to stand in that windy place in the cold early morning, but when I hesitated, Glen prodded me ahead of him.

"Start climbing," he said. "Don't be timid. It's not slippery. This face of the rock is clear of snow and ice. I'll come up behind you. It's an easy climb. Don't be afraid."

He did not know that I had been up to his secret place before, and I did not tell him. I fitted my mittened hands into the hewn places in the rock and went up, step by step, until I crawled out into the sheltered place at the top. There I forgot Glen for a moment and stepped to the parapet wall to look out at the sun rising over the lake, gilding every snowy tree branch with yellow light. Down on the ice an early skater was out, and I was reassured to see that it was Trent. He was a long way off, skating where snow had blown away, but if I needed him he was there. Not that I would need him in handling Glen. I had no fear. Not yet.

The air was sparkling clear and cold and I filled my lungs with it before I turned back to watch Glen climb up after me. I did not feel afraid until I looked down into his face.

He had unbuckled the leopard skin jacket so that it fell open as he came up and I saw that he had put on his Christmas gift chain of gold links. It was not the one Glynis had given him, however, but his own gift to her—gold links with the gold medallion of a leopard's head. The face he lifted toward me had changed. There had been some subtle metamorphosis. Now I felt what Jezebel had sensed. They were so alike—those two! Yet this was Glynis who climbed toward me! I knew it with some sixth sense. I knew it before Glen spoke to me—and then I knew it all the more. The voice was faintly husky, but not with the huskiness of a man's voice. It was Glynis's voice that spoke to me from Glen's mouth in that high place on Gray Rocks.

"Do you think *I* don't know what happened?" the voice said. "Do you think I can't tell you every detail of what happened? Oh, you can forget what we said about Trent. That was a ruse to get you here. But now you're going to face up to what you've done, Dina darling.''

He climbed up beside me, stood in the open, very close, yet not touching me. On one side was the rock wall, on the other the sheer face up which we had climbed. He was Glen—and he was not Glen. I did not believe in *possession*—of course I did not. Yet his expression had changed, his voice had changed, and it was Glynis who looked out of his eyes, Glynis who toyed with me—and had used, eerily, that pronoun ''we.''

I sprang away from him to the parapet wall and looked over it toward that skating figure on the lake. I cupped my hands about my mouth and shouted Trent's name, shouted for help. I saw the skater slide to a stop, saw him look toward the rocks upon which I stood—and then wave an arm. I had no chance to wave back because Glen swung me around, pulled me away from the parapet. It did not matter. Trent was too far away to help me. No one could help me now. I could deal with Glen—but not with Glynis.

Glen's hands held me from struggling. The pressure on my arms was painful as the soft husky voice went on. ''Now I'll recall you to exactly what happened that day when you went skating out there on the lake. You played the same trick that drowned our mother, didn't you? You skated out onto the dangerous part because your light weight wouldn't crack the ice. And when we came out to rescue you, the ice broke and we went through. Then you pretended all that bit of using a scarf to save us from drowning—but when the time came, you pulled the scarf away. You carried it back to the house and hid it among Colton's things, knowing he might not look for years in that old chest of junk.''

''No!'' I cried. ''No—Glen, it wasn't like that at all. Glen, *Glen!*''

But he could not hear me because *she* was interposed. She watched me warily, cunningly, through his eyes and smiled with *her* smile, spoke to me with her voice.

He let me go, and I cast about wildly for whatever help I

could find. I could not see Trent now. And what loose slabs of rock lay about were all outside the parapet, so I could not snatch one up for a defensive weapon. Both twins had always been far larger than I, and now their strengths were somehow combined and I knew my own helplessness. Nevertheless, I had to fight him if I could.

"Don't touch me," I warned. "This is no place for a fight, but if you lay a finger on me, I will fight—even if we both go off the edge."

"We won't touch you." He spoke almost pleasantly. "Don't worry—there won't be any fight. Because you are going to do what you have to do yourself, Dina darling. You're going to climb over that parapet. You're going to climb over it because you don't want to live any longer. You can't live with your own guilty conscience, can you? How could you bear to live knowing you've lost everything you care about? You've lost your husband forever, you know. And you've let a woman die out there in the lake. How cunningly you slipped the scarf away and let her flounder when she was tired and unable to fight for life in icy water. But you can't get away with it. We'll see to that."

"Glen!" I cried again. "Glen, come back to me!"

It was no use. He had gone into some dark hiding place of the disturbed mind where I could not reach him.

"Come now, Dina," he said. "I'll give you a foot up to get you over the wall. Just step into my hand—gently now."

I kicked out at him hard, and he caught my ankle in his grasp.

"If you're going to play rough, we'll play rough too. Up you go now." Again he used that dreadful first person plural.

He reached to take hold of me and force me to the wall, but at that moment a rifle cracked and a bullet spat against a rock nearby. Glen let go of me and we both looked around in astonishment in the direction of the shot.

Keith McIntyre had climbed to the twin pinnacle of Gray Rocks, and he sat astride a ridge of rock, almost on a level with us, his rifle at his shoulder.

"Put that gun down!" Glen said, but again the voice was

Glynis's, and I saw the boy wince. Nevertheless, the rifle did not waver.

"I'm a real good shot, Glen, and you know it," Keith said. "So get out of the way and let Dina come down. If you make one move in her direction I'll shoot."

Glen was not afraid. "You won't do that, boy. You're not going to hurt us, you know. Why should you? What does Dina matter, Keith—when she's the one who killed your mother?"

"I know who killed my mother!" The boy's voice trembled, but he held the gun steady. "I know how furious you were when I did as Dina made me understand I must do and told you how Glynis got me to crack that head and set it up in her room so it would look as though Dina broke it when she opened the door. Then I went over the balcony rail and back inside through Aunt Nomi's sitting room. I had to do what Glynis said—I had to! She said she wouldn't take me with her to New York if I didn't. But I've seen you carrying those witch balls around the house, pretending it was my mother placing them about."

"It was your mother," Glen said.

"I tried to get even with you that day I climbed up there and shoved down a slab of rock. But I couldn't make myself really hit you."

The boy was almost crying and the rifle wavered out of range. I stumbled toward the descent notches, but Glen caught me by the arm and for a moment I thought I was going over headfirst onto the stony saddle far below. Keith raised his gun and it cracked again. Glen fell back with a cry and I saw blood stain his shoulder, saw him clasp his hand to the wound.

"Come down, Dina!" Keith shouted. "Come down off that rock—quickly!"

At once Glen moved toward me, wound or no, and once more Keith fired. The boy was an expert shot. Glen stumbled and slid helplessly to the floor of the rocky space.

"I don't want to kill you!" Keith sobbed. "I don't want to kill you, but you've got to let her go."

Both wounds were in the same arm. Glen pulled himself up with his good arm and rolled himself between me and the handhold niches hewn in the rock. His face looked ghastly pale and there was no Glynis there to stare out of his eyes. For a breathless, agonizing moment, he looked up at me.

"I'm sorry, Dina," he said. "Sorry for so many things."

Then, quite deliberately, he rolled himself to the edge and went over the lip of rock. I stood frozen where I was, helpless and stunned. He struck the saddle with his body, bounced off and went crashing down the precipice toward the base of Gray Rocks.

Glen had faced his own reality.

Only then did I start frantically down the hand and foot stair and heard Keith's cry echoing over my head.

"I didn't want to kill him! I didn't want to! But I had to stop him. I had to stop *her*."

Her, he had said, and the hair on my scalp seemed to move. Keith had seen it too—that dreadful possession of one twin by the other. The boy clambered down from his rock and reached the saddle before me. He stared at me a moment, his look a little wild, and then he leaped down to the hillside and climbed around the rocks to the place where he could make a safe descent. I would have followed him down, but Trent called to me from the shore below.

"Don't come down, Dina. There's nothing you can do. Keith and I will get him home. Go and warn Nomi."

I did not ask—I did not dare to ask whether Glen were dead or alive, but I think I knew. No one could have survived that fall. It was what, at last, he himself had wanted. Now he would be forever free of Glynis. I climbed up to the path and fled along the very tracks we had made coming out. Double tracks, edged by a third pair—Keith's as he had followed us.

Nomi came to meet me before I reached the house. She had heard us go out, and she had dressed and come after us because she was worried. She had heard the shots, and I think she knew the worst by my face the moment we met in the woods. Her expression did not change. She simply muffled her coat collar higher about her head and turned back with me toward the house.

"Whatever he did," she said to me, "it wasn't as himself."

"At the end he was himself. What he did at the end was by his own choice."

Nomi shook her head vigorously as she walked beside me. "Never! Glynis had to repay him for her death. Somehow I always knew she would."

"Keith said—" I began, but again Nomi shook her head in denial.

"Keith never knew. He was only guessing. *I* knew. I was there near the rocks. I saw it happen."

As we approached the house she told me, speaking in a curious monotone, as though all emotion had been drained from her. On the day when Glynis had died Nomi had gone for a walk around the lake, and her return lap had brought her to a place below High Rocks where she saw Glen come down from the high path and go to his sister struggling in the water.

"He was wild with anger," Nomi said. "Keith had just told him what had happened about the alabaster head, and then Keith had left him and gone home. Both twins had dangerous tempers when they were enraged. That alabaster meant more to Glen than anything else at that moment, and his sister had spoiled everything for him because she was jealous of his work. He might have let you off to some extent because what you did was an accident. What she did was deliberate destruction, using Keith as her weapon so she could swear to Glen later that she had never touched the head. When he saw her in the water he went down to her in a rage and began to tell her off. I heard the whole thing. I saw it. She screamed to him to help her, and he would not. Instead, he untied the scarf I'd given you from about the stump and pulled it from her hand. I'm not sure he really meant her to die. Sometimes I think he believed her invulnerable and only expected her to struggle harder, have a greater fright, before she got free.

246

"At any rate, he left her there and went off carrying the scarf. I went after him. You had stopped below us and gone back when you heard him shout, so we were able to hurry along the upper path and reach home before you did, with your slower movements. Glen was in his studio again by the time you got home. I followed him, but I didn't go near him. Not then."

"And the scarf?" I spoke the words numbly.

"I don't know. I thought he might have put it among Glynis's things, but we didn't find it there. I suppose he hid it where Keith found it."

"I knew Glen was afraid," I said. "But I didn't understand why. It was only his conscience that was frightening him."

Nomi shook her head with conviction. "No—it was Glynis. It was Glynis, using the entry of fear that he gave her, convincing him that everything that had happened was your fault."

I had nothing more to say. It would do no good. They were all a little mad—the winter people of High Towers.

"Poor Colton," I said, remembering him for the first time. "To lose his daughter and then his son, within a month's time."

We had reached the house and Nomi went up the steps ahead of me. "Colton will survive," she said dryly. "He will survive because he has himself. He's already talking about closing High Towers and selling everything on this side to Pandora. But I have myself too—so I too will survive. Never trust anyone, Dina. Never open yourself to love."

I felt only pity for her rigidity. Her course was not for me.

We went into the house together. A doctor was telephoned and then Nomi went to Colton's room to break the news to him.

When Keith and Trent brought Glen back through the woods by means of an improvised stretcher of tree branches, he was taken into Nomi's sitting room. Jezebel remained by the fire, placidly washing her face, unperturbed. Glynis had gone from our midst for good.

247

I got Keith out of that room as quickly as I was able. He looked white-faced and ready to crack up completely.

"I killed him," he told me. "It was my fault."

We stood in the hallway, speaking softly in the dim light. I did not want to take him into the drawing room where the twins' picture hung.

"No, Keith," I said. "You woke him up. You made him stop being Glynis. But his own guilt was too much for him, and he couldn't live with it any more. It had to happen that way, I suppose. If you hadn't come to my aid, I would have been lying at the foot of the cliff by this time. You saved my life."

His smile surprised me. It was uncertain, but warming. It asked my friendship and forgiveness. I put a hand lightly on his shoulder and took it quickly away. I dared no further caress at the moment.

Trent came out to us from Nomi's sitting room and there was praise for his son in his look. "We'll go home now," he said. "The three of us. I've told Nomi you're leaving, Bernardina, and she understands. Go pack a few things and we'll wait for you."

He must have talked to Keith while I ran upstairs because the boy looked less sick-at-heart when I came down. Father and son had drawn closer in the last hour than they had been for a long while. We went down through the woods together and across the frozen lake to the stone house. There Pandora, prepared by phone, waited for us with a hot, strengthening breakfast, and a fire roaring in one of the big fireplaces that had once served an inn.

High Towers was left behind, but the shadows cast by the house and by Gray Rocks would last for a long time. They lay heavily across my spirit, though Trent would not let me be. He stood for reality in a world that had crumbled around me.

After breakfast he took me into the big living room where the lighted Christmas tree made a symbol of happier times to come. He wasted no time on words, but drew a big chair before the fire and sat in it, pulling me into his arms. He held me there with my head on his shoulder and it was as it had been that long ago rainy afternoon in California. Only this time there was no wistful, make-believe about it. I was no longer sixteen, but a woman.

"Bernardina," Trent said. "Don't fight me any longer. It's time to forget the past and begin living now as the woman you've become."

I pressed my head against his shoulder and gave myself into his loving hands.

About the Author

Phyllis A. Whitney was born of American parents in Yokohama, Japan. Today she lives in Virginia. She has always worked with books—as a librarian, bookseller, reviewer, teacher of writing and, of course, bestselling author. She is one of America's most successful writers of romance and suspense. All her books have been bestsellers and major book club selections.

Bestselling Writer
of Romance and
Suspense...

PHYLLIS A.
WHITNEY